Praise for Mar

Bruno, Chief o

"Rich in atmosphere and personality. . . . It's impossible to read a Bruno novel without getting hungry and thirsty."
—*The New York Times*

"With Bruno in charge, there's always time for one of those classic feasts that make this series such a mouthwatering treat."
—*The New York Times Book Review*

"Culinary mystery aficionados won't want to miss this."
—*Publishers Weekly*

"Unashamedly lavished with warmth. . . . The ubiquitous atmosphere of [Walker's] books is of undisguised affection for the towns, villages, their people, their wine, and their food of the Dordogne."
—*Forbes*

"Walker concocts a satisfying dish featuring an intriguing lead character who moves through enviable settings and enjoys wonderful meals while tracking down criminals."
—*Booklist* (starred review)

"While a brilliantly conceived plot builds up to a climax that James Bond might envy, there is pleasure to be had in Martin Walker's sensitive portrayal of a tight-knit community where friendship and mutual support count for more than expediency. Bruno is a hero for our troubled times."
—*Daily Mail*

"[A] charming French village, great food, eccentric characters, and a mystery to nudge things along. . . . Savory indeed."
—*The Seattle Times*

"Bruno Courrèges may be France's . . . answer to dapper James Bond."
—*Minneapolis Star Tribune*

"It is a delight to dip into [Bruno's] sun-baked world."
—*The Observer*

"Martin Walker plots with the same finesse with which Bruno can whip up a truffle omelet."
—*The Christian Science Monitor*

"Highly satisfying."
—*The Boston Globe*

"While I am an avid fan of one-sitting, page-turner books . . . I am also quite taken with books that force me to pause every few pages or so to savor and reflect a bit before continuing—to enjoy a deft turn of phrase or imagine the smells and sounds of the locale. Martin Walker's books fall squarely into the latter category."
—Bruce Tierney, *BookPage* (starred review)

"As readers are drawn into wine-stomping parties, truffle omelet dinners, and the aged dignity of a French hunting hound, the narrative tension gathers."
—*Houston Chronicle*

"A satisfyingly intriguing, wish-you-were-there read."
—*The Guardian*

"Falling-off-the-bone French at its ne plus ultra."
—*Kirkus Reviews*

Martin Walker

To Kill a Troubadour

After studying at Oxford and Harvard universities, Martin Walker served as a foreign correspondent for *The Guardian* in Africa, the Soviet Union, the United States, and Europe and was also the editor of United Press International. In 1987, he was awarded Britain's Reporter of the Year prize for his work in the Soviet Union. He was a senior scholar of the Woodrow Wilson Center and senior director of the Global Business Policy Council, both in Washington, D.C. He now shares his time between the United States, Britain, and the Périgord, where he writes, chairs the jury of the Prix Ragueneau cooking prize, and is proud to be a grand consul of the wines of Bergerac. He enjoys writing a monthly column on wine for the local English-language paper, *The Bugle*, and with wine-making friends produces an agreeable and unpretentious red wine, Cuvée Bruno. He has been awarded the Gold Medal by the French Republic for his services to tourism, and, in 2021, he was awarded the Prix Charbonnier by the Federation of Alliances Françaises for his services to the French language and culture.

brunochiefofpolice.com

To Kill a Troubadour

To Kill a Troubadour

A MYSTERY OF THE FRENCH COUNTRYSIDE

Martin Walker

VINTAGE BOOKS

A DIVISION OF PENGUIN RANDOM HOUSE LLC

NEW YORK

FIRST VINTAGE BOOKS EDITION 2023

The Library of Congress has cataloged the Knopf edition as follows:
Names: Walker, Martin, [date] author.
Title: To kill a troubadour: a Bruno, Chief of Police novel /
Martin Walker.
Description: First Edition. | New York: Alfred A. Knopf, 2022.
Series: A Bruno, Chief of Police novel
Identifiers: LCCN 2021053752 (print) | LCCN 2021053753 (ebook)
Classification: LCC PR6073.A413 T6 2022 (print) |
LCC PR6073.A413 (ebook) | DDC 823/.914—dc23
LC record available at https://lccn.loc.gov/2021053752
LC ebook record available at https://lccn.loc.gov/2021053753

Vintage Books Trade Paperback ISBN: 978-0-593-31398-5
eBook ISBN: 978-0-593-31980-2

vintagebooks.com

Printed in the United States of America
10 9 8 7 6 5 4 3 2

To my colleagues in SHAP,
La Société Historique et Archéologique du Périgord,
with my gratitude and respect

Mai no esborraran tots els nostres poemes.
Mei van a silenciar les nostres cançons.
Mai poden eradicar tota una cultura.
Els nostres somnis de trobador son massa forts.
Un poble que canta es un poble que viu.
I un poble viu mai mor.

They will never destroy all our poetry.
They will never silence our songs.
They can never wipe out our whole culture.
The troubadours' dreams are too strong.
A culture that sings is a people who live.
And a people who live cannot die.

To Kill a Troubadour

Chapter 1

Bruno Courrèges, chief of police for the small French town of St. Denis and for much of the Vézère Valley, was taking a late evening patrol around the garden with his basset hound, Balzac, when the phone at his waist vibrated. Although it was nearly time for bed, the screen showed that it was his friend J-J, head of detectives for the *département* of the Dordogne, who was calling, so Bruno thought he'd better answer.

"Glad you're still up and about," came the familiar voice. "I'm coming to your place right away. I want to show you something and then you can tell me how worried I should be."

Commissaire Jean-Jacques Jalipeau was a large and bustling bear of a man who had not been distracted from his duty when he was shot making an arrest. Some called him a cop "of the old school" in that he wore ill-fitting suits, smoked a pack of Gauloises a day, seldom polished his shoes and did not treat the media with the deference they had come to expect. His prisoners did not fall "accidentally" downstairs while handcuffed nor were their fingers caught in car doors. Female cops on his team almost never applied for transfers and he refused to play the usual turf wars with the gendarmes or to sneer at the municipal police.

Bruno went indoors and put out some glasses for drinks in the living room. Then he checked the latest regional news on his phone for any clue to J-J's unexpected visit. A few minutes later, the headlights of J-J's big Peugeot flared, and Bruno went to the porch to welcome his friend. Josette, J-J's driver and aide, reversed into the driveway and stepped nimbly out. J-J took more time to extricate himself from the passenger seat. He emerged carrying a small evidence bag.

"Welcome," said Bruno. "It's too late for coffee, but do you want wine, or something stronger?"

"I'll have a glass of your homemade *vin de noix,* since I know it has wine plus eau-de-vie," said J-J. Josette asked for mineral water.

Once installed in Bruno's living room with his drink, J-J tossed the bag toward Bruno.

"You're the military man with the Croix de Guerre," he began in his usual, abrupt way. "What can you tell me about that bullet, beyond the fact that it's a twelve-point-seven millimeter caliber and one hundred eight millimeters long, with what look like Russian letters stamped into the base?"

Bruno managed to catch the bag without spilling his drink, surprised not only by the unexpected nature of J-J's inquiry but also by his friend's confident expectation that Bruno could answer all questions concerning war, weapons and the military in general. Then he recalled that it was many years since all young Frenchmen had been required to do at least a year of military service, and by going to university and then enrolling in the police, J-J had been spared that. The tradition launched by the French Revolution for every male citizen to be trained as a soldier and ready to fight for France had gone for good. Bruno knew that modern weaponry and warfare demanded far more than the ability to fire a simple gun, fix a bayonet and throw a grenade. But he sometimes regretted the passing of the principle that every citizen owed a duty to the homeland and of that egalitarian mood of national integration that bonded young men together in their drills, mess halls and barracks. Bruno supposed that he was the former soldier that J-J knew best.

"It's a bullet for a Russian heavy machine gun, often used en masse for antiaircraft fire, but it also has the power to blast through body armor, vehicles and buildings," Bruno explained, weighing the bag in his hand. "The Russians pioneered their use in specialist rifles for snipers, and now everybody else has copied them. With one of these, a trained sniper can kill at a great distance. The current record is a confirmed kill at just over three kilometers by a Canadian in Iraq. The Americans have developed a similar version in their half-inch caliber, almost the same size."

"Is that what you were shot with in Bosnia?" J-J asked.

"No, thank God," Bruno replied, surprised at how little J-J knew about military firearms. "A bullet that size would have torn my leg off and probably half my pelvis. I was hit with a standard round, the usual NATO caliber of seven point sixty-two millimeters, half the length and almost half the caliber of this bullet. And even that put me in the hospital for months. So how has this bullet suddenly turned up?"

"In a stolen car, an old Peugeot that crashed and was abandoned. The bullet had rolled down into the spare-tire housing. It was in a ditch on a small road running parallel to the N21, north of Castillonnès and close to Issigeac. It had fake license plates. We're trying to identify the car now from its serial number."

"Any other car involved?"

"No, it hit and killed a deer and then went into the ditch, lost a front wheel. No sign of the driver. We think there might have been a passenger. There were two different brands of cigarette butts in the ashtray. Though, of course, they could be old."

"A trained sniper wouldn't leave butts," Bruno said. "Was there anything else in the car?"

"No bags, no papers, but one of the cops at the scene is a hunter and says he could smell traces of fresh gun oil on an old blanket. So the owner of the bullet might have had the weapon in the car with him. That's what worries me," J-J said. "*Putain,* you tell me this thing can kill at three kilometers?"

"In the hands of a trained sharpshooter, yes." Bruno had seen armored cars immobilized by a few of those heavy rounds. "Almost certainly he'd have to be military trained, and with the right kind of sights. I imagine they could be picked up in war zones like Iraq, Afghanistan, Ukraine and Syria, anywhere they used Soviet or Russian weapons. It's likely that such sniper rifles could get out into the illegal arms trade. There would certainly be a market for this kind of weapon."

"How do you mean?" J-J demanded. "Terrorists?"

"Yes, there's that, but some criminals would love to have them, or they could be sold for serious money to passionate big-game hunters. And we can't rule out the possibility of assassinations. I think you'd better contact the security guys, and maybe also the military police."

"What about the weapon itself, the gun that could have fired this bullet?"

"There are different models," Bruno said, "but they're all big, well over a meter long with a massive shoulder butt and special muzzle brakes at the end of the barrel to cut down the recoil. Without those muzzle brakes you could never fire the big rounds without breaking your shoulder. Mostly the sniper versions are single shot, bolt action, and always with a bipod to hold it steady. Barrett makes them in America, and there's a Canadian manufacturer whose name I forget. In Russia, Kalashnikov and Dragunov both make them, and then there's Snipex in Ukraine, Zastava in Serbia—"

"*Putain,* Bruno, where did you learn all this?"

"Ever since I was shot by a sniper, I've had a special interest," he replied. "When I was convalescing in the military hospital the psychologists had the bright idea of bringing in one of our own snipers to talk to me about how I'd been shot. I'm glad they did. I stopped thinking about me and my wound and began thinking about the sniper, almost as an intellectual problem."

"There are machine-gun versions, you say?"

"Yes, it's the classic Soviet air defense system: send up missiles to force the enemy aircraft low and then use massed machine guns to try to bring them down. The Iraqi Medina Division used them to break up an attack by American Apache helicopters, one of the few Iraqi successes of that war. The Vietcong used them to shoot down five U.S. helicopters, and when a colonel flew in to see what had happened, they shot him down, too. But the machine-gun versions need special reinforced mounts. They can't be fired from the shoulder like a sniper rifle."

"Thanks, Bruno, I'll keep you informed," J-J said as he stood up.

"J-J, there are some other things you really have to know about this weapon," Bruno said urgently. "Snipers like these never work alone. They need spotters. The sniper can't afford to be lifting his head and staring around. He almost has to be in a Zen state. I've known some of these sniper guys, and they are very special, almost mystical, almost religious. It is just them, their sights, their gun and their spotter. The target becomes almost irrelevant."

"*Putain,* Bruno, you sound almost romantic," J-J said after a moment, his voice not quite succeeding in making a joke of the remark.

"There is one more thing, J-J. At these shooting distances the sights have to be very powerful and calibrated to that particular weapon."

"Are they easy to find?" asked J-J.

"For hunters, yes. But at extreme ranges you want some special sights like AccuPower from Trijicon that cost around three thousand euros. Look, J-J, you have a serious problem here. It would have to be a high-value target, maybe even presidential level. And remember that snipers are accustomed to doing their job under extremely hostile conditions. We have to find them before they locate their target and fire, J-J, and it's not easy to find someone who's two or three kilometers away from the target before you even know the poor bastard he shot is dead."

J-J emptied his glass and led Josette to the door. "Thanks for the drink and the insights. We'll talk again tomorrow."

Bruno stood in his garden beneath the stars, Balzac patiently sitting beside him, and watched the big car leave, thinking about the difference between him and his friend. Bruno had been through the military and J-J had not, and in that way he resembled most of the new generation of French people who were younger than Bruno. Bruno understood the idealism that lay behind the idea that the new Europe had grown beyond war. But the bright and peaceful new world that had followed the Cold War had changed, become darker, and brought back some of the old fears. It was not simply the new challenges of terrorism but the old and traditional forces of national ambition. As the new Russia flexed its military muscle and used the new technologies to interfere in Western elections and to poison its social media, and used nerve agents to kill defectors in England, could Europe still hope to continue in its placid, pacifist ways?

Bruno thought of the emergent superpower of China and its blunt assertion of power in Hong Kong and Xinjiang, and of an America more focused on its domestic challenges than on the makeshift global peace and order it had sustained since the end of World War II. Could this great and lasting peace be maintained, or would future generations of Frenchmen, Germans, Britons and others have to gird themselves and train and mobilize to protect themselves and their people against hostile threats? The world, Bruno thought, was becoming dangerous again.

Chapter 2

Bruno still tended to think of himself foremost as the chief of police of St. Denis, but because of his increased responsibilities he had recently changed the route of his morning run so that he could see not only his own town but also a long stretch of the river and the great cliffs that led to Les Eyzies and beyond. His authority now extended all the way upriver to Montignac and its new museum featuring the prehistoric cave paintings of Lascaux.

He began his run on the trail through the woods around his home, then turned off along the wide ridge that offered magnificent views. He reached his favorite vantage point and waited for Balzac to catch up just as the sun rose fully over the horizon. The valley itself was still shrouded in mist over which the church spire of St. Denis seemed to float weightlessly in the still air. He stood watching the brightness steal steadily over the slopes below as the sun started to burn away the haze, revealing the top of the arches of the old stone bridge. He lay down on the grass, the fine dew already steaming in the sun's rays, and watched his dog's ears flapping as he loped up to clamber onto Bruno's chest and slather his master's neck and jaw with exuberant canine affection.

Bruno hugged his hound, then rose and set off back to his

house at a gentle trot so Balzac could keep pace. When the truffle oaks around his home came into view, Bruno, as always, ended his run with a sprint for the last two hundred meters. He watched Balzac lumber toward him and bent down to fondle his dog's long, furry ears before turning to feed and water his geese and chickens. Then he stripped off his running gear and left the kitchen door open for Balzac. He put the kettle on to boil, turned on his radio and headed for the shower. Balzac was slurping water from his bowl when Bruno, shaved and dressed in his summer uniform, returned to the kitchen to grill the remains of yesterday's baguette, poach two eggs and make coffee.

He checked his phone for messages. There was one from J-J, reporting that the crashed Peugeot had been identified from its vehicle identification number by a Spanish tourist who had reported it stolen from a multilevel car park in Bayonne two days earlier. Bruno shrugged and returned to his breakfast, knowing that J-J would call if there was more news.

As an experiment, Bruno used two pans for the eggs, one with water to which he'd added a teaspoon of apple cider vinegar, and the second using tarragon vinegar. The news on France Bleu Périgord was predictable, so he was barely paying attention as he tried to decide if the eggs had a slightly different flavor. Maybe there was something more subtle about the tarragon vinegar, he thought. Then came the final news item, announcing that the Spanish government had banned a song, or rather a recording, made by a local Périgord group of folk musicians called Les Troubadours, whom Bruno knew well.

Banned? Bruno looked up at the radio in surprise. The newsreader explained that the ill-fated attempt by the regional Catalan government to declare independence was still provoking angry reactions from the government in Madrid. Some members of the

Catalan government had been imprisoned, and others had fled into exile. Harsh sentences had triggered mass protests and a general strike. An uneasy calm had settled, but tensions remained. Even though the other countries of the European Union had declined to recognize Catalonia, the underlying question of the right of a region to declare independence remained unresolved. That was why the offending piece of music, "Song for Catalonia," was henceforth outlawed on Spanish soil.

Bruno asked himself how Madrid could possibly hope to enforce that command. Presumably the song could be banned on Spanish radio and TV, but people could hardly be arrested for singing it or whistling the tune or listening to it online or downloading it onto their phones. Nor could Bruno see how Madrid would be able to close down the internet. Human nature being what it is, the song would probably now enjoy much wider circulation than it would otherwise have received. Whatever the public's reaction, clearly the Madrid government was far more nervous about the Catalan issue than it pretended.

Since he knew Les Troubadours well, Bruno suspected that he was likely to become involved. They had performed the song in French, but then repeated the verse in Catalan as well as its close cousin, the old local Occitan language of the Périgord and of most of southwestern France. Bruno respected the devoted, although small, group of local enthusiasts who nurtured the Occitan tongue. These days it was spoken as a first language only by a handful of the elderly, but many of the words were still commonly used in farming and in the markets. Some of his friends used an Occitan greeting on their phones, and more and more bars and restaurants seemed to be adopting Occitan names.

Bruno had a special fondness for Les Troubadours, who performed agreeably modernized versions in Occitan of the old medieval songs of love and war and chivalry. He'd been looking forward to seeing them at the end of the following week, when he'd booked them to perform at one of the regular free concerts he arranged on the riverbank of St. Denis in summer. Bruno's role as impresario of such civic events—fireworks displays, concerts, agricultural shows and fishing competitions—was one of the unexpected delights of his job. Never before, however, had the concerts become politicized as this one now threatened to be.

The Catalan bid for independence had not at first received much support or attention in France, even in the southwest of the country, where there were some historic ties across the frontier marked by the Pyrenees. On the Atlantic coast the traditional Basque lands stretched from the Ebro River in Spain to the Garonne River in France. On the Mediterranean coast the old Catalan-Occitan culture stretched from south of Barcelona and as far north as Limoges and east through Languedoc to Provence. Indeed, there was some admiration in France for the generous degree of autonomy the national government of Spain had granted to their Basques and Catalans. In France there were Basque, Corsican and Breton campaigners who sought similar status for their own regions. Bruno had recently heard that a small group had emerged to campaign for an independent Alsace as a small new European state on the Rhine between France and Germany.

The attempt to ban a song struck Bruno as both foolish and provocative in this age of social media when anyone could parade their outrage over just about anything. He wondered how many listeners to the radio that morning were now planning to download the song onto their smartphones, as he intended to do. Once the news and weather had ended, the morning show began playing the outlawed "Song for Catalonia." It was a simple but memorable melody, with echoes of a half-remembered hymn. It was easy to hum or whistle, and it took him a while to realize what the radio announcer had meant when he'd said the three verses that were sung were the same song but in three different languages.

Bruno recognized the voice of Flavie, the woman who led the group and played the citole, a medieval version of the guitar. She usually performed with three men, one of whom played a three-string rebec, a kind of early violin played with a bow and small enough to be tucked into the elbow. A second player achieved flutelike sounds from an ancient recorder, and the third beat time with the tabla, a double-ended cylindrical drum that lay in his lap. The wider end gave a deeper, almost bass sound and was played with the hand. The narrower end was played with a small drumstick, aptly named since Arnaut, the drummer, used the bone from the leg of a goose.

Vincent, the rebec player, was a music teacher who lived with his partner, Dominic, whose instrument was the flute, which he called by the medieval name of a gemshorn. Dominic worked as a licensed tourist guide in the summer and spent the rest of the year running a small publishing company that produced local histories and guidebooks and the occasional collection of Occitan poetry. He had begun working from the apartment he shared with Vincent, but his expansion into compact discs of local musicians, including Les Troubadours, had been sufficiently profitable for them to move to an old farmhouse just outside Sarlat.

In partnership with Arnaut they had converted a barn into a recording studio. Arnaut, a qualified electrician who ran his own small company, had set up a small recording studio with a grant from the *département*. The studio could burn a dozen compact discs at a time for Les Troubadours and for other local bands and then sell them at their concerts. The studio employed two school assistants, had a deal with a local designer and printing plant and made a modest profit. Their business was probably going to have a spectacularly successful year with "Song for Catalonia," Bruno thought.

It had long been plain to Bruno, and probably to everyone else, that Arnaut was hopelessly in love with Flavie. But he was short, squat and unusually hairy, the kind of man who had to shave twice a day. His nickname at school had been Tal, short for "Neanderthal," after the ancient people who had lived in this valley forty thousand years ago until they were replaced by the Cro-Magnon. Despite Arnaut's business acumen and his crucial role in the fortunes and growing success of Les Troubadours, Bruno knew that Flavie had made it clear that she saw him only as a valued friend.

With a Roman nose and heavy jaw, Flavie was not a conventionally beautiful woman, except onstage, where her long, dark hair, lithe figure and eyes that looked enormous under good lighting all combined to show her off to great effect. Her speaking voice was almost as compelling as her singing one, soft, low and sexy. She had perhaps the loveliest hands Bruno had ever seen on a woman and, on- or offstage, she moved with a kind of flowing grace. Her conversation, however, could be tedious, since she always wanted to talk politics, and her own were relentlessly green. Still, she loved to eat meat and was a keen huntress and an excellent shot. She vowed never to have children, since the world was already overpopulated, and she tried to eat only organic food. Bruno, she often declared, was one of her favorite male friends, since his garden and chickens made him the most self-sufficient person she knew. His main flaw, she maintained, was his failure to install solar panels all over his property, and not just over the side of his barn that could not be seen from the house and garden.

Bruno took her nagging in good spirit and usually enjoyed the group's company. He always gave them a quickly prepared supper at his home after their annual concert in St. Denis: his own homemade gazpacho followed by spaghetti with meatballs and a salad from his garden. To finish he would make a dessert that his friend Pamela had taught him called apricot fool. Before leaving for the concert he would halve a kilo of apricots and stew them gently for fifteen minutes with the juice of two fresh oranges, a small jar of honey and three cinnamon sticks. Later, when the fruit was cool, he added the zest of two lemons to a kilo of Greek yogurt, took out the cinnamon sticks, folded the apricots into the yogurt and served it in wineglasses.

When the song on the radio ended, Bruno sent Flavie a text saying he was looking forward to seeing them perform next Friday night, and he expected a record turnout. Then he washed his breakfast dishes, put Balzac onto the front seat of his police van and set off for the riding school to exercise his horse, Hector. Before he reached the bottom of the lane, his phone vibrated, and Flavie's name came up.

"Congratulations, you have a hit on your hands," he began, but she stopped him at once, something close to panic in her voice.

"Bruno, I'm frightened, in fact I'm terrified," she said. "You have no idea of the stuff that's hitting our website, even death threats. A whole bunch of people are attacking us on Twitter and claiming we've declared a cultural war against Spain."

"They are just idiots, bored teenagers sounding off," Bruno said, vaguely recalling some article he'd read saying that abuse on social media was almost always just short-lived noise.

"No, there's a headline from some nationalist newspaper saying exactly that. They call it an act of cultural war and accuse us of inciting Catalans to revolt. They're demanding that the French government close us down. And the attacks on Joël, who wrote the song, are even worse. There's another newspaper that has his photo as a wanted poster, and it says, 'Is this man Spain's most dangerous enemy?' That's not bored teenagers, Bruno. That's a national newspaper."

"I sympathize, Flavie. This must be horrible for you and the band, and for Joël, but I don't know how seriously you should take this," he said, though it hardly sounded convincing, even to himself. "To put your mind at rest, we can lay on extra security for the concert. Where are you now?"

"In Bordeaux, at the TV studio of France Three, recording and then doing an interview for their news show. They put together a collection of some of the worst abuse that's come our way—it made me want to throw up. And now the Spanish government is involved. Can you imagine a government in Europe banning a song? It's surreal, Bruno. We're all stunned, and I'm not sure we'll even go ahead with the concert."

Even as Bruno tried to reassure her, the memory came of J-J handing him that specialist sniper's bullet in its evidence bag, from a car stolen in Spain and turning up here in the Périgord. If he mentioned that to Flavie, she'd probably cancel the concert at once. It seemed outlandish to think such a terrifying weapon could be connected to a simple song. But what if this was more than just a bizarre coincidence? Could his friends really be in mortal danger? His rational mind almost scoffed at the very idea, but his instincts stirred and that old sniper wound in his hip began to ache, something that had never happened before in summer.

Chapter 3

Pamela, Bruno's former lover and still a dear friend, was saddling up the Warmblood when he arrived, and they were soon joined by their usual riding companions, Fabiola and Gilles. Miranda, Pamela's partner in running the riding school, was helping her two children onto their ponies, and her father, Jack Crimson, was there to wave them off. Each of the adults took a leading rein for the other horses, and Pamela led them up the slope on the usual path to the ridge that offered a decent run and a splendid view of the Vézère Valley and the old stone bridge to St. Denis.

"You know this troubadour group, Bruno, the one you're friendly with," Gilles said as the riders paused to admire the vista. "There could be a story for me in this ban by the Spanish government. You can't buy that kind of publicity."

Bruno had known Gilles for many years, since their first encounter during the siege of Sarajevo when Bruno, still in the French army, had been assigned to the small force of United Nations peacekeepers and Gilles had been a reporter for *Libération*. Since then, he'd moved on to *Paris Match*, France's most popular illustrated weekly, and had been pleased to come across Bruno when covering the murder of a local heiress. Then Gilles had met Fabiola, a doctor in St. Denis, fallen in love and decided to stay in the Périgord. He was now writing books, but still wrote for *Paris Match* on occasion. Bruno gave him Flavie's number and said her group was booked to perform on Friday in St. Denis.

"This Catalonia business will bring out the crowds, so we'd better get there early, or, Bruno, maybe you could reserve us some seats?" said Pamela.

"I'd already been thinking we'll probably need some extra seats for the media and local politicians," said Bruno, making a mental note to consult his colleague Yveline about getting some of her gendarmes to help with crowd control.

"You might get a demonstration," Gilles added. "Some of the Catalans could well see this as a good opportunity for a demonstration, and we're only, what, three or four hours from the Spanish border?"

Bruno nodded, thinking that demonstrations often inspired counterdemonstrations. He'd better keep an eye on social media to see if Flavie's concert triggered serious interest from across the frontier. Meanwhile, Fabiola was exclaiming in disbelief as she looked at her smartphone. She was extraordinarily adept at using it, far more skilled than Bruno, and her thumbs flew across the screen whenever she sent texts. Bruno still hunted and pecked with a single finger.

"This is unbelievable—so many people are trying to download the song from the radio station that they've crashed the Périgord Bleu website," she said. "Let me check what's happening on Spotify." Her fingers danced over the small keyboard. "Wow, downloads are going off the charts. We're experiencing the first social-media megahit in the history of St. Denis. The band's website is overwhelmed, too."

"It's all over Twitter as well," said Gilles, intent on his own phone. "*Mon Dieu,* there's some vicious stuff here in Spanish, a lot of it aimed at Joël Martin, the songwriter. I interviewed him years ago, when the Catalan troubles first blew up. People are describing him here as a mortal enemy of Spain, an apologist for Catalan terrorism and a tool of the French government, which wants to weaken Spain by supporting Catalan independence." Gilles looked up, adding, "But we don't support it, do we?"

"We refused to extradite some of the Catalan ministers, but I think that was because European law did not accept the Spanish government's definition of 'treason,'" Fabiola said.

"I think I'd better get to the *mairie,* brief the mayor and the gendarmes and decide whether we have the capacity here to host the planned concert," said Bruno, turning his horse to head back to the stables.

"Don't forget the tennis tournament. You and I have a match tomorrow," Pamela said. "If you're dealing with computer stuff on this concert business, you might want to involve Florence," she called after him.

Bruno waved and nodded as he trotted back down to the stables. Florence, science teacher at the local *collège,* was by far the most digitally skilled person in St. Denis. The computer club she had launched for her pupils at the junior high school, between twelve and sixteen years old, had been a striking success. She had begun by rescuing abandoned and outdated computers from the local recycling center and showed the schoolchildren how to overhaul and upgrade them. Their first project had been to set up a LISTSERV for Bruno so that he could with one email contact all the other municipal police and gendarme offices in the *département.* Then they had crafted for him another, so he could reach all the tourist offices, hotels, campsites and rental agencies, and then yet another for all the media outlets.

The schoolkids' first attempt at making a computer game had found no buyers but had inspired a well-known games company in Paris to let Florence's club take over their old computers each time they needed upgrading. Florence had hopes of eventually steering some of her pupils into the company, once they had graduated from senior high school, the lycée, and perhaps even arranging some internships for them. Bruno had developed great respect for this impressive woman, and he'd become almost an honorary godfather to her young twins, Daniel and Dora.

Sometimes when his and Florence's glances met, Bruno felt a spark between them, but he had firmly repressed it, trying to stick to his old rule of never starting a liaison with a woman who lived in St. Denis. He had broken that rule in the case of Pamela, and while he'd never regretted it, he knew he had been more than fortunate in the finesse Pamela had displayed in steering their affair into a close and enduring friendship. Florence, he suspected, was not that kind of woman. Younger and with two children and an early divorce behind her, she struck him as a mother who would require, for her children as much as herself, nothing less than complete commitment. And as long as even a sliver of his heart remained in thrall to Isabelle in Paris, that was not something Bruno felt it was in his power to give.

Once in the *mairie* Bruno arranged a meeting with Yveline so that he and the gendarmes could prepare the necessary crowd-control measures if the concert went ahead as planned. Then he briefed the mayor, who was already interested in the concert after hearing the morning news. The mayor was proud of his fluency in Occitan, which he claimed secured him the votes of the rural elderly. Bruno knew the mayor loved the old medieval poems and songs, many of which he could recite by heart. It had been the mayor who first suggested offering a concert booking to Flavie and her group.

The mayor had heard them perform at the annual dinner of SHAP, the Société Historique et Archéologique du Périgord, shortly before he'd persuaded Bruno to join the group of scholars and enthusiasts who met monthly in an elegant medieval town house in the heart of old Périgueux. The society's interests stretched back for millennia to the Neanderthal and Cro-Magnon people who had settled in the region, but perhaps more attention was paid to the medieval period when the region had largely governed itself as the duchy of Aquitaine. Indeed, despite repeated attempts by kings in Paris to assert control, it was not until the reign of the Sun King, Louis XIV, in the late seventeenth century, that the French crown could be said to have achieved full authority over the region.

"Ah, Bruno, so we face a new *vergonha*," the mayor greeted him, relishing the word and grinning as he saw the baffled expression on Bruno's face. "You should know the word, Bruno. The *vergonha* was the monstrous shaming of our people, still within living memory, when our grandparents and great-grandparents were humiliated and punished in their schools if they dared to speak our own language, our Occitan, which is older than French. Now they want to ban our songs."

Bruno took a seat, not at all displeased to prepare himself for one of the mayor's history lectures. They were always interesting, and he usually learned something.

"Why did the Parisians try to ban the Occitan language?" Bruno asked.

"It began with the church, of course, which never forgave us here in the southwest for harboring the two great heresies that challenged the Catholic faith, the Cathars in the Middle Ages and Protestantism after the Renaissance. Then came the Revolution when that radical priest Abbé Grégoire tried to muscle in on the nationalist cause, insisting that we become one country with one language and a common set of laws. Napoléon was happy to oblige, at least in principle. But Abbé Grégoire wanted all the local patois banned—Breton, Basque, Occitan and Provençal— even though far more French people spoke their patois in those days than they did the French of Paris. And then after the Second Empire collapsed in 1870 during our war against Prussia, there came a new drive for a common tongue, insisting that we must all speak Parisian French so that our armies could understand the orders from officers—forgetting that the great victories of Napoléon had been won by troops speaking Occitan and Breton and everything else. They tried to tell us we should be ashamed of the tongue that had launched the poetry and song of France, the Occitan culture that civilized the feudal system and brought us chivalry."

Bruno coughed, a gentle interruption. Once launched in this vein, the mayor could go on for some time. "It's not the Parisians this time, Monsieur le Maire, nor the church. It's the Spanish government, so we can simply ignore them, but we might have a problem with extra crowds at the concert Les Troubadours are giving here."

"I know you can handle it, Bruno," the mayor said airily. "You know Occitan was the mother tongue of our great Aliénor, Duchess of Aquitaine, the only woman to marry a king of France and a king of England."

"Yes, I do, and I know she was also the mother of Richard the Lionheart."

"Whose mother tongue was also Occitan, even though he became king of England," the mayor replied, a note of triumph in his voice. "And he was himself a troubadour."

"Wasn't it de Gaulle who observed that England was an old Norman colony which had not turned out well?" Bruno asked.

"No, it was Georges Clemenceau," the mayor replied, looking at Bruno with a touch of suspicion. "You're not trying to tease me, are you?"

"Heaven forbid, Monsieur le Maire," Bruno replied, grinning. "As for the concert, since we're only a few hours by car from the Spanish border, I think we should take the security question seriously. We'll have enough of a challenge dealing with large crowds even if politics are not involved, and you're the one in charge of politics."

"The politics are what worry me," the mayor said. "There's a weak, minority government in Spain with elections on the horizon, probable changes coming among the party leaders as ambitious types start jockeying for position on both right and left. Each hopeful will be trying to show they can be tougher and more decisive than the incumbent. It could be a snake pit."

"That's why I leave politics to you," said Bruno.

"I'd better talk to the prefect, since she represents the government here. I'm counting on you to talk to your friends in security, in Paris as well as Périgueux. But let there be no doubt of the principle here. The Spanish government may try to ban a song in their country, but they are not going to tell us in France what we can or cannot listen to. Nor can they be allowed to censor what our people want to sing."

Chapter 4

Bruno was heading back to his office when Florence almost bumped into him. She had charged out of the elevator looking unusually flustered, brandishing an envelope of cheap brown paper as if it were a weapon.

"Bonjour, Florence," Bruno said, smiling and moving to embrace her. "I was planning to call you for advice on downloading some music. How are the twins?"

"They're fine, Bruno, but that's not why I'm here." She marched into his office, almost pushed him to take a seat at his own desk, closed the door and leaned back against it. "Read this," she said.

She thrust the envelope at him, and he saw that it had been sent from a prison near Lille, in the north of France. It was addressed not to her home but to the regional office of the teachers' trade union. That seemed unusual. He gestured for her to take a seat, withdrew the handwritten letter from the envelope and began to read.

Dear Florence,

I understand that since the divorce you have no wish to see me ever again but my sentence has been reduced for good behavior so I am to be released shortly. I would therefore hope to reach with you some amicable arrangement that would allow me to see our children in future on a regular basis.

Despite the divorce, I remain their father. At some point they are likely to want to know something about me. I suggest that for their sake, and perhaps for yours as well as mine, it would be better for them to know me sooner rather than later.

I have been working with the prison chaplain, a very helpful priest, who is hoping to arrange for me to work with the Action Catholique charity at their food bank in Bergerac. I read in a newspaper online that you have moved to the Dordogne and about your being elected to the executive board of the regional teachers' association. That's why I sent this letter to their address.

My warm and heartfelt congratulations on the new life you have built. Perhaps you would allow me to visit you and our children when I am released, to discuss what arrangement we can agree on for me to see them in the future.

Needless to say, I am very sorry for everything that happened between us and am now recovered from the alcoholism that led to our divorce and to my imprisonment. I have nobody to blame but myself for my foolish and self-destructive behavior. I know you to be a kind and generous woman but I cannot expect you to forgive me.

I understand that you may find it hard to think of me as a reformed character, but Father Parvin, the chaplain, and Monsieur Raspail, the prison governor, have told me that they would be happy to reassure you in this regard. I have

*been working as the prison librarian, helping other inmates
with their remedial education. I have also, thanks mainly to
Father Parvin, rediscovered my faith in God and his church.*

*Please find it in your heart to accept my most humble
and heartfelt apology for all the wrongs I did to you. I am
not seeking to return to our marriage. I accept that part of
our lives is over. But for the sake of the children, I hope that
you can begin, if not to forgive me, at least to allow them to
know their father, who is now a very different man.*

In great sincerity and affection, Casimir

Bruno read it through twice, the first time in surprise, and the
second time thinking that it had been very carefully drafted to
appeal to the judges of family courts. It was all news to him. Florence
had already been divorced when he met her, and she had never
spoken of her ex-husband. She'd been working in a dead-end job
in nearby Ste. Alvère as a technician at the truffle market, earning
minimum wage and struggling to ward off the unwanted atten-
tions of her boss. Florence had helped Bruno to uncover fraud in
the sale of truffles and a pedophile ring, which had to led to her
boss committing suicide.

When Bruno learned that she had a university diploma in
chemistry, he helped get her a teaching job in St. Denis, a move
that had transformed Florence's life. She was now a highly valued
member of the community and of Bruno's circle of friends who
dined together at Pamela's riding school each week, taking turns
to do the cooking. Bruno had taught her twins to swim and was
looking forward to getting them into the tennis classes he ran
for the local children. Sometimes he thought they might be the
nearest he'd ever come to having a family of his own, given his
habit of falling for independent women who had no intention of

tying themselves down to a husband and children. Only the local *notaire* knew that Bruno had changed his will to make Florence's children the main heirs of his modest estate, his home and his ancient Land Rover plus his shares in the town vineyard.

"You never said anything about the reasons for your divorce," he said, looking up at her. She used her maiden name, Pantowsky, and he knew she came from a Polish family in one of the coal-mining towns in the north. The letter had been signed "Casimir," a Polish name.

"Given what happened, I wanted to put it all behind me. Can you blame me?" she asked. "Besides, you and our friends were all too discreet to probe. I've tried to build a new life, so it's intolerable that he wants to come here and start interfering in the lives of my children. He's a violent, dangerous man."

"Do you want to tell me what happened?" he asked.

Florence set her jaw firmly and nodded. "At our university Casimir was a year ahead of me, studying biology," she began.

Casimir Maczek came from another Polish family in a neighboring mining town in northern France, she explained. Their parents knew one another through the local Polish club and church groups. They were all very devout, attending Mass each Sunday, and they all spoke Polish at home. Their grandfathers had both been in the Polish armored division that had fought alongside the British Army after D-Day, and each man had found work in the French coal mines after the war. When Florence arrived at the university, Casimir was already a star on the soccer and hockey teams, a good-looking and popular student. They began going out.

Florence paused, squared her shoulders, took a deep breath and looked Bruno firmly in the eye.

"I was a virgin when I met him, and I honestly don't know whether I fell in love with him, or just fell in love with the idea of being in love with a dashing young man," she said, and swallowed. "In my final year, when Casimir had graduated and was already working at a pharmaceutical company in Lille, I became pregnant. There was family pressure on both sides that we should marry, even though neither he nor I wanted to. In our families and our devout Polish community abortion was out of the question.

"We were not happy," she went on. "I was constantly sick, stressed out while trying to study for my final exams, living on campus and going to Casimir's little apartment on weekends. We each knew it was a mistake. Then he started drinking. Sometimes he'd hit me, always where it didn't show, and I was terrified he was trying to make me have a miscarriage. I spoke to my mother, but she said I'd made my bed and had to lie in it."

Bruno closed his eyes and tried to control his anger. "How did he end up in prison?" he asked.

"The drinking got worse and so did the beatings. One night I fled to a women's shelter in Lille where they looked after me. Then Casimir lost his job. He was fired when he was found drunk in the lab, so there was no compensation.

"Casimir got drunk at lunch one afternoon and went to a supermarket to buy food for the weekend," Florence continued, her voice flat, her eyes fixed on the window as though she could not bear to relate all this to Bruno's face. "Backing out of the parking spot, he lost control and slammed hard into an elderly couple who were loading their own purchases. He killed the man, and the woman lost both her legs. He fled the scene, caused a second accident and then fought the police when they arrested him. He attacked them with his hockey stick, put one of them in the hospital. He was sentenced to eight years.

"The women's shelter had a friendly lawyer on the board, and she helped me get a divorce, even though my parents insisted that I should stand by Casimir," she went on. "I refused. I'd had enough, of him and of them. Had I been the judge, he'd have gotten a lot more than eight years. I got my diploma, had the twins and told the lawyer I had to get away. I'd thought of Canada, but the lawyer had some family down here, and she helped me get the job in the truffle market at Ste. Alvère. The rest you know."

Bruno breathed out heavily, not sure what to say, and thought back to his first encounter with Florence at the small office in the truffle market. She had looked like a different woman then, plain and drably dressed, with a downtrodden air. It had taken him a while to realize that she hid her attractiveness in an effort to ward off her boss. Bruno recalled asking her at the end of their meeting whether she was being harassed at work. He could still remember the sudden blaze in her eyes that made her look like a different woman when she'd replied, "He's a pig, but he's also a coward. I can deal with it."

Since then, the new job and new life and new friends in St. Denis had transformed Florence. Pamela and Fabiola had taken her in hand, going together to Pilates classes, to hairdressers and spas and on shopping trips to Bordeaux. She now dressed elegantly, and the success of her computer club had boosted her self-confidence, just as the teaching job and the subsidized housing that went with it had made her financially comfortable. She was an attractive and capable woman, an exemplary mother to the twins, a much admired soprano in the church choir and a valued friend.

A memory suddenly came to Bruno's mind, from earlier that summer, when he'd been teaching Dora and Daniel to swim. When they had managed their first length of the pool, Florence, delighted at their success, had jumped into the pool to embrace him. He could still recall the sight of her in a green bikini and the feel of her breasts against his chest. Not that she had ever given him the slightest encouragement, perhaps because of his liaison with her friend Pamela. Or perhaps she'd been told of his occasional reunions with Isabelle, the policewoman with whom he'd fallen in love before she went off to build a brilliant career in Paris.

"Where are Daniel and Dora now?" he asked.

"At the *maternelle*," she replied. "School is out, but there are so many working mothers that they're keeping the nursery open, and the children all enjoy being together."

"Is this the first you've heard from Casimir since the divorce?"

"The first I've heard from him since he was arrested. I had to give evidence at the trial about his drinking habits, and about his beating me and my fear that . . . I'll never forget the look he gave me."

"So at his criminal trial the court knew about that?"

Florence nodded. "A policewoman came to the women's shelter to tell me Casimir had been arrested, and then I was asked to testify, and so was the woman who ran the shelter and the doctor she brought in to treat my bruises. The night I ran away he'd hit me in the face for the first time. He broke my nose and I lost a tooth. The prosecuting magistrate was a woman, and she assured me that bringing all that into open court would help me get the divorce."

"And now Casimir is back in touch, claiming to be a reformed character and wanting to see his kids," said Bruno. "That letter he sent you was carefully crafted, as though he wrote it with a family court hearing in mind. He accepts blame and responsibility. Do you think it's possible that he's a changed man?"

"I neither know nor care. I don't want him anywhere near my

children," she said fiercely. "Not now, not ever, whatever he says about finding religion. I don't want him back in my life. I came down here to escape him. I thought he'd never find me."

"I think we'd better talk to our friend Annette," Bruno said. She was the magistrate in the subprefecture who specialized in family law. "She'll know what the options are. May I make a copy of Casimir's letter and ask her advice? And I'll need the name of the shelter where you went, the doctor who treated you there and the lawyer who helped with your divorce."

Florence took out her phone, looked up the contacts and gave them to Bruno. He scanned a copy of Casimir's letter onto his own computer before turning back to Florence. Her face was blotchy, her jaw set tight as if she were fighting back tears, and her fists were clenched around a handkerchief.

"It looks as though Casimir has been trying to convince the prison governor and this priest that he's a new man," he said, as gently as he could. "With them on his side, he might be able to convince a court that he should at least have some access to his children."

"I should have gone to Canada when I first thought of it," she said. "With his prison record, they'd never have let the bastard into the country. Whatever it takes, Bruno, I want to keep him away from the twins and away from me. I don't trust Casimir and I don't believe he's become religious. He probably thought that was a way to get into the good graces of the prison staff."

"If he's succeeded in that, it could be a complication," Bruno replied. "Rehabilitation of prisoners is supposed to be the objective rather than just punishment. Prison officials tend to embrace any inmate who seems intent on going straight, so I presume they'll testify to the court or at least send letters of support. Any family court will want to take their views into consideration."

"You don't sound very hopeful." She sounded aggrieved. She'd obviously expected more from him.

"I'm just trying to think this through," Bruno replied calmly. "It's no use fooling ourselves that it will be easy to keep him at bay. Family courts usually support the principle of the father having some role in the lives of his children. And when the prison chaplain confirms that Casimir has found religion . . ." Bruno paused and saw Florence's expression darken as he went on. "Your own parents weren't happy about the divorce. Are you still in touch with them?"

"I send them Christmas cards with photos of the children, but I get colleagues to mail them from different cities. I don't want them to have my address because I'm sure they will share it with Casimir's parents, and I don't want him ever to find me."

"You might want to think about making contact with them now and trying to get their support, perhaps by taking the children to meet them. The last thing you'd want in a family court hearing is for both sets of grandparents to take Casimir's side. At the very least, the court would expect your parents to back you."

"Merde, merde, merde," Florence said, shaking her head in despair. "If Casimir has a priest on his side, that's all my mother will want to know. You've no idea how important the church is for my parents. She had a priest in the maternity ward to make sure the twins were baptized, terrified that they might die and be damned for all eternity." She sighed, and then murmured, "Maybe I should apply to immigrate to Canada."

"I hope not," said Bruno, his finger poised to dial the magistrate's office. "St. Denis would not be the same without you and the children. We'd all miss you terribly. The computer club would collapse, the school would go into mourning, and the mayor would probably blame me.

"You'd better think how far you want to go public with this," Bruno went on after a pause. "The whole town will be on your side, but everyone will know about this, and your children will probably get teased, maybe painfully, about their father. You know how cruel kids can be, even in a place like St. Denis."

"Damn it, that reminds me," she said, glancing at her watch and rising. "I have a computer club meeting due to start in five minutes. I have to run."

"I'll try to find out when Casimir is going to be released, and I'll text you about when we can see Annette."

Chapter 5

The mayor appeared in the doorway. "What on earth was that about?" he asked. "Florence ran out of here looking as if all the hounds of hell were on her tail."

"One hound, at least." Bruno beckoned the mayor inside and closed the door before explaining Florence's distress.

"That's the very last thing we want," the mayor said, aghast. "That computer club of hers is the best thing that's happened for the prospects of our youngsters since I first became mayor. What's this charity where her ex-husband hopes to find a job?"

"Action Catholique, the church's food bank in Bergerac," said Bruno. "Given Florence's importance to the church choir, we might want to talk to Father Sentout. He won't want to lose his star soloist. Presumably priests have their own networking system, so he should be able to contact this prison chaplain and find out more about the plans for Casimir."

"I'll talk to some old colleagues in the Senate," the mayor said, a light in his eye now that he had the beginnings of a plan. "There must be some committee or other that considers family law, and another that deals with prisoners and early releases. If need be, I can get some questions raised there. If the prison authorities held some kind of hearing on his early release without contacting Annette, we might be able to get that reversed. What about this woman Casimir crippled and whose husband he killed? Can we find out her name? Won't she have the right to address the court and say he should not be released early? And the policemen he assaulted? These people might want to tell the court they oppose an early release for this man. The more I think about it, Bruno, the more I think we have a lot of potential ammunition."

"The transcript of Casimir's trial is a public document, and as an ex-senator you should be able to get a copy from the justice ministry much faster than I can," Bruno said. "You'll probably need to get the date and place of the trial and Casimir's full name from Florence. I'm going to be tied up preparing for the big crowds we're expecting for the Troubadours concert."

In his office, Bruno emailed Annette explaining Florence's difficulty and asked if she could get any information about her ex-husband's release and whether it might be delayed. Then he went to find Father Sentout. After decades of hearing confessions from his churchgoers, he'd know how to keep a secret.

"Ah, Bruno, a pleasure to see you, although I don't suppose this is a social visit." The priest was in his study, pen in hand, a Bible open on his desk and a large notebook beside it. "What can I do for you?"

"I'm going to speak to you in confidence. It concerns Florence, and we don't want any of this to become public without her approval," Bruno said, and handed the priest a copy of Casimir's letter. "You had better read this."

Bruno took a hard-backed chair beside the desk as Father Sentout sat down and began to read in silence. "The poor child," he murmured. "How she must have suffered." He handed the letter back to Bruno. "I presume there is more you can tell me about the reason for his being in prison."

"It's a grim story," Bruno replied, and explained about the car crash, the beatings, Florence's flight to a women's shelter. "We're consulting Annette, the magistrate in the prosecutor's office in Sarlat. She knows family law. But I thought it might help to have your advice."

"In the eyes of the church, of course, Florence is still married to this man, and if it is true that he has found his way back to God, then there may be grounds for hope."

"I don't think she sees it that way, Father. Florence is determined to have no more to do with him and to keep him away from her children. She's prepared to emigrate rather than have him nearby."

"May God help us," Father Sentout said. Then he closed his eyes briefly and opened them to stare at the crucifix on the wall before speaking. "I think we have to keep her here in St. Denis. She's found a home here. How do you think I can help?"

"The prison chaplain seems to be a priest," Bruno said, and handed Father Sentout a card with the phone number. "I was wondering if you might talk to him, find out whether a formal hearing has taken place regarding Casimir's release. You might also talk to your colleagues at Action Catholique in Bergerac and see if they know when he'll arrive there."

"Of course, I'll do that, and anything else I can to help, but you should understand that I hope to see this family come back together in a spirit of forgiveness."

"I understand your position, but you had better talk to Florence about that, Father. I'm convinced you'll find her determined to pursue her life and raise her children without him."

Father Sentout grimaced and then murmured, "Saints preserve us." Then he looked at Bruno and nodded. "I'll try to find out what exactly is happening and let you know. I'll also talk to Florence."

Bruno shook his head. "I'd rather she didn't know you were involved until I can say that you helped us find out the timetable of Casimir's release and his expected arrival here. We want her confident that you're on her side in this."

"Of course I'm on her side, Bruno, as much as I can be given my duty to the teachings of the church. On that there can be no compromise."

Bruno's desk phone was ringing as he returned to his office, his mind still on Florence and her problems. He scrambled to focus when he heard J-J, telling him that the forensics lab had confirmed fresh gun oil on the blanket in the wrecked Peugeot. They had also found a golf ball in the car. The owner of the car had never played the game.

"If I were traveling with a sniper's rifle, I'd probably hide it in a golf bag with the clubs," Bruno said.

"That's what I thought, so I warned Prunier," J-J said, referring to the head of police for the *département*. "I told him what you'd suggested about potential targets. He spoke to the prefect who is checking on all planned ministerial visits to the region. I expect she's going to want a list of any VIPs down here on vacation, which could be a long one. The gendarmes are beating the bushes from Eymet to Issigeac and up to Bergerac for suspicious characters on foot."

"I presume the interior ministry is now involved," Bruno said.

"Prunier spoke to them and asked me to tell you to alert all the municipal cops in your valley. We've already been on to Musidan, Sarlat, Ribérac and Nontron, and we're checking on all new reports of stolen vehicles. We're also checking hotels, campsites, tourist offices and rentals for last-minute bookings."

"Get on to the hunting clubs, and ask them to report any sound of a heavy-caliber gun being fired. They'll know what you mean," Bruno said. "After a car crash, any good sniper is going to want to recalibrate his sights, so he'll have to fire his weapon. I can take care of that in my part of the *département*. And what about the media? Do we tell them anything about this?"

"Not yet, says the prefect. She doesn't want to start a panic," J-J said, and then paused. "There's something about this that doesn't feel right to me. It's a little too convenient—the crashed car, the special bullet, now the golf ball."

"You think we're being set up?" Bruno asked, prepared to take seriously the instincts of a cop as experienced as J-J.

"No, but maybe we're being steered in a certain direction. Or maybe I'm just getting old. Stay in touch."

Bruno drafted an email asking for reports of last-minute bookings and sent it out on the system Florence's computer club had made for him. It went to all the hotels, campsites, tourist offices and rental agencies in the Périgord Noir for which he was responsible and all the way east to Lalinde and north to Périgueux and Terrasson. Then he sent out another email to all the hunting clubs. He called his colleagues, Juliette in Les Eyzies and Louis in Montignac, to alert them.

Then Bruno opened his diary, knowing that the week ahead was going to be a busy one. There was the St. Denis tennis tournament in which he was playing, which included a feast of roast wild boar which he would help cook. Then there was the extra security to be arranged for the concert of Les Troubadours. After that would be the town's annual fair for the feast day of St. Louis, celebrated to commemorate the only French king who became a saint. He also had to arrange the hunting club dinner and the trials to pick the first and second teams of the rugby club for next season. And now he had Florence's problem with the prospect of Casimir's return, plus the new security alert. Why did everything always have to happen at once?

He called Annette at the prosecutor's office for the subprefecture of Sarlat and explained Florence's predicament. Annette agreed to meet them both for a drink after work that evening. She'd drive to St. Denis, Annette said, to spare Florence having to find a babysitter when most of the teenage girls she normally used were working in various bars, cafés and tourist sites during this peak season.

To remind himself of the main area of J-J's alert, Bruno glanced at the map of Nouvelle Aquitaine on the wall, a product of the latest reorganization of France into administrative regions. This new region now included twelve of the traditional *départements*. It stretched from the Spanish border in the south up to the port of La Rochelle in the north. It included the cities of Bordeaux, Angoulême, Poitiers and Limoges, and in the east stretched to the Massif Central. The region covered an eighth of France and was home to more than six million people. He got up and looked at the tiny triangle between Eymet, Issigeac and Bergerac. He glanced down at Bayonne, where the car had been stolen, almost at the Spanish border. He recalled his recent conversation with J-J about a possible setup. The connections were too vague, but something was going on here. He phoned J-J.

"Have you heard of the fuss being made by the Spanish about Les Troubadours' song, 'Song for Catalonia'?" Bruno began when J-J answered. "The group has a big concert next Friday in St. Denis. The song has jumped to the top of the charts, and we're expecting a lot of people. The Spanish government has just banned the song, and social media is full of furious Spaniards condemning it and the songwriter. I was wondering if there might be a connection with the car stolen in Bayonne, down by the border. It's a long shot, but—"

"I can see a few drunks in a bar deciding to come over the border to beat up the band," J-J interrupted him. "And I know that our radio and TV are having fun mocking Spain over this song, or being outraged that Madrid should try to tell us what we're allowed to hear. But given what you said about the bullet and the kind of sniper who'd use such a gun, I hardly think that a concert on the riverbank at St. Denis is the target. I respect your hunches, Bruno, but don't let your imagination run away with you."

Chapter 6

No sooner had J-J ended his call than Bruno's phone rang again. This time it was Gilles, saying that he was writing a piece for *Paris Match* and needed a quote from Bruno about the concert going ahead, in defiance of Spain. Bruno told him what the mayor had said, that it was up to the people of St. Denis, not any foreign government, to decide what they wanted to hear. Within twenty minutes, Gilles's story was the lead item on the *Paris Match* website, and then the *mairie*'s phone never stopped—*Sud Ouest,* the local newspaper, called first, followed by *Le Monde,* Agence France-Presse, *Le Figaro,* then Reuters, *El País* of Spain and *The Times* of London.

Bruno knew that any link between Les Troubadours' concert and the mysterious sniper was no more than his own wild speculation. But the idea nagged at him. He considered whether to use his informal connection to General Lannes and the security officials in Paris to alert them to the possible connection. In any event, he told himself, he needed some advice on handling the Catalan problem. He could call the personal phone of Isabelle, the police inspector with whom he'd fallen in love. She had chosen her career over him by accepting a job on the staff of the interior minister. They remained friends and occasional lovers, but their strongest bond now was Balzac, the basset hound puppy she had found for him when his old hunting dog, Gigi, was killed in an antiterrorist operation in which Isabelle had been involved.

Isabelle was now in charge of the Paris office that coordinated liaison with the security staff of the other European countries. That meant she would probably become involved anyway, given the way the French media was focusing angrily on Spain's attempt to ban the song. The midday radio news was quoting opposition politicians demanding that the French government stand up for the freedom of song. She'd probably already be in contact with her opposite number in Spanish security. Bruno decided to call her.

"Bruno! Bonjour," she answered, that trill of lightness in her voice that he'd always loved. "How is our wonderful Balzac?"

"He's fine, as ever. He misses you."

She laughed. "But I bet you're not calling about him?"

"You're right. Do you remember that concert we went to by Les Troubadours on the riverbank, the singers with the medieval instruments?"

"Of course I do," said Isabelle. "It was a perfect summer evening, and we were falling in love. But now I'm thinking of them in a very different context. We had a worried report overnight from our consul in Barcelona, and what I've just heard from my Spanish colleague on the EU Security Committee has me even more concerned. Joël Martin was already controversial, but now with this song he seems to have become a real object of hate, possibly even an assassination target for some of the extreme nationalists."

"And have you heard about the sniper's bullet J-J found in a crashed car, stolen at the Spanish border?"

"Yes, that's why I called my Spanish colleague. He's a sensible guy and says there are some real crazies among the militant nationalists, including ex-soldiers. Because of the sniper factor the security guys at the Élysée are also interested, and so the army's new cybercommand is already looking into the social-media surge that seems to have triggered all this. They've now been brought in officially with all their magic tricks to see what's behind it. Is Les Troubadours' concert going ahead next week?"

"The band is worried, but the mayor wants it to happen, so I think we'll go ahead with some extra security."

"Knowing the minister I'm pretty sure he won't swallow the idea of some other government presuming the right to say what music we can listen to in France. Even less would he like to see newspapers criticizing him for caving in to the Spaniards."

"What's the background on Joël Martin?" Bruno asked. "I'm friendly with the band, but I don't know him personally. Why's he of interest?"

"There was some diplomatic fuss about him," she replied. "He's a French citizen, born in Bergerac, married a Catalan woman, lived with her in Barcelona and was a cultural adviser to the Catalan government. His wife was a member of the Catalan parliament, voted for independence and was then killed in a car crash during the violent events around the general strike. She's become something of a martyr. He was making a lot of noise on Catalan social media, and the Spaniards wanted to extradite him. We suggested to Madrid discreetly that this wouldn't be a good idea if they wanted to keep French goodwill. We put him on the security watch list. It would be a big help if you can find out more about him. I have to go, sorry, Bruno. But stay in touch. You're on the scene, so please keep me informed. Bye now."

Bruno's heart gave that little jump that Isabelle always inspired; by now he'd learned to assume it always would. Each of them knew there was no future for them, but neither one could resist the opportunity to rekindle the passion they had shared in the glorious summer when they had met. She had been a rising star among detectives, being groomed to succeed J-J as chief detective for the *département.* But then she had caught the eye of the interior minister, been transferred to his staff in Paris and was launched on the brilliant career that was always her ambition. Sadly there was little room in it for Bruno, and although their occasional reunions were passionate and sweet, their partings always left him miserable. He wondered if they would ever be able to make the transition to the kind of trusting friendship that Bruno felt he now enjoyed with Pamela.

He dragged his thoughts back to the present and considered what little he knew of the Catalonian crisis. He recalled a close election with a narrow parliamentary victory for the pro-independence parties, and another narrow vote for independence in a referendum with a low turnout. He used his computer to refresh his memory. Many Catalan voters had boycotted the referendum vote when the Madrid government had said it would be illegal under the Spanish constitution. Catalan independence had been declared in principle but suspended in practice by the regional government pending negotiations. This strange half-life of a new Catalan state lasted only briefly before Spain seized back control.

Some of the Catalan ministers had been tried and sentenced to ten or fourteen years in jail. Several more had gone into exile, and Madrid had demanded their extradition under European arrest warrants. German courts had refused to enforce the warrants, saying they did not share the Spanish courts' definitions of "treason" or "sedition." The exiled leader of the Catalonian government, Carles Puigdemont, had since been elected to the European Union's legislature and was living in Germany.

"Madrid Wins an Ugly Victory in the Battle for Catalonia but May Still Lose the War" was the headline over one assessment in *Le Monde.* "It Was the Economy, Stupid!" read another in *Le Figaro,* tracking the way opinion-poll support for independence had begun to soar after the euro crisis, and the recession sent youth unemployment in Spain soaring close to 30 percent.

Bruno had not formed much of an opinion on the matter, which until now had seemed of little relevance to him or his work. He had a vague suspicion of plebiscites and referendums, thinking they were as likely to reflect current moods about the economy as they were to foster serious consideration of the matter at hand. Simple majorities of those voting were hardly conclusive for any important issue like breaking up a long-standing nation-state. Pamela, he recalled, had been outraged that she had been robbed of her European citizenship and her life had been transformed when fewer than 40 percent of Britain's registered voters had opted for Brexit in the referendum, since only 70 percent of the electorate had bothered to vote. Seeing the impact on a level-headed and sensible woman like Pamela meant that Bruno had some insight into the passions and anger that referendums and nationality could provoke.

His phone vibrated again, and this time it was Flavie, saying the band and songwriter had decided the concert should go ahead.

"Glad to hear it," he replied. "The mayor was outraged at the idea of some foreign government telling French people what songs they were allowed to hear. But we thought it best to leave the decision to you."

"You and St. Denis would hire us when nobody else would, so we're not likely to let you down now that we've made it onto the Spotify charts. We won't even try to raise our fee."

"We're expecting a lot of people, so we're thinking of moving the venue to the big park across the river here so we can make the concert more secure," Bruno told her. "You might want to talk to your technical guys about amplifiers and extra loudspeakers. We can put you on the back of a big truck, and we'll rig up curtains and spotlights; we might need a rehearsal for all that. And if you have to pay extra for more speakers, we'll cover that, too. Will that be okay?"

"That will be fine. Would you object if we pass some buckets around the crowd to raise money for the Catalan defense fund?"

"Could be tricky with the politics of this. Why not pass the buckets around for the Occitan society instead?" Bruno asked. "They're always short of funds, and there would be no political fallout."

"Okay, it's a deal. I'll talk to the tech guys and get back to you about the sound system. And check out the TV news this evening. We're on it!"

Bruno dragged his thoughts back to Florence. On his computer he found an outline of family law that had been drafted for police and gendarmes. The old Napoleonic code, firm on the succession of property rights, paternal authority and the legitimacy of children, had been modernized over the years, not least because of the impact of the judgments of the European Court of Human Rights. He thought he should brush up on the law before meeting Annette and Florence. As he thought, there was a presumption that each biological parent should have the right of access to the children, and the children also had a right to build relationships with both parents. Once a prisoner had served his or her sentence, the debt to society should be considered paid, and the ex-convict had the right not only to vote but also to run for office and enjoy all the other civic rights, including the right to a passport.

He checked whether prisoners on early release for good behavior qualified for full civic status, at least until the time set in the original sentence had expired. That depended on whether a court had decreed a commutation of sentence, in which case all civic rights were restored. The situation was less clear if the prison authorities and a *juge de l'exécution,* a special enforcement judge, had approved an early release. That was conditional on the subject staying out of trouble, and his wearing an ankle bracelet to monitor his movements. He'd have to check how far that might affect Casimir's status. He read on, trying to see if there was some special provision that might let Florence block his access to the children. He wasn't looking forward to telling her that he had failed to find one and that, even if she went to Canada, Casimir might be able to get a passport and follow her.

Chapter 7

It was time to meet Yveline to talk about security for the concert. Bruno donned his cap, told the mayor's secretary where he'd be and walked down the stairs to the main square. Yveline, in uniform, was coming up the street from the gendarmerie. He grinned and touched his cap.

"I was coming to see you," he said, and fell into step beside her. As well as being the best colleague among the various young officers who had been assigned to command the gendarmes of St. Denis, she'd become a friend.

"I assumed you would be, but I thought we should take a look at the site. The usual riverbank area won't be nearly big enough for the numbers we're expecting."

He nodded as they set off across the bridge over the Vézère. "I thought we might use the big space on the far bank," Bruno said. "We can move the camping cars away and set up a big truck as the stage, like we did with Rod Macrae's comeback concert. Security should be easier, with more space to erect barriers."

"I don't see why not. The local businesses will be annoyed if we don't give them the opportunity to make some extra cash. Do you have any idea how many gendarmes will be available?"

"I've asked for a full brigade, four squads of a dozen each plus a headquarters group," she replied. "Plus my own team."

"The rugby and hunting clubs will provide volunteers for stewards," he said. "We'll need a medical tent, some lighting rigged up and a tent for the performers to use. There's no admission charge, but they'll pass around a bucket to raise money for the Occitan society."

"Very much like last time," she said. "It's becoming routine. And the nearest we'll ever get to show business. I already spoke to Périgueux about bringing in reinforcements and also some traffic cops to help manage the parking."

"By the way, does the name Joël Martin ring a bell, a guy from Bergerac who got involved with the Catalan business through his Spanish wife?"

"Joël Martin the poet?" Yveline raised her eyebrows. "*Mon Dieu,* Bruno, what century are you living in? The guy is huge, he's become like the voice of Catalonia."

She pulled out her phone from its pouch on her belt, turned it on and called up a Twitter feed to show Bruno. "With the publicity today, he's going viral. He's on Instagram, WhatsApp, TikTok, all over."

"Is he making himself into a symbol of the government in exile of Catalonia?"

"No, he doesn't seem to be much into politics," Yveline explained. "He's a poet, writing in Occitan, and he loves the language and its history and wants to promote it."

"So it's more than just the song?"

"He's got a lot of content: short lectures about Catalonia and its history, lessons in how to speak Occitan and how close it is to Catalan. I didn't know most of this stuff about how Paris tried to stamp out the local language in the Périgord, it's really interesting.

Did you know Paris got the pope to launch a Crusade against the people down here on the grounds that we were heretics? They brought in the Inquisition, burned people at the stake and everything. In fact, that's when they invented the Inquisition. I thought all that just happened in Spain."

Her fingers darted over the screen of her phone. Bruno could not tell which app she was using, but it opened to the image of a man with curly red hair and a pleasing manner, speaking directly from the screen and asking, "Do you know the role that this region of Occitania played in the great legend of King Arthur and the Knights of the Round Table?"

"That's Joël," Yveline whispered.

"We first hear of it as a history of King Arthur and Merlin the wizard being recounted at the court of King Henry the Second of England," the man on-screen was saying. "He was the husband of our own Eleanor of Aquitaine. Her grandfather, Duke William, was one of the first troubadours, and Eleanor and her husband were great patrons of their music. The tale of Sir Tristan and Iseult is written for Eleanor by a poet, Thomas of Britain. Then a Breton poet, Béroul, turned it into a dramatic tale of love and adultery."

As the man spoke, images of nineteenth-century Romantic paintings appeared on the screen—of medieval knights and their ladies, of King Henry's castles in France and in England, of Eleanor's palaces in Bordeaux and Poitiers and her tomb at Fontevrault.

"At Eleanor's court, another poet known as Wace embellished the poem with the idea of the Round Table, where the king and all his knights would sit as equals. Eleanor's daughter, Marie, became the patron of Chrétien de Troyes, who brings in Sir Lancelot and his love for Queen Guinevere, and Sir Perceval and the quest for the Holy Grail. That in turn becomes the opera *Parsifal* after

German poets take up the story from the courts of Eleanor and her daughters.

"This is not just the stuff of legend, it is the birth of our poetry, of chivalry and the taming of the brutal feudal system. If you want to know more about Eleanor, click on the image of her below. If you want to know more about Duke William and his Crusades, click on his image. And for more on the Occitan poets, click the image of the manuscript."

Bruno was fascinated, itching to reach out to Yveline's phone and click one of the links to learn more.

"You see how good he is at getting you into the story and making you want to go on looking further?" Yveline asked, closing her phone. "I've been caught up in this for hours at a time. Before you know where you are, you find that you're hooked. Nor does he stop at social media. He also publishes his own short books. Then there are his own poems, in Occitan with French translations, and whole lectures on the troubadours and their songs, with bits on the medieval instruments and the themes they wrote about, including some raunchy ones."

"Do you have any idea how many people are watching this material?" Bruno asked.

"He's got close to a hundred thousand followers on Twitter alone, but I don't know about the other media like Instagram and WhatsApp and the rest. He seems to be everywhere."

Bruno pursed his lips, thinking that this put the Spanish banning of the song into a totally different context. Joël Martin was running what seemed to be a successful propaganda campaign beneath the surface of conventional media. Bruno had seen nothing in the press and had heard nothing about it until the radio news that morning.

"How did you learn about him?" he asked Yveline.

"A friend from the hockey team I used to play for. She knows I'm based here, and she texted me to ask if I knew anyone who spoke Occitan and if I'd run into this Joël Martin. She was on vacation in Barcelona when they had some big demonstration for independence and she got interested."

"And have you? Run into him, I mean."

"No, but some of his poetry is good. He writes in Occitan, but he always puts up French translations, and I found myself intrigued by the history he posts about, so I started following him."

"From what you say, he must spend all his time posting this stuff," Bruno said.

"Maybe at first, but now he's got so many followers it's like a rolling snowball, and there are endless links to other stuff about Catalonia and human rights and Occitan. It's interesting. I never knew that French poetry started here, that Occitan has a thousand-year-old culture and a language that was spoken in the royal courts of Europe."

Bruno looked blank. "How do you mean, he has so many followers?"

Yveline gave an indulgent smile. "You really live a sheltered life, Bruno. There are people, superstars, on social media who have tens of millions of followers, on Instagram or on Facebook, like the Kardashian family in America who are famous simply for being famous. One of them charges half a million dollars to companies who want her to post something nice about their products. It's a whole industry."

"*Mon Dieu,* half a million?" Bruno asked, startled. "We're in the wrong business. So it's like advertising."

"Not quite advertising. It's more like getting a personal recommendation from a trusted friend. People always say that word of mouth is the best recommendation, so through social media they're trying to mass-produce it."

"Does it work?" Bruno was skeptical.

"I don't think people would pay half a million dollars if it didn't," she replied. "But it's not just advertising, it's entertainment. Joël Martin may be small on the global scale, but he's big in France and getting bigger."

"Does that mean he's making some serious money out of this?"

"I don't know. He doesn't seem to advertise anything except Occitan and Catalan culture, along with his own books and poems. But you could say he's making a subtle kind of political propaganda, which I suppose explains why he's got Madrid worried. And he's started a revival of interest in Occitan."

"How did this happen? I mean, how could it be that this is all new to me?" Bruno asked. He didn't add that he found it strangely worrying, although he wasn't sure why. Certainly J-J didn't seem to have been aware of it, but J-J was close to retirement. Bruno imagined Isabelle would probably be familiar with it. He knew something about it from the press stories of the Russians using social media to plant fake stories to whip up extreme views and interfere in American elections and in the Brexit referendum. Bruno had never paid much attention, thinking that such high-tech trickery didn't have anything to do with him, nor with the people of St. Denis.

Perhaps he should have paid more attention, he told himself. The educational potential of what Joël was doing with the history and poetry was impressive. If Bruno had been taught history in that way rather than having to learn by rote the names of kings and dates of battles and various French revolutions he would have become far more interested. But a technology that could be used for such useful purposes could also be misused.

"You aren't of the generation that grew up with a smartphone in your hand," Yveline replied, "nor am I, but my little sister is. And there are millions like her in France. So however many people you thought might be coming for this concert on Friday, you should double the number or maybe even triple it. This guy is a real star."

Chapter 8

Bruno drove to the *commissariat* of police in Bergerac. At the front desk he asked to see Peyrefitte, the deputy *commissaire* in charge, whom he knew slightly, and asked him if he knew the whereabouts of the crashed car that had been found with the sniper's bullet inside. It was in the garage, he was told, having been examined by the forensics team. Bruno was welcome to take a look.

"What about the deer it hit?" Bruno asked.

Peyrefitte shrugged and checked on the report for the name of the gendarme, Tarichon, who had found the crashed car and called in the report. Peyrefitte was with the Police Nationale, and the gendarmes were a separate body. Bruno called the office of the gendarme general in Périgueux and explained that he needed to talk to Tarichon. Five minutes later, as Bruno was examining the crashed car, still dusty with fingerprint powder, the general's aide called back to say that Tarichon was manning a roadblock on the Route Nationale 21 at the turnoff for Bergerac airport.

"He'll be with you in a few minutes at the *commissariat* garage," the general's aide confirmed.

The old Peugeot was not a write-off, but close to it. The front-passenger-side wheel was gone, the hood caved in and the headlights smashed. Bruno saw streaks of dried blood and a trace of fur on the broken glass. There was dried mud along the passenger's side of the car, and the rear wheel on that side was flat. It looked like the many other collisions with a deer that Bruno had seen. Then he looked at the front wheel housing and was less sure. Usually when a wheel was smashed off, the bolts that held it were broken or bent. These all seemed normal. He called over one of the mechanics and asked what he thought. The mechanic bent down, wiped the bolts clean with a rag he took from his belt and examined them closely.

"Looks to me as if it was taken off manually, rather than broken off in the collision or when it went into the ditch," the mechanic said. "But the forensics guys never ask us what we think."

"I'm looking for a local cop called Courrèges," came a voice, and Bruno turned to see a gendarme in motorcycle gear. "He's supposed to be in the garage."

"That's me," said Bruno, shaking hands. "You must be Tarichon. Thanks for coming. Do you remember this car?"

"Sure, the one where we found the big bullet in the back, down near Plaisance on the road to Castillonnès."

"Have you ever seen a wheel hub like that before in a crash?" Bruno asked. "All the bolts look normal to me."

"You're right," said Tarichon after bending down and looking at the hub for a moment. "But after searching the car and finding the deer, we just called it in and got a tow truck to bring it here. We put the smashed wheel in the back."

"It's not there now." Bruno turned to the mechanic. "Any idea where it might be?"

The mechanic pointed to the wall behind the car. A broken wheel leaned against a rack of shelves holding cans of oil and lubricants. "Forensics left it there. We have to keep it in case the insurance people want to check it. But a car as old as this, I don't think they'll bother. It can't be worth more than five hundred, even if they don't have to buy a new wheel. Still, those old Peugeots go on forever. Could be a good buy at five hundred."

"Take a look at that wheel, could you, and tell me what you think?" Bruno asked.

"The car went into the ditch for sure," said Tarichon. "You can see the mud."

"Yeah, but look at those bolt holes," the mechanic said. "They're smooth and round, just like normal, not scarred and ripped as you'd expect. This one looks to me as if it was taken off with a wrench."

Tarichon nodded. "Didn't notice at the time, but that's not our job. We just call it in and get the tow truck."

"I'm not blaming you," said Bruno. "I just want to be sure you both agree that this might have been a staged smash."

"Maybe," said Tarichon. "But what about the dead deer that was there. You can see from the front of the car that it was hit by a deer."

"So what happened to the deer?" Bruno asked.

"I took it to the old folks' home in Issigeac," Tarichon replied. "They appreciate a bit of free venison, and my wife's uncle lives there. Better than letting it go to waste."

"Good idea," Bruno replied. "Could you give them a call and ask if it's been eaten yet?"

Tarichon gave him an odd look but pulled out his phone. When it was answered, he said, "Giselle, it's Maurice. Can you put me through to the kitchen, please?" A pause, and then, "Marcel, it's Maurice. That deer I brought in, have you cooked it yet?" Another pause, and then Tarichon replied in a startled voice, "Are you sure?" Another pause, then Tarichon said, "I'm glad it turned out well."

He ended the call and turned to Bruno. "That's a funny thing. It's being roasted now, but the chef's a friend of mine and he says the deer had been shot. He found the bullet. He saved it so I could pick it up sometime."

"So we were conned," said Bruno. "They faked the crash. Could you call your friend again and ask him to hang on to the bullet. We might need it as evidence."

He pulled out his own phone.

"J-J, it's Bruno. That car crash where they found the sniper's bullet was faked. The deer was shot." He explained what he had just learned.

"Why would they fake the crash?" J-J asked.

"You remember when you told me about the golf ball?" Bruno said. "You suggested then that it all looked a little too convenient, the car crash, the sniper's bullet that happened to be left inside, almost as though somebody was laying down clues for us to find. What if it's a distraction?"

"A distraction from what?"

"I'll leave you to work that out, J-J. The gendarme who found the crashed car, Tarichon, he's getting the bullet from the retirement home. Should I tell him to deliver it to you?"

"Sure. But why would they want us to think they're planning to use a sniper if they have something else in mind?"

"I have no idea. Maybe they're already back in Spain while the real plot goes ahead."

Bruno heard a long sigh from J-J before the call ended. Next, Bruno called the general's aide to thank him for his help and said that Tarichon deserved the credit for checking on the deer and finding that the crash had been faked. He closed his phone and asked the mechanic his name. "Suchet," he was told.

"Right, I'll let the commissioner know you spotted that the wheel had been taken off manually. Thanks, both of you."

"Thanks to you, Courrèges," said Tarichon. "I didn't do anything."

"Yes, you did," said Bruno, turning to leave. "Both of you confirmed that we've been set up, so thanks."

Before leaving, Bruno called in at the deputy *commissaire*'s office to thank him and to say that Mechanic Suchet deserved a commendation. Bruno had learned in the army that sharing credit cost him nothing and gained him friends. So did sharing news. He called Isabelle and left a message that the crash had been faked.

Chapter 9

Florence had arranged the meeting with Annette at the riding school, where her two children were accustomed to play by themselves without needing babysitters. What's more, they wouldn't be able to overhear the adults talking. As soon as Florence's car arrived, Balzac was the first to run up to greet its occupants. He led Dora and Daniel to Hector's stable for them to give the big horse his customary apple. Pamela was leading a group of youngsters in a trot around the paddock, and Miranda was in the ring finishing a pony class for children not much older than Florence's twins.

"Thanks for arranging this, Bruno," Florence said. Once the three of them were gathered in Pamela's kitchen, Florence showed Annette the letter from her ex-husband and explained the grim story of the pregnancy, parental pressure to marry, the beatings and Casimir's alcoholism.

"I can't trust him getting involved in the lives of my children," she said.

"Did your lawyer never suggest that you apply for a *déchéance de la paternelle puissance*, stripping him of his legal rights as a father?" Annette asked. "That's what I'd have recommended, and if you'd gone to the family court immediately after the trial, it would probably have been a foregone conclusion. Now it may be too late."

"Where does that leave me and the twins?" Florence asked. "Would I have to give him regular access to them?" Her voice caught, and she swallowed, squared her shoulders and set her jaw. "Could he even move to St. Denis?"

"That would be for the court to decide," Annette said. "The principle is to seek the best interests of the child or children, and also to consider the rights of each parent. There's a presumption that the children should have the opportunity to know and develop a relationship with each of the parents. In this case, Casimir might do better to stay out of the hearing and allow his parents to seek right of access. The court will have to take note of the fact that you have not allowed either set of grandparents to see the children since their birth. I'm sorry, but that could work against you."

Florence looked aghast. "This is awful. His parents never tried to contact me, never came to the divorce court, even refused contact with my own parents. At Casimir's trial, they shouted that it was all my fault. The judge made them leave the courtroom."

"We're trying to get hold of the court transcripts, both for Casimir's trial and the divorce hearing," Bruno said.

"We'll need those," Annette broke in. "Particularly the evidence of his physical abuse of you when pregnant. Did that come up at the divorce hearing?"

"Yes, the lawyer for the women's shelter where I took refuge and the doctor who treated me, they each testified at the divorce hearing."

Annette closed her eyes. "I'm so sorry, Florence. It must have been terrible for you."

"How much of this old testimony can we bring into this new court hearing?" Bruno asked. "Casimir's abuse of Florence has to be a crucial part of the context, no?"

"That will depend on the judge assigned to the case," said Annette. "I might be able to find out which one and how he or she usually thinks."

"What about outside pressures?" Bruno asked. "I'm thinking of press reports about Casimir's brutality, courthouse protests by women's groups, maybe including the elderly woman he widowed and put into a wheelchair, bringing in the cops he assaulted. Could any of that help?"

"It could do more harm than good, depending on the judge," Annette said. "And, Florence, that will be up to you. If we go public with demonstrations and get women's groups involved, there could be implications for your children. You would probably face sexist attacks on social media from aggressive male groups. These things can go viral very fast."

Florence looked stunned. "I couldn't possibly put the children through that. I'm not sure I could handle it myself."

Annette leaned forward to take Florence's hand in her own. "I haven't had long to think about this nor to consult with colleagues, but we have time, Florence. I'll talk to people with more experience than me and see if they think you should apply for the *déchéance* to annul his paternal rights. At least then you'd be able to bring in all the evidence of his alcoholism and the beatings. That might be the way to send up a kind of warning sign to Casimir and his family that you're going to fight this."

"Can you find out whether there's already been a hearing on Casimir's release? If not, when it will be," Bruno asked. "From Casimir's letter, it sounds imminent."

"Isn't there some kind of probation board to decide on his release?" Florence asked. "If so, why was I not contacted for my view? And what about the woman he injured? Was she consulted?"

"Good question," said Annette, rising to go. "I don't know, but I'll find out." She put her hand on Florence's arm. "I understand how awful this must be for you, but you have friends and we're all on your side, yours and the children's. We'll do whatever we can."

"I'd better take the kids home and feed them," said Florence, after Annette had embraced her and left. "I have this terrible feeling that the odds are stacked against me."

"Don't say that," Bruno replied. "We're just beginning to organize ourselves, and we have a lot of cards to play. How much of this can I share with our friends? I've already told the mayor."

"Feel free," she replied. "I was going to tell them all anyway at next Monday's dinner, after the kids were in bed, but maybe it will be better coming from you. And thank you for your support."

"We're all on your side. You're important to us, you and the children, to us all, to your pupils in school, to the town. Most of all to your friends."

"That's why you deserve to know that I called the Canadian consulate today," Florence said. "They have a special program in Quebec for French speakers with qualifications like mine. Qualified science teachers with a chemistry degree are in demand. So I'll pursue that while you and Annette work on the legal side. I'm trying to decide whether I should contact my parents, but I want to sleep on that."

She rose and gave him a peck on the cheek. "Thanks for your help, Bruno. I'll round up the twins. By the way, the children want me to bring them to the tennis club to see you and Pamela and Fabiola play in the tournament."

Bruno headed for the stables where he found Pamela saddling

Primrose for the evening exercise. He'd given her a very sketchy account of Florence's situation earlier, just saying that her ex-husband was about to be released from prison and wanted access to the children.

"What did Annette have to say?" she asked. "Can this ex-husband be kept away?"

"It's complicated, but probably not. Annette will do what she can. We're still trying to find out the timing of all this, whether we can delay her ex-husband's release from jail and what the options are. Florence has already been in touch with the Canadians about emigrating."

"What's to stop him following her over there?"

Bruno shrugged as he saddled Hector. "I don't know, but his prison record probably won't help, not if the Canadians get to know about it, although legally we probably can't stop him from getting a passport." As they put on their riding boots, he asked, "Are Fabiola and Gilles coming with us?"

"They called just before you turned up to say they were on their way. We could save time if we saddle their horses for them. Do you think Gilles is ready for the Warmblood?"

"You're the expert," Bruno replied.

"Let's try it. I'll saddle him if you saddle the Andalusian for Fabiola."

They were slipping on the bridles when Fabiola's electric car, a Renault Zoé, peeped its horn as it drove in. She and Gilles were already in their riding clothes, and within minutes they were all circling the paddock where Gilles was looking nervous on the Warmblood. Bruno had to smile, recalling his own first ride on Hector, the largest and most powerful horse he'd ever known. He felt so high off the ground, so awed at the strength of the horse beneath him, yet now, nothing felt more natural than riding him. Soon, he thought, Gilles will feel just as comfortable with the Warmblood.

After a few circuits of the paddock, Pamela opened the gate and led them outside at a walk, heading up the familiar slope to the ridge that overlooked the valley. Gilles still looked nervous, and Bruno wondered if his uncertainty would communicate itself to his steed. But the Warmblood was a good-natured horse, accustomed to strangers, and he seemed to understand that his rider was no expert. Gilles gained confidence as their walk increased to a gentle trot and then to a canter. Pamela reined in as they reached the ridge, looked back at Gilles and smiled reassuringly.

"You're doing well," she said. "He's comfortable with you. We won't gallop this evening. Let's just canter along the ridge."

It was a subdued ride, partly because of the sedate pace that Pamela maintained for Gilles's sake, partly because Bruno was lost in thought. They were so slow that Balzac could not only keep up with them but he even ran a little ahead, then stopped, turned and gazed at them all reproachfully as if asking what was holding the horses back. Pamela and Fabiola laughed out loud at the dog's expression, bringing Bruno out of his introspection.

Back in Pamela's kitchen, with the horses unsaddled and rubbed down, a glass of wine in front of each of the friends, Bruno recounted the whole story of Florence's unhappy marriage, of Casimir's beatings and his desire now to have regular access to the children. He stressed that Florence at this stage wanted her news shared only with these close friends.

"It's a hell of a compelling story," Gilles said, staring up at the ceiling as if plucking something from the air. "A young woman whose life is almost destroyed by a violent man, and then she rebuilds it while raising her children. She becomes indispensable to her new town. And then the man comes back to threaten it all, claiming to be a reformed character. But is he? Dare she bet her children's lives on that? And does she have a choice? She must come to terms with the fact that it's not her choice to make. Instead, some impersonal thing—called the law—will decide."

"I don't think you should write anything without Florence's approval," Pamela said, and Fabiola swiftly agreed.

"They're right," said Bruno. "This isn't your story. It's for Florence to decide."

Gilles shook his head, as if to clear it, and looked around at the others before speaking again.

"I'd like to try to write the story but only if Annette and Florence agree that publicity would help. Judges are human; they keep an eye on the media and they are sensitive to outside pressures."

"That's what the mayor thinks," Bruno replied, explaining the steps he and the mayor were taking. "Frankly, I'm not so sure. Once this goes public all sorts of pressure groups could get involved, some of them hostile, and that could be grim for the kids."

"We should form a support group for her," said Fabiola. "We could get all the computer club kids involved, and their parents and families."

"And bring in the other teachers, and maybe the teachers' union," Pamela said. "And the mothers of all the other young children in the *maternelle*."

"Remember, nothing of this goes public until Florence says so," Bruno said, rising to leave, when Fabiola asked if Les Troubadours' concert would go ahead.

"People were talking about it at the clinic today," she added.

"Everyone was asking the same question: How can you ban a song these days? And one of the verses is in Occitan? An old lady was singing it in the waiting room and everyone applauded."

"Mon Dieu," said Gilles. "A half-dead language goes viral in *la France profonde.* The Périgord meets the twenty-first century. *Paris Match* will love this."

Chapter 10

Not long after seven the next morning, Bruno packed his tennis gear into his van, installed Balzac in the passenger seat and set out for Château Rock in response to a plea the previous evening from its owner, Rod Macrae. Macrae was an aging Scottish rock musician who had relaunched his career with a successful new song he'd first sung at one of the free concerts organized by Bruno.

"I have to fly to London tomorrow to negotiate a new record deal," Macrae had explained on the phone the previous evening. "Can you puppysit the Bruce for me? I'll be back Wednesday or Thursday."

The Bruce was one of the pups that Balzac had fathered. He was one of two that Bruno had received instead of a stud fee from Claire, who specialized in breeding pedigree bassets. Part of the sale deal was that Bruno would look after the pup when Rod was away. The pup's full name was Robert the Bruce, named after the legendary Scots king who had beaten the English at the Battle of Bannockburn in 1314.

Bruno was happy to agree and so, he believed, was his own dog. Balzac had met his litter about a month after their mother, the stately Diane de Poitiers, had given birth to nine pups.

Bruno had no idea whether Balzac fully comprehended his role in their appearance, but his dog had been delighted to renew his acquaintance with Diane and seemed, after considerable sniffing, to understand that the pups were hers. As he and Diane lay companionably together, Balzac had indulged the way the pups crawled over the pair of them. Bruno had picked out two pups, a young male for Macrae and a female for Yveline. Her dog was named after Gabrielle d'Estrées, a mistress of Bruno's favorite French king, Henri IV.

Gabrielle certainly recognized Balzac whenever she saw him in the market or strolling about with Bruno. Bruno was interested to see whether she would also recognize her brother in the coming days. The people of St. Denis, who had become deeply attached to Bruno's basset hound, had warmed to the frequent sight of father and daughter plodding along side by side with Yveline and Bruno.

"Let me pay you for looking after him," Macrae said when Bruno arrived. The Bruce darted in and out beneath his father's legs, patiently tolerated by Balzac.

"I wouldn't dream of it," Bruno replied, picking up the eiderdown on which the Bruce was accustomed to sleep, along with his familiar leash, feeding bowl and water dish. "I'm curious to see how the Bruce gets on with his father."

"Thanks for this, Bruno," said Macrae. "I'll miss the little fellow, but I know you and Balzac will take good care of him."

"Try to get back in time for the Friday concert. Les Troubadours will be playing their new hit, 'Song for Catalonia.'"

"Yeah, I heard about that," Rod replied. "I'll do my best. I downloaded the song onto my phone and I'll play it for my agent. Maybe they can get a British record deal out of it."

Back in St. Denis with Balzac and the Bruce, each on a separate leash behind him, Bruno headed for the Saturday morning market. A much smaller and more local affair than the big Tuesday market, it covered only the square in front of the *mairie*. There were perhaps twenty stalls, mainly selling local foodstuffs, although there were Vietnamese and Mauritian food stalls, and another selling specialist African coffees and chocolate. Bruno had a particular affection for the hardware stall, without which no rural market was complete, selling pins and needles, pots and pans and utensils, pocketknives, pan scrubbers and wraparound aprons.

Bruno knew all the stallholders and greeted them by name, grinning at the shouts of welcome for the new puppy as he headed for Fauquet's café, where the Bruce would be introduced to the best croissants in the region. Balzac loved them and picked up his pace to secure Bruno's favorite table by the stone balustrade overlooking the river and the quayside below. Fauquet came out with Bruno's coffee and a basket of croissants, *chocolatines* and *pains aux raisins*. As usual, one of the croissants that had been deformed in the oven, which Fauquet normally would not sell, was on top of the pile, specially selected for Balzac.

"Meet Balzac's son, called the Bruce," Bruno said. "I'm looking after him for a few days while Rod Macrae is in London."

"He's a little charmer," said Fauquet, breaking off two chunks of the oddly shaped croissant, one for Balzac and the other, smaller one for the puppy. The Bruce sniffed it suspiciously, then looked at his father to see Balzac wolfing down his own portion. The pup then gave his chunk of croissant a hesitant lick before devouring it. He looked up hopefully for more, but Fauquet had other matters on his mind.

"So what's this about Florence having a husband back from the dead or, at least, back from prison?" Fauquet asked, his voice low so that only Bruno could hear. "Eight years, he got, or so I heard."

"Where did you hear that?"

"From Rosalie, one of the cleaners at the clinic, Madame Eavesdropper in Chief."

"I always thought you were the king of gossip, Fauquet," Bruno said, buying time to think how best for Florence's sake to handle this inquiry. Rosalie must have heard, or overheard, Fabiola saying something.

Fauquet raised his head, almost proudly. "I have to be, don't I? Who wants to go to a café that doesn't have the latest word?"

"If what you hear is that her divorced husband is trying to come back after years in prison, you're missing the point," Bruno said, thinking that the best strategy was to be honest about the reasons for Florence's fear. "She's still afraid of him. He used to beat her, even when he knew she was pregnant. That's in the past, we hope, but the real issue is whether St. Denis loses Florence. She's thinking of immigrating to Canada as her only option to be sure of keeping him away from her and the children."

"Canada? Why there?"

"A Frenchwoman with a science degree, a trained teacher with two French-speaking kids, is just the kind of immigrant Quebec wants. They'll welcome her with open arms, a guaranteed job and free housing. And their gain is our loss."

"But it's freezing, covered in snow half the year."

"Depends on the alternative," said Bruno.

"Putain de merde," Fauquet said. "You know as well as I do that she needs more of a reason than that to keep her here, something personal and lasting. She wants a future."

"How do you mean? She has her future here."

"Bruno, don't be an idiot," said Fauquet, glaring at him. "Do I have to spell it out? What she needs is a father for those kids, a good man in her life, maybe another kid or two, a proper family."

"I think she's had enough of men after that ex-husband of hers."

Fauquet shook his head and continued staring at Bruno. Then he shrugged, sighed loudly and began clearing away Bruno's plate and coffee cup, angrily muttering something to himself as he stalked off.

"I'll have another coffee," said Bruno to Fauquet's retreating back. "Make it two and bring back the croissants. Here comes Yveline with Gabrielle."

He rose to greet Yveline and then bent to say hello to Gabrielle, who was already sniffing noses with the Bruce, clearly recognizing him. Then she sniffed Balzac, who responded amiably and then lay down to let the puppies clamber over him.

"I've arranged reinforcements from the gendarme general in Périgueux for the concert," Yveline began, sitting down and selecting a croissant. "And it looks like their mayor and the prefect will both be coming. I hope this doesn't interfere with the tennis tournament. By the way, are you playing today?"

"Yes, Pamela and I are in the mixed doubles, and we have a match this afternoon, but I'm not sure who the opponents are. How about you?"

This was the first week of the St. Denis tennis club tournament. Bruno had already been knocked out of the singles, and he and Gilles from the men's doubles. But he and Pamela knew each other's game so well that they had become a formidable duo on the court.

"I have a singles match this afternoon with some visitor who is supposed to be really good," Yveline said. "If I manage to win that, I'll be in the final. Are you helping with the feast tomorrow?"

The club had a tradition of roasting a wild boar for a communal supper on each of the two Sundays of the tournament.

The season to hunt boar began on August 15, but Bruno usually waited for the general opening of the hunting season in mid-September, when he could pursue the wily *bécasse,* which he found the most delicious of the game birds. That was what he'd trained Balzac to hunt. But he always joined in the roasting of the boar.

"I hope so, but the combination of Florence's trouble and this concert is taking up most of my time. But I won't let down Pamela for the mixed doubles. I'll manage somehow."

Bruno set out on a second patrol of the market, but the crowds had thickened in the rue de Paris, and the sight of the young puppy triggered an endless chorus of oohs and aahs, from the locals and the stallholders as much as the tourists. From the church he could hear the sound of organ music and then of chanting voices. It was choir practice.

He slipped inside and took a seat at the rear with Balzac sitting at his feet and the Bruce on his lap. Another dozen or so people were scattered around the church. One, sitting in the row ahead of him, turned and offered Bruno a program of the music they were rehearsing. It was Brosseil, the town's *notaire,* dressed in his usual formal style of suit and tie with cuff links. His wife sang in the choir, and his finger tapped the name of the piece the choir was singing, Vivaldi's *Gloria.*

"Florence and my wife are singing the two solos in the third movement, which comes next," he whispered, giving the Bruce a friendly pat before turning back to watch the choir.

It was cool in the church and Balzac sprawled at Bruno's feet, as if trying to get as much of his body in contact with the cold stone floor as he could. Bruno held the Bruce firmly and closed his eyes as the music started, a classic opening of brisk baroque before the two women's voices came in, now as if conversing and then the two of them singing in unison, Florence's soprano and the other voice a little lower. Bruno did not know whether Madame Brosseil was contralto or mezzo-soprano, but he knew it made for a marvelous balance. This was yet another reason to keep Florence in St. Denis, he thought.

As he enjoyed the music, Bruno's mind began to wander, exploring thoughts he'd never considered before, like Florence's presence in a church choir, singing most Sundays and being part of the service, when she had sounded so angry at the devout Polish Catholicism of her own upbringing. She had been outraged, furious at her own parents for insisting that divorce and abortion were unthinkable, mortal sins, and that marriage to a brutal drunk was to be suffered and endured in the name of holy matrimony. It was hard to believe that a mother could inflict so much grief on her own daughter in the name of a religion that maintained that God is Love.

Even as he sat in the familiar old church, where he'd attended weddings and funerals, and stood by the font at baptisms promising to abjure the devil and all his works, Bruno felt his own view of religion was a long way from orthodox Catholicism. He had never understood the insistence that priests should remain celibate, until a cynical fellow soldier had suggested it was all about property, to ensure that no priest could have legitimate children who could claim to be heirs. Everything should belong to the church. And yet that same soldier had babbled prayers, just like Bruno and every other man in the unit, when they took shelter from an artillery barrage in slit trenches. Though he did not go to confession, nor believe in an afterlife, Bruno still found something comforting and familiar in the church services he attended and in this glorious, uplifting music he was hearing now. Even the puppy in his arms seemed awed, and certainly calmed by it.

Looking around the church, Bruno wondered if Florence had

spoken to Father Sentout about the prospect of an unwanted ex-husband seeking to return to some shred of family life. He was a wise and understanding old man, the perfect priest for St. Denis, with his devotion to the pleasures of the table and his enthusiastic embrace of the special needs of a rural commune in the Périgord. Each year he held a service of blessing for the local hunting club, and his loyalty to the town's rugby team was legendary. The good father would have a very early lunch on Sunday to be there in time for the match of the second team and remain at his place in the front row of the stands, whatever the weather, until the end of the first team match some four hours later. If a match ran into extra time, there would be a line of people waiting for him to hear their confessions before the evening Mass. This, of course, was not unwelcome, since the sinners knew that in his haste to rattle through his duties, Father Sentout would issue only the briefest of penances. So Bruno was quietly confident that whatever his views on divorce and ex-convicts, Father Sentout would act in the best interests of St. Denis.

Reluctantly, but with a sense of duty tugging him to his feet, Bruno left the church, blinking as his eyes adjusted to the bright sunshine. The crowd was even thicker now, so he kept the Bruce against his chest and headed back up the Grande Rue toward the *mairie.* He'd have to find somewhere secure for the puppy before the main market on Tuesday. Perhaps he could leave him in one of the vacant stalls at the stables, with Balzac to keep him company. Then he glanced up at the *mairie.* His office had a balcony with a stone balustrade—that might work.

He went up and opened his office window. He climbed out, lowered the Bruce to the ground and helped Balzac over the low sill. Back indoors he filled the water bowl he kept for Balzac and put that and Balzac's sleeping cushion onto the balcony floor. The gaps in the balustrade were too narrow for Balzac but perhaps not for a puppy; luckily they were too high for him to reach. Pleased at finding a solution, he closed the window and went back downstairs to make a more thorough patrol of the town. Wandering up an alley to a quiet residential quarter, he saw the mayor and his partner, Jacqueline, at work in the shaded part of their garden.

"Ah, Bruno, come in, come in—you provide a perfect excuse to pause for a drink," said the mayor. "How does a glass of cider sound?"

"It sounds great, Monsieur le Maire." He embraced Jacqueline and shook the mayor's hand before they went to sit under the awning by the kitchen door.

"All quiet in the market?" the mayor asked, returning with a bottle and three glasses. "Where's Balzac?"

"With his son, Rod Macrae's puppy, on the balcony outside my office. I should never have tried walking him through the market, he's too little."

"Another day bring him here, we'll happily look after him," said Jacqueline.

"Thank you, I will. Tell me, have either of you heard of a man named Joël Martin, an expert on Occitan culture? Apparently, he wrote the song all this fuss is about."

"Of course I know him, and so do you, Bruno. He's a fellow member of SHAP, wrote a couple of decent articles for the journal on Bertan de Born and the other troubadours."

"Do you know where I could find him?" Bruno asked.

"You've been a member now for what, three or four years," the mayor replied. "Joël spent a lot of that time in Barcelona, but I heard he was back, living with some relatives in Urval. He used to live in Bergerac, teaching at the lycée, before he met that Catalan woman and married her. I had wondered if we might be able to get him a teaching post here. I don't know what he's doing for money."

"This song of his has become quite a hit, so I assume he gets royalties, and I gather he has thousands of followers on social media," said Bruno.

"Mon Dieu," exclaimed Jacqueline, who was thumbing her smartphone. "He's all over the place. This is interesting—he's got some separate websites, one of poetry, another on Périgord history, and there's even one on how to teach yourself Occitan. I'd very much like to meet him. What's he like?"

"He's tall with curly red hair," said the mayor. "He wrote one article that I recall about Duke William IX of Aquitaine, the first troubadour whose work had come down to us, and grandfather to our own Eleanor of Aquitaine."

"A duke who was also a troubadour?" asked Bruno, grinning. "I thought these grandees sat back at their groaning tables and waited for lesser mortals to entertain them."

The mayor eyed him beadily. "You are letting your politics peek through your judgment, my boy. Duke William was a character after your own heart, a soldier who fought with the Spaniards against the Moors, and Joël suggests that he became a troubadour after hearing the Arabian music there. He kept some of the captives he took in Spain at his court in Bordeaux while waiting for their ransom to be paid. And that was supposedly where Eleanor of Aquitaine developed her own love for the music and poetry of the troubadours. She became their greatest patron."

"I imagine SHAP will have Joël Martin's phone number," Bruno said. "I'd like to get in touch."

"He has an email here, OccitanJoel.Martin at orange.fr," Jacqueline replied, and Bruno took out his notebook and scribbled it down. Meanwhile the mayor was calling somebody on his own phone.

"He's getting death threats," Jacqueline said in alarm as the mayor ended his call. "*Mon Dieu,* there's some vicious stuff about Joël Martin on social media, and about that Troubadour group of yours, Bruno."

"That's why I need to brief the mayor," Bruno said. He explained the concern of the security staff in Paris that Joël might be a target.

"Would that have anything to do with that email you sent to the hunting clubs about some heavy rifle that you're interested in?" the mayor asked, passing Bruno a note. "Here's Joël's mobile number. The SHAP secretary had it. So, should we be worried here in St. Denis?"

"I don't really know, but there's a local alert about keeping our eyes and ears open for any evidence of a heavy-duty rifle. A special kind of bullet was found in a faked crash of a Spanish car. The security people promise to keep us in the loop," Bruno replied calmly.

He did not want to say more. The mayor was discreet, but Jacqueline was not. He called the number the mayor had given him, got an answering service and left a message explaining that he wanted to discuss the St. Denis concert and asking for his call to be returned. He declined Jacqueline's offer to share their lunch, pleading that he'd rather not play in a tennis tournament with a full stomach.

Chapter 11

When he returned to his office to liberate Balzac and the Bruce, he saw through the window that they were contentedly snoozing together, the Bruce curled up against Balzac's tummy. Quietly, he took a photo with his phone and emailed it to Isabelle in Paris. Within moments, his phone rang as he'd hoped it would.

"I'm going to blow it up, get it framed and put it by my bed," she said. "Which puppy is it?"

"Robert the Bruce. I'm looking after him while Rod Macrae has a business meeting in London. Balzac is being an excellent father, even when he had to cope with two of them. Yveline's puppy joined us for croissants at Fauquet's." He paused. "I thought I might be hearing from you before this, on that official matter."

"I'm in the office but is your line secure?" she asked.

"Yes, the green light's on."

"My Spanish counterpart says the new government in Madrid just wants to let the dust settle, no dramas, no extradition demands. He was as surprised as we were by the banning of the song. He assumes it has to do with internal politics in the coalition, but he's trying to find out more."

Isabelle explained that there had been an organized campaign to spread fake news on Spanish social media, some of it linked to Russia's Internet Research Agency, which had launched a major effort to stir up divisions in Europe. After fake-news campaigns on Ukraine and on allegations of NATO rearmament and aggression, Europe was the main target of the Russian campaign, even more than its better-known incursions into American politics.

"As well as bailing out our Front National with a nine-million-euro loan from a Moscow bank, the Russian internet guys did it to us over the *gilets jaunes* protests, putting up fake documents on blogging sites like *Medium* and then recycling them on dozens of different websites," Isabelle went on. "They've been doing the same over Catalonia, claiming Catalan extremists are preparing for a terrorist campaign. At the same time, they've been pushing other stories on different websites claiming that the Spanish government has set up a dirty-tricks group called the Novios to target the independence movement."

"Novios, does that mean 'new guys' or something like it?" Bruno asked.

"No, it means 'bridegrooms.' It stands for the Novios de la Muerte, the bridegrooms of death," she replied. "It's the old name for the Spanish Foreign Legion, which General Franco used to command in the 1930s. It was his elite force in the Spanish Civil War, so there's a fascist connection which the fake-news campaign is stressing. There's been nothing yet about the concert in St. Denis, but we're keeping an eye on it. I'll call you back once I know more."

"Thanks," he said, and then had a sudden thought. "Do you have access to the justice ministry's database? I need to find out the release date from prison of the ex-husband of one of our teachers."

"No, I don't, but you have a friend who does. That jazz singer who did the Josephine Baker concert, Amélie. I had a drink with her the other day and she's doing some part-time work with the ministry, helping with some commission on prison reform. She'll have access."

"Good idea, thanks, I'll call her."

He had met Amélie when she had come to St. Denis as part of a study on local policing. They had become friends after he'd heard her sing, and he invited her to give one of the town's summer concerts. It had been a triumph. Then he'd arranged for her to perform at a special gala concert of Josephine Baker's songs at the Jazz Age superstar's old home in the Dordogne Valley, Château des Milandes.

"Bruno!" said Amélie. "How nice to hear from you. I was just thinking about you when I heard this Catalonia song that's going viral. I looked up the group's website and saw that they're giving a concert in St. Denis next week. I might have guessed you'd be involved."

"Come on down for the weekend. I'll get you a ringside seat, and you can meet them and see lots of your old friends. We miss you, Amélie."

"I'll try to get away, but I have a new boyfriend."

"Bring him, too. You can both stay at my place."

"We're not quite that close yet," she said, laughing.

"Alone or accompanied, you're always welcome. But that's not why I'm calling." He explained about Florence's ex-husband and his need to find out Casimir's release date.

"I'll be happy to help, Bruno, but it will have to be tomorrow. Right now I'm heading home to change and then straight out on a date. Email me the details and I'll check him out in the morning."

Bruno had some time before going to the tennis club, so he opened his computer and launched a search for "Catalan terrorism." There were several newspaper articles on the arrest of several members of a group called ERT, standing for Technical Response Teams of a Committee to Defend the Republic. The committee claimed to be committed to nonviolent ways to resist the Spanish police. The press reports said that nine members of the ERT had been arrested for possession of explosives and maps of government buildings. But then the cases against them had not been taken seriously by the courts; half of the alleged "terrorists" had been released. Another press report identified neo-Nazi groups chanting *"Sieg heil"* and using baseball bats as they attacked demonstators among the crowds protesting against the arrest of the Catalan government ministers. The report added that other groups involved in violence were singing "Cara al Sol," the anthem of the Spanish Falange, the fascist movement in the 1930s.

The usual story, thought Bruno; claim and counterclaim. Except that this time the courts had dismissed the charges on possession of explosives. He plowed on with his research, interested to find that there was a Spanish equivalent of the Front National in France, called Vox. They were intensely nationalist, opposed to Islamic immigration but welcoming migration from Latin America "to help repopulate Spain." They were also opposed to what they called "radical left-wing feminism" and called for a return to traditional gender roles. They wanted to annul the self-governing powers of Spain's regions like Catalonia. This was not his country, not his cause and not his fight, Bruno concluded. But the concert and the presence of Joël Martin could bring this foreign quarrel to St. Denis.

It was time to head to the tennis club. Bruno drove first to the riding school and put Balzac and the Bruce in Hector's stall to see how the puppy would react. Bruno had been a little nervous about the tiny dog and the enormous horse, but the Bruce seemed content as long as Balzac was there, and sniffed back politely when Hector nuzzled him.

"A pity humans aren't so sensible," Bruno said to Pamela as he held open the door of his van for her. She was already dressed in her tennis whites. He put her sports bag in the back beside his own and drove to the club.

It was a futuristic building, a series of stepped pyramids, all covered in solar panels and with huge containers to collect rainwater for the club's vegetable and herb garden. There were male and female changing rooms and an impressive kitchen with a well-stocked pantry and freezers. The main room, with a bar in one corner, was supposed to be a clubroom where board meetings could be held, but it was mainly used for dining. Each evening during the tournament, volunteers prepared dinners for those who signed up. Sliding glass doors opened onto three hard courts and a covered court where the regulars played in winter.

Bruno and Pamela were warming up on the far court when their opponents, Horst and Clothilde, arrived. Horst was a German professor of archaeology, now based in the Périgord at the prehistory museum of Les Eyzies, where Clothilde was a senior curator. Pamela and Bruno had each been witnesses when the two archaeologists, after two decades of an on-and-off love affair, had finally been married by the mayor. They tossed a coin for the choice of ends and, given the heat of the day, they agreed to play only a single set.

Serving well, with a high kicking bounce that spun the ball away from the receiver, Pamela won the first game easily. Bruno received Clothilde's smooth, competent serve and played it back fast down the middle. Horst scrambled for the return, scooped it high, and Pamela put away the smash. Pamela played the next serve back at the feet of Clothilde, who tried to play it wide of Bruno; he was there for the easy volley. And so it went, Pamela scoring most of the points until it was five games to one, and Bruno had to serve for the match.

"Good luck, Bruno," came a familiar shout, and he turned to see Florence and her children standing by the side netting. He raised his racket in salute and hoped he wouldn't disappoint Daniel and Dora.

A little more pressure was just what he didn't need, Bruno thought. Almost inevitably, he double-faulted. Feeling like a fool he apologized to Pamela. His next serve was little better. Horst fired it back, but Pamela seemed to have all the time in the world to run in and make the volley.

"You're winning this game on your own," Bruno murmured to his partner as he went back for his next serve.

"No, you're lulling them into a false sense of confidence," she replied, smiling.

Maybe that was what made his next serve his best of the day, an ace that scorched past Horst. Forty–fifteen. Match point. His next serve was competent, but Clothilde's return to him was better, and his ball hit the net. Forty–thirty.

"You are not nervous," he told himself as he walked back to serve to Horst. He bounced the ball, wondering whether to try to repeat his previous ace but doubting whether he could. He tried it and heard Clothilde's call, "Out!" His second service was a deceptively slow ball with a lot of spin that forced Horst to run in and scramble to scoop it high. Again Pamela was there to take the easy smash. Game, set and match, most of it thanks to Pamela, as Bruno told the other couple when he went to the net to shake hands.

"You'll have to struggle in your next match," Horst said. "It's those traveling professionals, the ones with the camper in the parking lot."

The tennis clubs of southern France that offered a decent cash prize to the winners of their tournaments had become increasingly popular with young European players from other countries. Strong amateurs or semi-professionals spent a couple of months on the small-town circuit, earning enough to pay for their summer vacation. They could use the club kitchens and bathrooms and play every day, swim in the town pool and use the laundromat. Usually it was a young couple or two male friends. But this camper contained two couples, and they were entered in every part of the tournament: male and female singles, male and female doubles, and mixed doubles. If they won all the matches, they'd walk away with five hundred euros between them.

Bruno knew they had made similar sums at Ribérac and at Nontron, and they were entered in the big tournament at Périgueux, where the prize money was larger. Tennis had never been like that when Bruno was their age.

"Old age and cunning can sometimes outdo youth and inexperience," said Pamela.

"Not on a tennis court," said Horst, grinning. "But we wish you the best of luck. You played well today, Pamela."

There was some scattered applause from the score or so of spectators seated outside the clubhouse as they walked in, and Bernard, the club secretary, gave Bruno a punch on the arm, saying, "Only one double fault today. You're coming along!"

Bruno ordered four glasses of beer at the bar, orange juice for Florence and her children and signed the chit. It was customary for the winners to pay for the drinks, despite Horst's kind offer. He took the drinks out to the others, standing to watch another game in progress. One of the young visitors was playing against Yveline, the female club champion. It looked to be a fairly even game, then Yveline hit a terrific shot to a far corner, winning the game and the set.

Bruno was looking forward to the decisive third set when he heard his phone ringing in his sports bag. He'd changed the tone from the "Marseillaise," which too many other people used, to the "Chant des Partisans," the anthem of the wartime Resistance whose opening drumbeats were unmistakable. He pulled out his phone, and the screen showed it was J-J calling.

"Why is it that when I'm checking on someone who's on the special watch list, I find out that the last call to him was from you?" J-J began.

"Because I was trying to meet him ahead of the concert at which his Catalonia song will be played," Bruno replied. "Why is Joël on the watch list?"

"Because a few months ago Spain wanted to extradite him," J-J answered. "His sister called to say he hadn't been home and she was worried. The sniper alert means we take it seriously."

"Anything unusual at his house?"

"No signs of trouble, doors locked, front and rear. His alarm hadn't been triggered. His car is here, but his bicycle has gone. His sister says he always tells them when he's going, but she hasn't heard from him since yesterday morning."

"Have you called his friends in the band?" Bruno asked, putting a hand to his free ear to reduce the sound of applause from the spectators watching Yveline's match. Damn it, he thought, convinced he was missing a memorable game.

"His sister did that already, and they have no idea, at least the two guys she reached."

"Give me a minute and I'll try." Bruno hung up and called Flavie's mobile. It took a while, but she finally answered, sounding sleepy.

"Flavie, it's Bruno. We're trying to find Joël. It seems he's been missing since yesterday, and his sister called the police. They want to be sure he's all right. Would you have any idea where he might be?"

She didn't answer at first but seemed to put her hand over the phone, since he heard a muffled conversation in the background before she spoke again. "Let me try and reach him. I think he's got a new mobile. I'll try to get him to call you."

"Okay, thanks. It's pretty urgent." Bruno wondered if that muffled conversation had been with Joël and whether he'd spent the night with Flavie. That would annoy J-J, who could be caustic if he felt his time was being wasted. Bruno checked the scoreboard. Yveline and the visitor were tied at three games each. His phone rang and his screen told him the number calling him was unknown. He answered with his rank and name.

"This is Joël Martin, and I think we know each other from SHAP," came the voice. "Flavie just called to say you'd been trying to reach me. What can I do for you?"

"It's not just me trying to reach you, Joël, but also your sister, who sounded the alarm. There's also Commissaire Jean-Jacques Jalipeau, head of detectives for the department. Because of the threats being made against you and the band, he dropped everything to visit your home to see if you were all right. Do you understand how serious this is for you, for Flavie and the others?"

"It's just politicians scoring points, amplified by social-media blowhards, lonely jerks who think they're somebody because they screech out crap on the internet."

"You may not take this seriously, and given your reaction I wish I didn't have to, but we police have no choice but to follow this up for your own protection," Bruno said, his own anger putting an edge into his voice. "I don't know what the cost of all this is in police time, but it could make a big hole in your song's royalties. And this false alarm makes us less eager to help if there's a next time."

"I'm sorry, Bruno, but something suddenly came up. I should have called my sister."

"I suggest you call Commissaire Jalipeau first to apologize and then your sister." He recited J-J's number from memory, and then added, "I wanted to reach you anyway to talk about the concert next Friday. Were you planning to say something to the crowd?"

"Yes, of course. I need to put the song into its political context of the Spanish repression of Catalan independence and ask people to support our freedom."

"If this looks like it's becoming a political event, rather than the Occitan concert that Les Troubadours have been giving for years, the mayor may have to cancel it. That's not what the residents of St. Denis are paying for. Talk about Occitan all you like, but if you want a political rally you should organize your own meeting."

"You want to ban us?" Joël's voice was suddenly aggressive, almost hostile.

"I don't want to ban anything, least of all Flavie and Les Troubadours, whom I admire and enjoy. But I know the mayor and the town council, and a lot of the people who'll be turning up. They want a concert and they're not interested in offering political platforms."

"But my 'Song for Catalonia' is itself political," Joël replied sharply. "This Spanish attempt to ban it rips the mask off the Madrid government and shows them for what they really are, nationalist bullies who reject a referendum vote for independence."

"I understand what you're saying, and the mayor doesn't want any other country trying to decide what music French citizens are allowed to hear," Bruno said, forcing himself to be patient. "So feel free to talk about the importance of keeping the Occitan tradition alive. But don't abuse the town's hospitality, after all these years we've backed Flavie. Think about her and the band, Joël, and their hopes for the future."

"What do you mean?" Joël asked less aggressively.

"This isn't just about politics, it's about people, Flavie and her band," Bruno said. "This could be the concert that gives them the chance to take off. That's what your song has given them. Don't wreck it to play politics and get yourself booed off the stage."

"I see what you mean," Joël said after a pause. "I'm sorry about wasting police time."

"Tell that to Commissaire Jalipeau," said Bruno, not mollified but pleased that Joël had apologized. As always when Bruno was angry, he calmed down quickly, and told himself there was much about this man to admire. "We can't afford to lose what you're doing on Périgord history," he said.

"Thanks, I'm glad. Look, Bruno, I'm sorry for causing this alarm."

"Well, you can expect a real tongue-lashing from Jalipeau," Bruno said. "Bear in mind that if anything happens to you, it will be him and his team who get into trouble. The least you can do is keep him informed."

"I promise to call him right after this and apologize, and I'm sorry to have caused trouble. Perhaps I could take you to dinner one evening this coming week."

"I'd like that," said Bruno. "After a concert I usually invite the band to my place for supper. Perhaps you'd like to join us on Friday evening?"

"That would be great, thanks, but I'll hope to see you before that. Now I'd better call your commissioner."

Chapter 12

Bruno put Joël's number into his phone's memory and went back outside to watch what remained of the tennis, only to see Yveline sprawled on the ground and Fabiola with her medical bag attending to her.

"Sprained ankle," Fabiola said grimly, coming over to him when she'd done. "I told her to stop, but she wants to play on."

The visitor applauded Yveline when she limped back to receive the next service, which was decent of her. However, she made no allowances for Yveline's injury, deliberately alternating her strokes between one side of the court and the other so that Yveline had no chance to reach the ball, far less return it. Her opponent briskly took the next three games to win the match, and then ran courteously to the other court to shake Yveline's hand. Bruno joined in the applause as Yveline limped back into the clubhouse where Fabiola had already prepared a bag of ice to strap to her ankle.

"Well, barring a miracle cure, it looks like I just lost my partner for the ladies' doubles," said Pamela. "And if the guy that young woman plays with in the mixed doubles is as good as she is, I think we'll be knocked out tomorrow. Do you think it makes sense to have these open tournaments, or should we restrict it to members of clubs in this *département*?"

"You can argue it both ways," Bruno replied. "It's frustrating for us to know we're going to get knocked out of our own tournaments by these visitors, but I think being open to outside players helps to raise the quality of our tennis overall. You're a good example of someone rising to the occasion. If we always play the same people, we don't improve."

"Hmm." Pamela sounded unconvinced. "What were those calls that took you away? Police business?"

He nodded and grinned at her. "The law never sleeps."

"Nor do the tennis club volunteers," she replied. "We have work to do, getting this evening's buffet supper ready. I checked with Xavier, and he says we have twenty-four signed up, and we always get some extras. We'd better plan for thirty."

To raise funds, the club members volunteered to take turns to prepare a simple meal each evening. Charging fifteen euros for the food and three euros for a glass of wine, they usually took in more than enough cash to provide the tournament's prize money. The surplus went into the travel fund that paid for the junior team's transport to away games.

"It's all under control," Bruno said. "I brought some salad, peppers and tomatoes from my garden and put them in the fridge. We'll have gazpacho to start with, then chicken with baked potatoes and various salads, then apple pie. I checked and we have some ten-liter boxes of wine still unopened, and Gilles said he'd give us a hand to prepare the salads, so I think we'll be fine."

His phone gave the ping of an incoming text message. It was from Flavie, saying, "I heard what you said to Joël. Thanks, Bruno."

So Joël had been with Flavie, as Bruno suspected. That could cause some trouble with Arnaut, her admirer in the band. People's love lives, he reflected, could cause just as many problems as politics, an experience to which he knew he was not immune.

He took a bowl of hot water and cleaning liquid into the main room and began to wash down the four long tables where they would eat. His hunting friend Stéphane, who was also the local cheese maker, was manning the bar, but with everybody watching the matches he came to give Bruno a hand, opening the folding chairs to set them at each table. Pamela prepared bouquets of the wildflowers she had brought, putting them into small glass yogurt pots.

The three of them stood back to admire their work, when the drumbeat of Bruno's phone began again. This time it was Father Sentout.

"Bruno, I reached Father Francis in Bergerac and asked about Florence's husband. He's there already. He arrived yesterday, and he's been helping to pack boxes at the food bank. I thought you'd like to know. Father Francis spoke well of him and tells me Casimir is hoping eventually to go to a seminary to become a teaching brother, probably with the De La Salle order."

"You mean he's going to become a priest?" Bruno asked.

"Good heavens, no. There's not a bishop in France who would ordain him. In the eyes of the church he's still married to Florence. There may be some churches in other parts of the world who might turn a blind eye to married priests, but not here. No, he would be a lay brother, dedicated to teaching, which would probably mean leaving France. Almost all of the De La Salle schools are abroad."

Bruno thanked Father Sentout and looked back along the front of the clubhouse to where Yveline was sitting with her leg propped on a stool. Florence was beside her, both of them smiling as Dora put smacking kisses on Yveline's strapped ankle.

"She's kissing it better," said Daniel. "That's what *maman* always does when we get a bump."

Bruno felt a lump rise in his throat. No, he couldn't ruin this moment by telling Florence that her ex-husband was now out of prison and in Bergerac, just forty kilometers away. He walked a little way off and called Annette to inform her. There was no reply, so he left a message, thinking how much harder it would be to curtail Casimir's newfound freedom than to prevent his release in the first place.

"You look like you've had bad news," said Pamela, coming up from behind him, carrying a box filled with tomatoes, cucumbers and lettuces for the buffet. Behind her came Miranda with her children and their grandfather Jack Crimson.

"Sorry, some police business," Bruno replied, taking the box from her and heading for the club kitchen. He took his own vegetables from the fridge and began to wash and chop everything. Jack came in and unloaded various cheeses from a large bag while Miranda put a dozen *pains,* the double-sized, fat baguettes, onto the kitchen counter.

The three of them began preparing bowls of salad while Bruno started to load the food mixer with chopped peppers and cucumbers to make his summer soup. He added a small wineglass of olive oil, another of white wine and some crushed garlic. Pamela began blanching the tomatoes for peeling before adding them to the soup. The mixer could make ten bowls of soup at a time. Once each batch was made, Bruno poured it into a jug and put it in the fridge to chill. Bruno had brought six jars of his venison pâté and in the club's refrigerator were six chickens for roasting. Fauquet had promised six apple pies.

Once the salads were done and all the potatoes wrapped in tinfoil, Miranda and her father strolled out to watch the tennis, leaving Bruno and Pamela to prepare the chickens. Bruno stuffed three with a mix of onions, sage and garlic, and Pamela stuffed her three with lemons and sprigs of thyme. They loaded them into giant roasting trays and put them all with the potatoes into the oven.

Bruno helped Pamela to wash up.

"That call you said was police business," she said. "You looked really shaken."

"I was," he replied. "Still am, for that matter. It's about Florence's ex-husband. I just heard he's been released already and is in Bergerac. I didn't want to spoil the day by telling her, not without talking to Annette about what we might do now."

"Poor Florence," she said. "You'll have to tell her at some point."

"I know, but I'm worried about her. I think you or Fabiola ought to be there when she learns that he's out."

At that moment Bruno's phone rang again. This time it was Amélie calling from Paris. He could hear the clicking of laptop keys as she explained what she had found on the database.

"I thought you were going out on a date this evening," he said.

"It got canceled," she said briskly. "Don't ask."

"So, here we are. Casimir Maczek was released Thursday morning with a travel warrant to Bergerac, an approved job awaiting him at the Action Catholique food bank and an approved address at the presbytery of St. Jacques-en-Bergeraçois," she said. "There's a note saying that he has to wear an ankle bracelet that records his location at all times. After completing a successful year on this probationary release, he can apply for the rest of his sentence to be suspended."

"Does he have to stay in Bergerac, or can he move around?"
Bruno asked.

"Under supervision and if required for work, yes, he can travel
but not stay away overnight. He has to sleep at the presbytery in
Bergerac."

"I thought there had to be a hearing with a judge."

"The hearing was on Monday at the prison. It was thought to
be in the interests of his children, and there were letters of support
from both sets of grandparents."

"But nothing from the mother. Isn't that unusual?" Bruno
asked.

"Very unusual, almost unprecedented. But there's a note on
file from the prison chaplain saying that nobody had an address
for the prisoner's ex-wife."

"Well, Casimir was able to send her a letter, care of the teachers' union," Bruno said. "Apparently because of the computer in
the prison library he'd come across a press release naming her as a
new member of the executive board."

"If he didn't let the court know how to contact her, that was
deliberate deception. Annette can use that to file an appeal against
his release and for a restraining order to stop him visiting St.
Denis. I'll let you know about coming down to see you all."

"Thanks for this, Amélie. How was your concert last night?"

"I did a couple of Josephine Baker numbers as well as my usual
torch songs, and the concert went really well," she said. "But I'm
not so sure about the new boyfriend, since he decided he had better things to do tonight. So if I come down, I'll be alone."

"In that case, he doesn't deserve you."

"Listen, Bruno, don't get your hopes up about getting this
thing with Casimir reversed," she said. "The prisons are so full
right now, they're desperate to reduce the overcrowding."

"I understand. Let me know about the weekend and thank you again for your help."

He took Pamela well out of earshot of the group on the terrace and explained what Amélie had said and that he'd wait until tomorrow to tell Florence.

"Does Annette know about this yet?" Pamela asked.

Bruno shook his head. "I left a message for her to call me. She's already preparing to apply for a restraining order to prevent his coming to St. Denis."

"Do you think Florence is being realistic about this?" Pamela asked. "I mean at some point in the future her twins are going to be curious about their father, probably want to meet him. Would that be so bad, under controlled circumstances, perhaps with you there or some other friend? I mean, if he is turning over a new leaf."

"You're probably right, but I think that has to be Florence's decision," he replied, and then sighed. "Is there anything more we have to do in the kitchen?"

"You were going to make hummus and hard-boil the eggs while I'm finishing the mayonnaise," she said.

He put two dozen eggs on to boil while he made the hummus, breaking off to poke a finger into one of the bowls of mayonnaise Pamela had just made, stuck it in his mouth and nodded approval.

"Don't do that, it's not hygienic," she said. "You're not in your own kitchen now. When you get back from fetching the dogs, you can set all the tables to make up for it."

He grinned at her, gave her a swift hug and drove off to the riding school. There he found Félix, the stable boy, saddling the horses for the evening ride with some of the guests who were renting Pamela's *gîtes*. Bruno had seen them all ride and knew that with Félix the horses would be in safe hands. He gave Hector his usual carrot, put Balzac and the puppy into his van and drove back to the club. Florence's children at once abandoned watching the tennis to swoop upon the two dogs as Pamela called out, "Bruno, you have work to do!" He gave her a mock salute and took piles of plates out to the long tables and began to fold thirty sets of knife, fork and spoon into individual paper napkins. Just as he finished, Fauquet arrived with the apple pies.

"The match of the day is about to start, the semifinal of the over-sixties, the baron against that English friend of yours, Crimson. I wouldn't be surprised if one of them has a heart attack," he said. "Where do you want me to put these pies?"

"In the kitchen, please. We should have two to each table," Pamela replied. "Come on, Bruno, this is not a match I want to miss."

The terrace was full, and other spectators were already gathering as the two elderly men began. Each one had been a good player in his day, and they struck the ball solidly with graceful, easy strokes. The baron was older, perhaps more cunning, but there was little to choose between them. Each man kept winning his service, and at five games to four, Jack Crimson was serving to save the match. The over-sixties were only expected to play a single set.

They reached deuce, and the two men were visibly tiring as their years caught up with them. Crimson's next serve went into the net. His second serve was too easy, and the baron's return was beyond Crimson's reach. Match point for the baron. Crimson served a ball almost beyond the baron's reach, but he somehow got it and played a feeble stroke. It seemed doomed to go into the net, but it hit the top and fell slowly over it into Crimson's court.

"No, no, that wasn't fair," the baron said. "Let's play the point again."

Crimson was standing in his own court, leaning heavily on his racket and panting, his face bright red. He shook his head. "No, you win," he said. "You deserved to win, and I'm not sure I could play another point."

The two limped to the net to shake hands and then left the court arm in arm to the cheers and applause of the audience.

"Well done, Grandpa," called out one of Miranda's children.

"Best game of the day," Bruno called out, and went to the bar to order two beers for his tired friends.

There was one other doubles match still underway, but the sun was sinking behind the ridge that ran from St. Denis to Limeuil, and those who had booked a place for supper were beginning to drift into the clubhouse, keeping Stéphane busy as he served drinks, mainly beers, white-wine spritzers or pastis and water. Florence came in with her children to kiss her friends goodbye before taking the twins home to put them to bed, saying she'd see them all the next day. Bruno took the dogs into the kitchen to feed them and left them sharing a large bowl of water.

"So, after my triumph today, whom do I have to play next?" said the baron, joining them, his gray hair still dark from his shower.

"Whoever wins the match between Horst and the mayor," Bruno said.

The diners began to take their chairs. Fabiola and Jacqueline had helped Pamela and Miranda to load the counter between the dining room and kitchen with bowls of salad. The *pains* were all sliced and put into large baskets on the tables with the *oeufs mayonnaises,* the hummus and venison pâté. The chickens were being carved, the roast potatoes piled high in another basket, and then the four women began to bring out the bowls of Bruno's version of gazpacho.

Bruno and his friends left the bar to make way for the diners, lining up to buy wine, with Stéphane calling out, "Three euros a glass, ten euros for a carafe that contains a liter."

The town vineyard sold ten-liter boxes of their wines for twenty-five euros, so the bar was making a very good profit. Pamela had saved a table for her and Bruno's friends, and the mayor stood a moment before taking his place. He surveyed the crowded tables and the throng at the bar, raised his glass and declared, "Here's to the best tennis club in the Périgord and to the volunteers who made tonight's dinner. *Bon appétit* to all!"

As he was about to take his seat, Bruno heard the familiar double ping of an incoming text message. It was from Isabelle, and it read: "New dramas on Spain, Russia. Your presence required for meeting at prefect's house Périgueux tomorrow noon."

Chapter 13

Bruno woke with the dawn and had a short run with the dogs before he showered and shaved. Remembering the meeting at the *préfecture,* he'd put a fresh uniform shirt and trousers on a hanger in his Land Rover before heading down to the clubhouse to help his friends start the fire to roast the wild boar. But first he'd gone into his garden to cut down some branches of bay leaves, a dozen sprigs of rosemary and more of thyme and put them into his largest wicker basket. The bay leaves would be tied to a long pole to make a brush with which the boar could be basted, and the other herbs would go into the empty stomach cavity before the boar went onto the fire. He remembered to take a spool of wire to sew its stomach closed.

The car radio was tuned to France Bleu Périgord, and the lead item of the local news was the fire at the recording studio in the barn belonging to Dominic and Vincent, two of Les Troubadours. They had been performing at the night market in Audrix, where they had eaten afterward, and had then gone directly to bed. They had been awoken by the glare of the flames and the smell of smoke. The *pompiers* had arrived in time to stop the fire from spreading to the house and other outbuildings, but the barn itself, its recording equipment and CD printer, had all been destroyed.

Bruno stopped the car and called Albert, the head of the *pompiers* in St. Denis. They were still awaiting a formal report from the fire inspector, but the word was that it had been deliberate.

"I spoke to Fernand at the Sarlat station who said he could still smell the gasoline," Albert said. "One Molotov cocktail at the double doors and another through the window, he thought. Do you think it might have something to do with this Catalonia song that people are talking about, Bruno?"

"That's what worries me, because if you're right, this may not stop with the barn," Bruno replied. "Could you be sure to give me a call when you hear what the fire inspector says?"

Albert agreed, and Bruno drove on thoughtfully to the tennis club. When he parked outside, he took a moment to send Isabelle and J-J a text message reporting Albert's suggestion of arson. The baron and Jack Crimson were already at the club when he joined them just before seven, along with Stéphane, Raoul and Marcel from the market. The club coffee machine was working nonstop, and they were all tucking into a stack of croissants and *chocolatines*. Bruno thought he'd better not discuss the fire until the inspector made a formal finding of arson, so he joined them at the table and gave Balzac and the Bruce each his own corner of croissant. Then Hubert arrived with the boar in the town vineyard's delivery van. He was followed by other members of the tennis and hunting clubs. The last to arrive was Dougal, the Scotsman who ran the town's vacation rentals agency, carrying the bottle of scotch whisky that he had made a regular feature of these boar roasts.

First, they carried two tables from the clubhouse and covered them in sheets of thick plastic. Then all of them were needed to heave carefully from the town vineyard's delivery truck the elderly bathtub in which the two-hundred-kilo boar had been marinating all night in ten liters of wine. They placed it on one table, and on the other Bruno and Hubert began to make the basting sauce with honey, chopped garlic, thyme and some wine from the bathtub. Balzac and the Bruce patrolled around the table, hoping to catch some droppings from the men's work.

The others started building the fire in the deep pit by the parking lot. Once it was blazing heartily, they began to prepare their own concoctions of stuffing and basting sauce. Stéphane liked sage and onion bound together with moistened stale bread, sausage meat and red *piment d'Espelette*. Hubert liked to add quartered apples and oranges that had been soaking in brandy, but he always saved one apple for the boar's mouth.

Once the stuffing had been inserted, Bruno began to sew together the skin over the boar's stomach with baling wire, using pliers to pull it tight over the bulging stuffing. Now came the most delicate part of the operation, pushing the long, pointed bar of iron into the beast's mouth and then carefully through the length of its body to emerge, if the men all working together had done it right, beneath the tail. The baron and Marcel covered the boar in the basting sauce. Hubert checked whether the fire had burned down low enough for the roasting and decided it needed another half hour. While waiting, they started preparing the *haricots couennes,* the wonderful blending of white beans and rind.

Marcel had soaked the white beans overnight. Bruno and Stéphane put a steel bar onto the supports for the spit, and Raoul hung a large metal pan from it. They had saved the skin from another boar and now sliced it into long, thin strips. These were tossed into the steel pan where they quickly began to sizzle and give off a splendid aroma which boded well for the eventual dish.

Marcel used a garden fork to turn the strips of skin, and when he declared them ready, he and Raoul donned protective gloves and removed the pan from the fire. They gave Balzac and the Bruce each a strip to taste. Balzac gently pushed the puppy aside until they were cool enough to eat.

The baron had meanwhile cleaned three *fait-touts,* the big enamel-covered pots that held twenty liters of liquid and were normally used to make jams or *coq au vin.* He had filled each one halfway with the white beans, then Marcel doled out the contents of the great pan between each of the enamel pots. A healthy slug of eau-de-vie was added to each one, the remainder of the beans divided among the pots, and Marcel, Raoul and the baron stirred each one thoroughly so that the strips of skin were well mixed. Allowance was made for different tastes, so the baron added chopped tomatoes and red peppers to his version. Marcel added chopped leeks and onions to his, along with a handful of sage, while Raoul embellished his with the scrapings from a mostly devoured ham bone and the remains of Bruno's venison pâté from the almost emptied jars of the previous evening. The jars were then given to the dogs to lick clean.

The fire was now judged to be low enough, and Lespinasse started the old engine, which would be attached to the spit with an ancient leather belt. It turned as expected. Now came Dougal's part of the ceremony. He lined up glasses, one for each man, and poured a generous slug of scotch into each one. Perhaps a quarter of the bottle remained, and this he poured slowly over the seam in the stuffed belly that Bruno had sewn, muttering something that he claimed was an ancient Gaelic prayer.

The final drops went onto the boar's head. Hubert stuck the apple into its mouth and two men took each end of the long metal bar on which the boar was impaled. Bruno with Stéphane and

Raoul with Charlot the plumber edged carefully toward the rim of the firepit to place it onto the spit supports. Finally, Lespinasse checked that the bar was properly placed on the spit mechanism, pulled a lever to disengage the engine, put the leather strap back on the spit and pushed the lever back. For a moment the strap turned without gripping the bar, but then it held and the boar slowly began to turn.

The sound of applause came from behind Bruno, who turned to see the four tennis players from the camper clapping and cheering. He recognized the young woman who had beaten Yveline the previous day. Bruno and his friends smiled and waved their thanks, and Balzac and the Bruce trotted over to the camper to make new friends. Bruno called across to ask if they would be joining the feast that evening.

"Yes, of course," said the taller of the two young men. "Can't wait. These are wonderful dogs, by the way." His French was correct, but Bruno picked up a foreign accent.

"They are basset hounds, hunting dogs," he told them. He glanced at the license plate of the camper. It was Spanish, and it carried a bumper sticker with a heart between the words YO and CATALONIA.

"Are you from Barcelona?" he asked.

"No, from Manresa, the heart of Catalonia," came the reply. This time it was Yveline's young adversary who spoke, a dark-haired, sturdy woman who looked older than the others.

"You missed the feast at the club last night," said Stéphane, pointing at Bruno. "Our friend here made a great dinner, cheaper and better than a restaurant."

"We went to the night market to hear the music, because we heard the group that does 'Song for Catalonia' was playing," the man said. "I'm Jordi and we look forward to the roast boar."

"I'm Alba," said the other young woman, slim and pretty in a girlish way, who had squatted down to play with the puppy. "And we didn't miss your supper. When we got up this morning, the men who were cleaning said we could have some of the gazpacho, hummus and bread that was left over. It was really good." She had pale, blonde hair, and her French was excellent.

"Thank Bruno here," said Marcel. "He's the cook."

By this time the two groups had gathered together, and Bruno complimented the woman who had defeated Yveline on her tennis. Her name was Jacinta, she said, and Yveline had given her the hardest game she had yet played in France.

The second young Spaniard darted into the camper and came out brandishing a bottle of Spanish brandy. "My name is Iker and I saw you put the whisky on the boar. Maybe we could add a little of this to give it a Catalan touch."

"Good idea," said Marcel, and Iker poured out a glass, came as close as the heat allowed to the firepit and tossed the contents onto the slowly turning boar. Some drops fell into the pit, and little blue flames leaped briefly from the ashes.

They all got chairs from the club, and a large pot of coffee that had been percolating as they worked. Iker added a dash of brandy to everyone's coffee, saying they called this a *carajillo*. The blonde woman, Alba, brought out a large almond cake, which she cut into slices. They all began chatting happily together, Alba enthusing about the group that had played at the night market.

"Did you know Les Troubadours will be giving a free concert here in St. Denis on Friday evening?"

"Really?" Alba's eyes lit up. "Will Joël Martin be there, the songwriter? It was so sad when his wife was killed. There are a lot of rumors about that."

"What do you mean?" Bruno asked.

"You should ask Jordi," Alba replied, tucking her fair hair behind her ears. "He's much more involved in the politics of all this, and he says that it was deliberate. A heavy truck smashed into the car she was in, and the police refused to charge the driver. Jordi says they didn't even conduct a serious investigation. There was a lot of violence during the general strike, people from Madrid trying to provoke trouble in what was a peaceful demonstration. At least, that's what he says. But he'll be so excited to think he might meet Joël Martin. Unless we're knocked out of the tournament."

"No fear of that," said the baron. "I saw some of you play, and you're very good. Are you professionals?"

She laughed. "No, we're all students. We play for our university and we heard we might be able to pay for our vacation by winning some prize money at local tennis tournaments in southwestern France. It's been a lot of fun."

"Where are you studying?" Marcel asked.

"We are all at the University of Lleida, the oldest in Catalonia, founded in 1300, but the Spaniards closed it. When we got autonomy, the new Catalan government reopened it, so we are all for Catalan freedom."

She and Jacinta were training to be food scientists, she explained when the baron asked about their studies. Iker was doing forestry, and Jordi was in computer science.

"So what does a food scientist think about our roasting wild boar?" Bruno asked.

Alba grinned at him as she stroked the puppy's ears. "I think it will be delicious and will make many people happy. We spoke of this in the camper when we saw what you were doing. You should ask Iker, the forestry expert, what he told us."

She called him over from where he was kneeling beside Balzac, one hand stroking the dog and watching the drops of fat from the turning boar fall sizzling into the ashes below. Iker was heavily built with thick forearms and broad shoulders. Bruno could imagine him wielding an ax to cut down trees. Alba asked him to tell the French cooks what he'd said about the fire they had built.

"I could see you were using offcuts," he said, in decent French. "They must be cleared from woodlands to stop the spread of forest fires. So, it's good for this purpose."

"So you see, we can say you were using sustainable energy," said Alba, smiling, cradling the Bruce on her lap while Balzac snoozed contentedly alongside.

"Thank heavens for that," said Bruno, rising. "I'm afraid I have to go, but I'll see you all later today. I think I might be playing against some of you this afternoon. But in the meantime I have work to do." He checked his watch. It was almost eleven, so he'd be in good time to drop off the dogs at the riding school before the meeting in Périgueux.

"May we look after the dogs while you're gone?" Alba said. "I so much miss having our own dog around. We have a Labrador at home."

Bruno glanced across to the baron, who nodded reassuringly, before agreeing. Bruno went into the club, took his uniform into the changing room and emerged a few moments later dressed as a policeman, which drew some startled looks from the Catalans.

"Don't worry," said the baron. "He's not really a cop. He's our village policeman."

Chapter 14

The prefect's house in Périgueux was a classic, small, eighteenth-century château in the Palladian style, as befitting the official representative of the French Republic in the *département* ever since the role had been invented by Napoléon. It stood on a gentle slope behind the main *préfecture* building, separated from it by a formal French garden with gravel paths between the lawns and flower beds. Appointed by the president of France, the prefect had local responsibility for the national interest, the state's administrative procedures, coordination of the various arms of the police, and was expected to take charge in all emergencies.

Word had come from Paris that an emergency had arisen which involved the police, the security services, the foreign ministry and the president's staff in the Elysée Palace. The prefect should therefore host a meeting for local officials involved. It took place in the library, where a large screen dominated one wall for videoconferences. Bruno knew the others who were present around the long table: Contrôleur Général Prunier, head of the Police Nationale for the *département;* his counterpart for the gendarmes, who held the rank of general; J-J as chief detective; the prefect's chief of staff and Bruno, the man with the local knowledge. Salutes were exchanged and coffee and mineral water offered as the prefect explained that they awaited the internet connection with Paris.

The prefect was fresh to the job, since each new government had the right to appoint its own supporters among the prefectoral corps, most of whom had served as subprefects in other regions. Bruno thought she could only be an improvement on her predecessor, a man who had tended to dither, to blame his underlings and to worry too much about what Paris might think.

"What do we make of this fire, Bruno?" Prunier asked. "The Périgueux fire chief said his Sarlat colleague suspects arson, two gasoline bombs."

"My *pompiers* in St. Denis say the same but suggest we'd better wait for the fire inspector's report," he replied. "I doubt that it's kids. Les Troubadours are too popular, and most local people seem proud of their success."

The screen flashed and then cleared, flashed again, and Isabelle appeared. Even though he'd heard her voice on the phone earlier as he drove to the meeting, he still felt a thrill at seeing her face over the video link. He smiled inwardly at her almost boyish short hair, her lack of jewelry and the merest hint of makeup around her eyes. She was wearing a shirtlike blouse in what looked like a cream silk.

"Bonjour, Madame Préfet, *messieurs,* I am Commissaire Isabelle Perrault, France's representative on the European coordinating committee for security and antiterrorism. I'm sorry to interrupt your Sunday, but the Elysée made this a priority after the briefing I received late yesterday from my Spanish counterpart."

Among the extremist and possibly violent groups on whom Spanish security kept a discreet watch, she explained, were some nationalists of the far right. Some of them were linked to the new Vox Party, which had broken away from the more moderate conservatives of the Partido Popular, the People's Party. The new party had surged in the polls after demanding tougher measures against Catalan independence. Vox leaders had called for a new *reconquista* of Spain, which, Isabelle noted, was a reference to the first Reconquest in the Middle Ages, which sought to drive all the Muslims from Spain. Vox opposed what they condemned as the Islamization of Europe and wanted women to return to their traditional roles in the home. They claimed the European Union was infringing on Spain's national sovereignty, revered the late General Franco and sought to end the autonomy that the Catalan and Basque regions had been granted.

"Some of the Vox members are ex-military and extremely militant. They are our concern today," she said, and held up photographs of two tough-looking men in camouflage uniforms standing against a background of sandbags and military gear. One of them was carrying a very large weapon.

"These are the two men who worry Madrid," she said. "The one with the specialist sniper weapon is Sargento Primero, or Senior Sergeant, Luis Eduardo Jaudenes, reputed to be the best sniper in the Spanish military. The other is Comandante, or Major, José-María Garay. They were both members of the Spanish Legion, in the Nineteenth Special Operations Group known as Maderal Oleaga. They served in Bosnia, Iraq and Afghanistan and were trained in special operations at Fort Bragg in the United States. They left the army in disgust after the new center-left government withdrew the Spanish military contingent from Iraq.

"These two men are as of today at the top of our wanted list, and their images and fingerprints have been sent to all French law enforcement agencies and to the media with an urgent request for maximum visibility and prominence. This is a nationwide manhunt." Isabelle paused to let that sink in.

"Let me explain their background," she went on. "After the new government pulled out the Spanish troops, Sergeant Jaudenes and Major Garay found their way back to Iraq as highly paid security consultants, or mercenaries. They returned to Spain in 2008 with over a million euros and started a security company which prospered as the economic recession made wealthy businesspeople seek protection. The Partido Popular won the election of 2011, with Major Garay as one of their candidates, but he failed to get elected. Two years later, the two men were part of the split in the Partido Popular that launched the far-right Vox Party, which now has more than twenty deputies in the national assembly and close to four million votes.

"Even the Vox Party seems a little tame for our two ex-soldiers, and our Spanish sources tell me they are involved in the clandestine group known as the Novios, from the old battle cry of the Spanish Legion, *los novios de la muerte,* the bridegrooms of death." Isabelle put down the photos and paused. Bruno remembered her mentioning the Novios in their earlier phone conversation.

"On a historical note, these two men are both fourth-generation members of the Spanish Legion," she went on. "Their great-grandfathers fought with Franco in the civil war, and both went on to volunteer for the Spanish División Azul, volunteers who fought for Hitler on the eastern front. They both died there, but not before fathering the fathers of our two Novios, who disappeared from their usual haunts in Madrid almost a week ago."

Now she smiled. "They told their staff they were going to explore new business opportunities in Europe, but without specifying where. We've been sent copies of their fingerprints from Spanish military records, and although the crashed Peugeot was wiped clean, we have a partial match—not enough for certainty and not enough for a court—a partial match of Sergeant Jaudenes's thumbprint on the catch that adjusted the passenger seat."

"That all seems a little too convenient to me," said J-J. "Leaving a specialist sniper's bullet, a golf ball and then carefully not wiping a place we'd be sure to look for fingerprints. And anyone who watches TV knows the way to get rid of any traces on a car is to burn it. Why didn't they do that?"

"Perhaps because it was a diesel," said Prunier. "They don't burn easily. And these guys are ex-soldiers, not professional criminals."

"Who do you think is his target?" J-J asked Isabelle. Bruno picked up a little hint of the affection J-J had for her as the young detective he'd trained and had hoped would be his successor in the *département*.

"We don't know," she replied. "There are some obvious targets. The most prominent is the former president of Catalonia, Carles Puigdemont, now a member of the European Parliament. He had been living in Germany, but he has recently rented a house outside Brussels in the commune of Waterloo, so I'll be briefing my German and Belgian colleagues later today."

"Waterloo is an interesting choice of residence," said the prefect, glancing around the table. "Hardly likely to endear him to France."

"The other obvious target is your particular concern, madame," Isabelle said coolly when the laughter around the prefect's conference table had died down. "Joël Martin, the Occitan enthusiast, poet and writer of the now famous 'Song for Catalonia.' The Elysée suggests that we offer him protective custody, either in a gendarmerie barracks or on a military base."

"What if he refuses?" the prefect asked.

"That's his choice," Isabelle replied. "We can't legally detain him, but he should be briefed on the risks. If need be, the offer of protection could be made public."

"Would that include going public with this news about the two former Spanish Legionnaires and their sniper gun?" J-J asked.

"The Elysée doesn't want to start a public panic about a sniper on the loose. And of course there are other former Catalan officials in exile."

Bruno wondered how many of these videoconferences Isabelle had gone through in her new role, which clearly involved regular contact with her security counterparts across Europe. She handled them well, being cool and professional, but her evident competence was made less intimidating by the occasional smile and a slight cock of an eyebrow when she mentioned the Elysée, as if to suggest that she knew her fellow security professionals across Europe probably shared her skepticism about their political masters in the various capitals.

"I can see why these two guys might want to target the Catalan politicians in exile," said the gendarme general. "But why go for this songwriter? I realize he's a symbol, but I don't think these ex-Legionnaires are into symbolism. Shooting a French citizen throws up diplomatic complications."

"That was initially our thinking, as well," Isabelle responded with a slight smile. "So let me now bring in the colleague who changed our mind, Colonel Richard Morillon of CALID, the defense ministry's analysis center for cyberwarfare."

The screen split into two, Isabelle shrinking to one half while in the other half appeared a slim man with iron-gray hair cut short and a friendly smile. His look was military chic, a well-pressed army camouflage jacket over a khaki T-shirt that appeared freshly ironed. He was sitting behind a desk with a blank wall behind him that seemed to flutter. Bruno guessed this was a security screen, lowered to conceal whatever maps or whiteboard might be behind.

There had been very little public information about CALID, except that Bruno had heard from Yves, the Police Nationale computer expert on J-J's staff, that they had hired a thousand specialists from universities and research centers and had a budget of 1.6 billion euros. They had tried to recruit Yves, but neither he nor his wife wanted to move from the Périgord to Rennes, in Brittany, the main base of Comcyber, France's new cyberdefense command.

"Bonjour, Commissaire Perrault, General, *messieurs-dames*. By chance, one of our team of cybernauts here hails from Perpignan, has family across the border in Catalonia and is interested in Occitan culture. He had heard of the 'Song for Catalonia' last week, several days before the Spanish government announced its ban, and was startled when he downloaded it to his private phone to see just how much demand there was for it. Looking more closely, he found there was more to this than met the eye. It was a bot surge, an automated system to mimic thousands of individuals seeking to download the song at the same time. He mentioned this to a colleague who reported it to me. It seemed unusual enough for us to take a look.

"For the past few days, this bot surge has continued, not only for the song but for the associated websites of Joël Martin on the Occitan language and culture," Morillon went on. "We found that much of it was coming from the dark web, hidden behind wall after wall of security. France's national institute for computer science research had been a pioneer in cracking some of these Tor and BitTorrent encryption systems. We really stepped up the work after the attempt by APT28 to interfere in our presidential election in 2017," he added, with a touch of pride.

"Excuse me, Colonel, perhaps you could explain APT28," Isabelle suggested.

"It stands for advanced persistent threat 28 and is also known as Fancy Bear and Pawn Storm," Morillon said. "We believe it is run by Russian intelligence. Two days before the runoff election that put President Macron into the Elysée they published a massive data dump of material from the Macron campaign, including internal staff emails and so on, apparently meant to damage or embarrass the campaign, along with faked documents claiming Macron had private bank accounts in the Bahamas. We're pretty sure it was Russians because some of the metadata in the faked documents was drafted on computers with Russian-language operating systems. Fortunately, they did not seem aware of the French rule of no new political reporting for two days before an election, so it had very little impact. However, it made the Macron team in the Elysée Palace extremely sensitive to this kind of operation and to cybersecurity in general."

"So the Russians are behind this attempt to make 'Song for Catalonia' into a gigantic hit?" asked the gendarme general.

Bruno could not be sure whether the general was genuinely as illiterate as Bruno in these matters, or whether he was trying to ensure that the prefect and the others around the table understood exactly what Morillon was trying to say.

"We believe so," said Morillon. "Most of the recent downloads of the song and the other material on history appear to reflect genuine public interest, but the Russians gave it a massive initial push. They have become very good at this. Another of their operations was disguised as coming from the Lazarus Group, which is a North Korean cyberwarfare unit. That was an attack aimed at the Tokyo Olympics, from which Russia had been banned after a cheating scandal, and this latest effort is using some of the same computer code. We've also been picking up some strongly encrypted phone calls here in France over the past three days."

"Do you think you can crack the encryption?" the general asked.

"Not quickly. I've told my superiors that we might want to consider asking the British or the Americans for their help on an informal basis, but we've had no official response so far. Nor do I know whether the Spanish government has been informed that somebody, somewhere, is running this bot surge against them. We could do that."

"Thank you, Colonel Morillon," said Isabelle. "Are there any other questions, or can we let our cyberwarrior return to his electronic battlefield?"

The room was silent. Bruno for one had no idea what to ask, beyond the obvious question: Who might want to encourage the Catalan cause, to embarrass the Spanish government and to drive a wedge between Spain and France? To his surprise, that was the very question that the prefect now asked.

"I don't think that question is within my field of competence, madame," replied the colonel.

"Nonetheless, you must have thought about it," the prefect said in a friendly tone. "Any ideas? Could a Catalan government in exile have this kind of capability?"

"I very much doubt it," Morillon said. "The Spanish government has only recently developed its own cybersecurity strategy and is still building capabilities, and I would question whether even they could do it. We'll keep looking, but we are almost certain it's the Russians." He paused. "If you can get me authorization to liaise with the British and the Americans, we might do better. We're starting to think most of the Russian cyberwar people are part of a GRU operation—that's Russian military intelligence—called Unit 74455, or the Center for Special Technologies. We know where they are, at 22 Ulitsa Kirova in Khimki, a Moscow suburb. That's where they launched the operation that closed down the Ukrainian electricity network and tried to penetrate the British investigation into that nerve-agent attack in Salisbury, as well as the one against Macron. The FBI in the United States has filed formal charges against some of the named members of Unit 74455."

"How the hell did they get the names?" the prefect asked. At the same time the gendarme general demanded, "Why on earth would they help us?"

"They might help us because we helped them," Morillon replied. "We managed to get into the Russian car registration computer and suggested the Americans look at the owners of cars registered to the Ulitsa Kirova address. They got forty-seven names, which they then shared with us."

"Thank you, Colonel," Isabelle said quickly and at once closed his half of the screen, which made Bruno suspect that Morillon had revealed more of French capabilities than Isabelle had expected.

"Now you know why we think Joël Martin might be the target of these ex-Legionnaires," Isabelle went on smoothly. "Some powerful state or group, almost certainly Russian, has deliberately tried to make him and his song famous, to the embarrassment of the Spanish government and perhaps to provoke a crisis in relations between Paris and Madrid. We don't know why, but I think we need to find out. And in the meantime, we have to hunt down Major Garay and Sergeant Jaudenes. Contrôleur Général Prunier, as regional chief of the Police Nationale, do you have anything to report? I have already been informed by Chief of Police Courrèges of last night's fire, apparently deliberate, at the recording studio of Les Troubadours."

"No, nothing else yet. We're tracking new car rentals, purchases and thefts, checking hotels and campgrounds and golf clubs—"

"Why golf clubs?" the prefect interrupted.

"Because of the golf ball found in the wrecked car, and Bruno's suggestion that a bag of golf clubs would be a way to camouflage the rifle," Prunier replied. "Now I think J-J and I should get to my office to coordinate the hunt for these two men, and I'm sure the general will want to join us and do the same. And since Bruno knows Joël Martin and the performers of the song, I suggest he be assigned to persuade Martin to accept our offer of protection."

"What worries me is that Joël Martin may well be their preferred target," Bruno said. "But if he is under our protection and out of their reach, I suspect these two Legionnaires will settle for shooting Flavie and the other musicians who perform the song. We may need to protect them, too. In any event, should we cancel the concert?"

"I'm not sure about that," Isabelle replied. "These two ex-Legionnaires have their mission, and they are believers, perhaps even fanatics, in their nationalism. They have already taken serious risks; they are confident in their skills, so I don't see them stopping now even if the concert is canceled. They'll just find another target. Maybe letting this concert take place as planned is what we need to draw them out."

A stunned silence fell, then everyone spoke at once, protesting, objecting, saying the Elysée would never stand for it, that the media would crucify them; everyone, that is, except Bruno, who sat quietly, thinking what Isabelle might mean.

He knew that a sniper needed a safe spot with a clear line of sight to the target, with an optimal range of between one and two kilometers, maybe a little more. Wind would be a problem. So would mist or strong light in his eyes. Maybe they could generate that fake smoke he had seen at other concerts, only this time send it up behind the crowd to block the sniper's vision. Or could he set up searchlights that would appear to be shining into the sky until the band appeared, and then they could play over the higher land where a sniper would be waiting? Or strobe lights onstage could temporarily blind any sniper looking through a magnifying sight. They could saturate the area with their own security teams from the military and perhaps use local hunting clubs to search out all possible sniping spots, mark them, even bring in French Special Forces to set up an ambush.

He tapped the table twice, three times, as the others continued their protests and objections, and he looked directly into Isabelle's eyes on the screen.

"Chief of Police Courrèges," she said sharply, silencing the others around the table in Périgueux. "You are our military veteran here. You wanted to say something?"

"Yes, Commissaire, thank you," he said, and all the others turned to stare at him.

"I know something of snipers, their abilities but also their limitations," Bruno began. "Of course, it will be a risk, but there might be a way to make this work."

And he began to explain what he had in mind.

Chapter 15

As Bruno drove to Flavie's house south of Siorac, he noted the unusual presence of a police control point at each of the main roundabouts on the way from Périgueux. Two motorcycle cops, a van with three armed gendarmes, one with a submachine gun, and all wearing flak vests signaled a high level of alert. Despite his police van and uniform, Bruno was stopped like every other vehicle and his face checked against the photo of the two ex-Legionnaires.

"That was quick," he told his old friend Sergeant Jules at the checkpoint by the bridge at St. Denis. "I've just come from a meeting at the prefect's house where I saw those mug shots for the first time."

"We got an all-points radio alert about an hour ago, and the photos came through on the gendarme net," Jules told him. "We just printed them out, set up the checkpoint, and the motorcycle cop arrived a few minutes later. Somebody pulled out the stops to set this up so fast. And they've canceled all leave and days off."

"What about Yveline with her bad ankle?" Bruno asked.

"She's holding the fort back at the gendarmerie. Are you involved in all this, too?"

Bruno smiled and nodded. "I'm heading for Siorac to try to persuade two people at risk to accept protective custody."

"Anyone I know?"

"Yes, Flavie, the singer with Les Troubadours, but keep that information to yourself."

"Will do, and I'll buzz the control point at Siorac to let them know you're coming. Marcel from St. Cyprien is in charge there. You know him well enough. Take care and I'll see you at the feast tonight. We've been put on twelve hours on and twelve hours off, and I've been on duty since seven this morning."

Bruno was waved through by Marcel at the Siorac checkpoint and turned off to the small hamlet of Pech-Bracou. Flavie lived in a converted barn which she had designed herself. The entire ground floor was a vast open space for living, for rehearsals and for the occasional chamber concert. Halfway down one side of the barn was a huge stone fireplace whose chimney rose majestically to the roof. Facing it was a set of double-glass sliding doors that led to the terrace and garden, with views down to the River Dordogne below. An open-plan kitchen occupied one end along with a bathroom and a pantry. Half of the barn was open all the way to the roof. The other half was reached by a spiral staircase that opened onto the upper floor, which housed two bedrooms, a bathroom and a kind of musicians' gallery where Flavie practiced her songs. Bruno thought it one of the best barn conversions he'd seen.

Bruno had been there for parties and dinners, to see the band rehearse and on one memorable winter's evening for a full concert followed by a party that had gone on until dawn. He had texted Flavie from his van when he'd been about to leave the *préfecture* parking lot to say he needed to see her and Joël urgently. She replied with a simple, "Okay, I'm home."

She met him at the door as he parked, looking relaxed in

flowing black cotton pants with a loose blouse in black silk, all held together by a belt made of woven white rope that matched her rope-soled espadrilles. Her hair was loose, tumbling over her shoulders.

"Welcome, you timed it perfectly for coffee, and I suppose you heard about the fire?" she said, proffering her cheeks for the *bise.* He nodded, offered the usual palliative about waiting for the formal report and followed her through the sliding glass doors to the terrace, where the telescope she used to scan the stars at night seemed to be pointing downward as though to watch something in the town.

Joël, barefoot in jeans and a light blue polo shirt, was sitting at a table loaded with cups, saucers and a *cafetière* and reading the *Journal du Dimanche.* He looked up at Bruno's approach, rose to shake hands and asked, "What's so urgent? Don't say you've come to tell us that after this fire your mayor wants to cancel the concert."

"Let him have his coffee first," said Flavie. "And maybe then, Bruno, you can explain this heavily armed police roadblock down at the bridge." She gestured at the telescope.

Bruno had considered on the drive the best way to break the news, and to raise the invitation of protective custody, and whether to appeal to Flavie if Joël were skeptical or resisted the offer. After all, Bruno knew her quite well and felt sure she would take the threat seriously. And presumably Joël knew enough about the passions involved in Catalan politics not to dismiss the threat out of hand. But men could be unpredictable in their reaction to the threat of personal danger. Fight or flight was the conventional view, but Bruno knew it was far more complex than that, particularly if a woman was involved. Joël's instinctive urge to impress her with a display of masculine courage would be balanced by the equally instinctive sense of duty to protect her, all the more so in these first, heady days of their love affair.

There was no point in thinking this endlessly through, Bruno had concluded. It was his job to lay out the facts that were known, the reality of danger, and then let them decide what to do. If he could, he'd stay with them while they discussed the matter.

"We're looking for two professional assassins from Spain who we suspect have come here to kill you, Joël," Bruno replied and took a seat.

"You're kidding, right?" Joël replied, with a nervous laugh. Flavie stopped pouring Bruno's coffee, put the cup down with a clatter and raised her hand to her mouth before sinking onto the chair beside Joël.

"I wish I were," said Bruno, taking a sip from the half-filled cup. "I've just come from an emergency meeting at the prefect's home in Périgueux with the heads of the police and the gendarmes. We had a video briefing from a senior security official in Paris on the imminent danger you're in. As a result, I'm authorized to offer you the protection of La République, whether on a military base or in a gendarme barracks."

"When you say professional assassins . . . ," Joël began, and then paused, swallowing hard.

"Two former members of Spain's Special Forces, ex-Legionnaires, are on the Spanish government's list of dangerous political extremists who need watching. They disappeared a few days ago. One of them is a trained sniper, and he's carrying a weapon that can kill at two and more kilometers. We have a fingerprint on a crashed stolen car that gives us reason to believe that they're in the Périgord. And thanks to security officials in Madrid we very strongly suspect that they're looking for you."

Bruno paused to let that sink in and gestured at the high

ground across the river and the wooded slopes to the south. "This is good country for snipers."

"So this was the official word from the Madrid government?" Joël asked, a touch of skepticism in his voice.

"As official as you can get, through the formal procedures of the European security coordination committee. It came from the Spanish delegate to the French one," Bruno said. "The Belgian and German delegates are also being informed, in case Carles Puigdemont is also a target."

"Have you any details on these assassins, which group they're from?" Joël asked.

"We believe they are two ex–Special Forces soldiers, with combat experience in Iraq and Afghanistan, both members of the Vox Party, and apparently connected to a militant breakaway group called Los Novios. This is what they look like." Bruno laid the photographs on the table. "Your government is taking it very seriously and is prepared to protect you at a military base, and Flavie as well, if you wish, while we do our best to round these guys up."

"When you say a military base . . . ," Joël said hesitantly, glancing at Flavie and putting a hand on her arm.

"There's the Mont-de-Marsan air base, which has a guarded perimeter; I have a cousin who is based there. And there's a secure army base for our own Foreign Legion at Castelnaudary, near Toulouse. I think they might be preferable to a gendarme barracks. The secure ones tend to date from the nineteenth century, so I don't recommend the plumbing."

"What about Puigdemont?"

"You probably know his whereabouts better than I do," Bruno replied. "I'm told he's renting a villa outside Brussels, but I'm confident the Belgians will be offering him protection, too."

"How would they know that Joël is staying here with me?

There's nothing to link him to this address," said Flavie, turning her face to Joël with a look of such longing that Bruno felt a twinge of envy.

"You're the lead singer of Les Troubadours," Bruno replied. "They'll certainly know everything about you that's in the public domain, with the interviews that have been all over social media. You're on the front page of *Sud Ouest,* and if I know my friend Gilles, you could even be on the cover of *Paris Match* this week. Didn't I hear that interviewer on France Bleu Périgord mention that you lived in a hamlet just outside Siorac?"

"*Mon Dieu,* yes, I remember that interview with Marie-Do, she was so nice." Flavie sighed. "I suppose there are very few secrets left."

"Do we have time to think about this, to discuss it ourselves?" asked Joël. "And after the fire we need to talk about it with the rest of the band."

"I don't want to put pressure on you," said Bruno. "So why don't I drive you to my place where you can relax without worrying about snipers hiding behind every tree and think about what you want to do. I have to go to the tennis club, so you'll have the place to yourselves while you talk it over. I'll drive there and you can follow in your car."

"I suppose we don't have much choice," said Flavie, standing up and starting to clear away the coffee cups.

"I'll do that," said Bruno, rising to stack the cups. "I think it would be better if the two of you were to use the time to pack some things. You can stay at my place overnight and let me know what you want to do in the morning when you've slept on it. Then we can talk again."

"That makes sense," said Joël, rising. "Can we stop at my place to get some more things, my laptop and a suitcase?"

"Why not ask your sister to do that for you and get her to drop off the case at the tennis club in St. Denis? From there I can bring it back tonight," Bruno suggested as he finished stacking the tray and turned to take it indoors. "Who knows, they might be watching your place already."

Fifteen minutes later, with Flavie and her suitcase in his van and Joël following in his own car, Bruno beeped to get Marcel's attention at the checkpoint before the bridge over the river at Siorac. He told Marcel the following car was with him, and they were waved through to the road that led to Coux. Instead of turning off through Audrix, Bruno drove on to cross the river again at Campagne, rather than use the better-known bridge at St. Denis. Then he turned off on the road to St. Cirq and Petit Paris, stopping to be sure he had not been followed, before taking the back way to his home.

He told Joël to park his car behind the barn, away from the view of casual visitors. Then he led the way upstairs to the two spare rooms that he had installed in the *grenier,* where the shepherds who had lived there in the distant past had stored their hay.

"You have your own bathroom up here, and there are clean sheets and extra blankets and pillows in the cupboard," he said. "Help yourself to food in the fridge and the pantry, and there are jars of pâté and preserves on shelves in the barn at the back. And help yourselves to fresh eggs in the chicken coop."

"This is very kind of you, Bruno," Flavie said, giving him a quick peck on the cheek.

"I'm touched by your hospitality, Bruno, and by what you've done over the years for Flavie and Les Troubadours," said Joël. "There's a question I've been meaning to ask. What do you think about Catalonia's right to independence after we won a referendum?"

"Exactly what I think about Breton or Corsican independence, or what I told my British friends about Scottish independence and their Brexit referendum," Bruno replied. "I think to break up a long-standing constitutional relationship is a very serious matter, and it needs more than a simple majority in a yes-no referendum of those who bothered to turn out to vote. I could never understand why the British locked themselves into Brexit with a minority of their people who were entitled to vote."

"Well, we got more than ninety percent for independence in 2017," Joël said. "That's a pretty clear verdict."

"Yes, but a lot of people didn't vote," Bruno replied. "Only about forty percent of the voters cast a ballot, so I don't see that as much of a mandate. It's like Brexit. I think the minimum sensible threshold would be at least half of all registered voters, and even sixty percent, just so that the will of the people was clear beyond doubt. The Americans require a two-thirds majority in both houses of Congress to amend their Constitution."

"But a lot of our people were blocked from getting to the polling stations," Joël said.

"True, and I'm sure you know a lot more about this than I do. I recall that the decision to hold the referendum was taken by a Catalan parliament which failed to get the two-thirds majority required for any change in constitutional status. And international observers called in to monitor the vote said it didn't meet their standards. That's why I think constitutional issues really need supermajorities."

"Yes but . . . ," Joël began, but Flavie cut him off.

"Stop it, Joël, the two of you are not going to agree on this, but Bruno has made a reasonable argument, and he's giving us the shelter of his own home, for heaven's sake! So let's just drop it."

Joël stared at her for a moment before nodding and saying,

"You're right, Flavie. I'm probably too close to all this, anyway. But what do you think Flavie and I should do, Bruno? Hide up in an army or air force base and wait, hoping you track these two men down? Or should we just stay here where we should be pretty safe and carry on with the concert as planned but under cover? Most of the crowd will be watching us on the big video screen anyway."

"That's something you should talk about with the rest of the band," said Bruno, intrigued that Joël's mind seemed to be working in similar ways to his own, to let the concert go ahead. "I have to go. I hope you'll be comfortable, but please stay out of sight."

"Could we use your internet?" Joël asked.

"Sorry, I'm afraid not. It's on a police net, so even if I was allowed to share the access code, it would have to be my computer with my own code and my fingerprint. Can't you get internet access through your phone, Flavie? I think Joël should be careful about using his, maybe turn it off and take out the battery. If he's being monitored, they can easily locate him."

"Yes, I can," said Flavie. "Don't worry. When should we expect you back?"

"Not before ten at the earliest. You have my and Commissioner Jalipeau's numbers. I'll let him know that you're here."

"Thanks for this, Bruno, I'm sure we'll be fine," said Flavie.

Chapter 16

Bruno arrived at the club to the usual enthusiastic welcome from Balzac, loyally supported by the Bruce. He was in time to take his turn basting the boar and helping the others rig the second spit that would take the lamb, offered as an alternative. So much smaller than the boar, it would cook faster. It was an unwritten rule in St. Denis that any public event involving a *méchoui,* the roasting of a whole lamb, had to be conducted by the town's acknowledged expert, Momu, the math teacher at the *collège.* Bruno was honored to be his usual helper and began by peeling ten fat cloves of garlic while Momu assembled his special rub for the meat.

Momu dried all his herbs himself and brought them to the task with ceremony, all in individual, corked glass jars in an ornately carved wooden box with brass fittings that was a family heirloom from Algeria. Its interior was almost as elaborate, divided into carved and cushioned sections, and fitting neatly over them was a carved brass bowl.

Sitting cross-legged on the ground and crooning an Arabic song or chant to himself, he put the bowl between his thighs and began to open the jars one at a time to take out his chosen herbs, closing and replacing each one when done. He began with a handful of oregano and then added a smaller one of rosemary. He crumbled them together by hand. To this he added some pinches of salt and paprika, two pinches of fenugreek and a secret ingredient that looked like pinkish-gray dust. As well as bringing a sense of ceremony to the making of the *méchoui,* Momu liked to keep his secrets. As always, Bruno and the other men watched all this with solemn attention, aware that they were observing a master. Balzac and the Bruce also sat facing him in silence, fascinated by Momu's careful movements.

Once the rub was complete, Bruno was directed to begin the basting sauce by grating the zest of eight lemons and hand squeezing their juice into a half liter of olive oil. He crushed half of the garlic cloves and added them while Momu added more paprika, two glasses of white wine and ended with a flourish of his antique black pepper grinder. He stirred it all carefully, added another secret ingredient, which looked to Bruno like some kind of meat stock, and then with his hands began to coat the empty stomach cavity generously with the liquid.

"Now," Momu said, without turning his attention from the lamb. Bruno brought to him the bowl of his magic rub, and Momu began patting this onto the moistened cavity walls. When this was done, he brushed his hands on the foreleg and instructed Bruno to sew the stomach closed.

As Bruno worked, Momu walked slowly and thoughtfully around the lamb, a large knife in one hand, the other reaching out to poke the flesh here and there, paying particular attention to the shoulders and haunches. He made a series of careful incisions, perhaps an inch or so deep, and pushed a pinch of his rub into each cut, closing it with a sliver of the remaining garlic.

Momu then inspected Bruno's sewing, cross-stitched as Momu

always required, and grunted a cautious approval before using his hands to spread the basting sauce over the whole of the lamb. Along the seam of Bruno's sewing, and in the crevices where the lamb's legs met the body, he patted the last of his special rub. Finally, he sprinkled sea salt over the lamb, stood back and said, as if to himself, "That should do it."

He and Bruno went into the kitchen to wash their hands, the room already filling with club members, who turned to greet them while doing their own bit for the supper. The old bathtub in which the boar had been brought to the club was being filled with potatoes wrapped in tinfoil, ready for roasting. Other volunteers were chopping lettuces and cucumbers and slicing red onions and tomatoes for the bowls of salad.

"Ah, Bruno," said the mayor, who was making a large bowl of vinaigrette for the salads. He drew Bruno outside to speak privately. "I had a long discussion with Annette this morning, and she'll file the case about Casimir in the family court in the morning. She helped me draft a formal letter saying that I as the mayor have reason to fear for the safety of Florence and her children if her ex-husband were free to come to St. Denis. So we asked formally for an exclusion order to keep him away, stressing that we would hold the court responsible in the event of any new attack on her. We're unlikely to get it, but it will remind the court that Florence has the community behind her."

"Led by an influential mayor," Bruno said.

"She suggested that I add a paragraph about my letters to my former colleagues in the Senate stressing that I was using my right to appeal personally to the justice minister," the mayor went on. "I gather that since this man is already installed in our *département,* matters have become extremely urgent. I just hope this other emergency that has cropped up won't keep you from giving

Florence's safety your personal attention. We really don't want her heading off to Canada."

"I'll do my best," Bruno said. "I thought I might drive down to Bergerac tomorrow to see the priest who seems to be some kind of sponsor for Casimir, just to let him know we're keeping a close eye on this."

"Okay. And I presume you're involved with the new security alert. I saw Sergeant Jules at the roadblock at the bridge. Is that because of the fire?"

"I was at the *préfecture* all morning discussing it on a video call from Paris, a meeting arranged before we knew of the fire." He lowered his voice as two of the volunteers came from the kitchen and stood nearby to light up cigarettes. "I can brief you later, but I don't want to talk about this in public."

"Fine," said the mayor, heading back to the kitchen and his vinaigrette. "I'll leave matters in your hands. Just one thing: please check out that Spanish camper vehicle."

Bruno looked at the mayor's departing back and then at the camper van, pondered a moment and then called J-J. He got his voice mail and left a message, saying that many of the tennis clubs in the area were likely to have campers staying unregistered and unnoticed in the parking lots using the tennis clubs' bathrooms and showers. They should all be checked, along with farms offering camping and *tables d'hôte*, which might also offer space to camping cars.

As he spoke, Bruno thought how he might have organized such an operation. He'd have flown from Spain to Amsterdam or Munich and rented a Dutch or German camper, come in that way and arranged to meet with the driver carrying the gun. He would never have allowed the weapon and the sniper to come into contact until they were in the target area in France. He passed this on to J-J as well.

Then he went to the area behind the reception desk usually occupied by Bernard, the club secretary, and opened the register to the page listing the entrants for the tournament. Beside each name was the club membership number and the license number from the French lawn tennis association. The four Spaniards had listed their license numbers from the equivalent Spanish association, and the secretary had also listed their national ID card numbers. Bruno scribbled all the details into his notebook, copied them onto his phone and sent them to General Lannes's in-box as Spanish visitors worth checking.

Pamela, already in her tennis whites, was sitting on the terrace outside the clubhouse watching the two young Spaniards make short work of two of the club's better players. They had won the first set six–two and were leading in the second by four games to one. Iker was serving, hitting a powerful stroke into a corner and then putting away the fumbled returns with a volley down the middle of the court, leaving his opponent flat-footed.

"I'm glad we're not playing against him," Pamela said, rising for Bruno's *bise* and then gesturing at Iker. "All the same, we're facing a tough match. And I don't think this one will last much longer, so you'd better change. Have you heard from Florence? Annette told her that her ex-husband is out of jail and she's in quite a state."

Bruno grimaced. "I'd hoped to give her at least one more day without that news landing on her. But what's done is done. Have you seen her since she learned about it?"

"No, she called Fabiola, who told me. Florence said she hadn't been able to reach you."

"I was stuck in a meeting at the *préfecture,* a new security alert. You may have seen the roadblocks."

"What is it? Terrorism again?" She gave him an impish look. "Or just plain crime?"

"A bit of both," he replied and then changed the subject. "Have you met any of these Spanish youngsters? They gave us a hand this morning, setting up the spit, and seemed very friendly. Apparently, they're all on their university team."

"I've been watching them play. They're very good, but not professionals. We'll be playing on the far court where that singles match is wrapping up, Fabiola against Clothilde."

Bruno went to change into his whites, and when he came out a few moments later, Florence and the children walked into the club, Balzac skipping happily between Dora and Daniel, who raced to be first to cuddle him. Then they squealed with delight as they saw the puppy and at once abandoned Balzac for the Bruce. Florence, by contrast, had a face like thunder as she confronted Bruno.

"Why didn't you tell me the bastard was free?" she almost hissed. "I only found out from Annette. And then you were nowhere to be found and not answering your phone."

"I was called up to the *préfecture* where we spent all morning on this new security alert," he replied. "You must have seen the armed police at the roadblock by the bridge."

"But you knew about his being freed yesterday and you didn't tell me," Florence snapped. "A fine friend you are."

Stung, Bruno retorted, "At least I spared you a sleepless night, and I can't spend all my time on your problems." As soon as the words were out of his mouth, he regretted them and tried quickly to apologize. But Florence's eyes blazed in fury as she turned on her heel.

"Bruno, get moving," Pamela called from outside. "The other game is over. We're on!"

Jordi and Alba were already on the court, opening giant tennis bags that looked intimidating, each one big enough to hold four or five rackets. They began hitting, and it was soon clear that while Jordi was at least as good a player as Bruno and possibly better, Alba seemed not to be in the same league as Jacinta, the woman who had beaten Yveline the previous day. After four rallies, all four of them met at the net for the toss.

"Best of three sets?" Pamela asked, and the Spaniards agreed. They won the toss and Alba opened the serving. Pamela slammed her first return right past her, and then, obviously shaken, Alba served Bruno a double fault. They won the first game at love, and Alba's game never recovered. Pamela won her service game in four straight points. Jordi's game went to deuce, but Pamela was playing like a woman inspired.

Bruno had time to admire her play, since she was making most of the shots, ruling much more space than her own half of the court, perfectly poised as if she had all the time needed to make each stroke. Although she must have been twice Alba's age, she looked magnificent, trim and toned from constant horseback-riding as she dominated the game with controlled aggression. She and Bruno took the first set by six games to one.

"We've got an audience," she said as they heard cheers and applause from a gathering crowd.

"I don't think I ever saw you play so well," Bruno said to her as they changed ends. "You'd win this match playing alone."

"Just keep the pressure on," she replied, glancing across the court with a merciless look. "They're cracking. Let's win this one for Yveline."

Jordi opened the second set, and Pamela's blazing return went right down the middle between the two Spaniards. The next service came easily to Bruno's forehand, and he drove it back hard just beyond Alba's outstretched reach. So it went, with Bruno sufficiently inspired by Pamela's example to serve several aces, and the crowd of club members on the terrace applauded each one. They took the second set six games to two, and Bruno felt he'd never played so well in his life. Pamela won the final point to clinch the match, leaping like a panther to jump on a scooped return that bounced high. She smashed it down so hard that the ball rose like a rocket and soared high over the netting at the far end of the court.

To the cheers of the crowd, Bruno hurried to congratulate her, and she gave him an enthusiastic hug that somehow turned into something more urgent. She whispered, "I'm off to take a shower. Why not join me back home in twenty minutes."

Never had Bruno bought and served the two losers a drink so quickly. Never had he been so inspired to fake an urgent phone call from police headquarters demanding his presence. Never had he been so cunning in pretending to take the road for Périgueux before turning back to the riding school and parking behind Pamela's house. And never had he been more eager as he leaped up her stairs and heard her voice from the bathroom over the sound of running water, inviting him to join her.

Chapter 17

"You should go back. Duty calls in the form of that boar, waiting to be carved," Pamela said sometime later, as they led the horses down the slope to the paddock and then to the stables. "And we couldn't possibly return together. Think of the gossip and the knowing glances."

"And your reputation," he said, grinning at her. "At least I'll rub Hector down before I change back into uniform. But I can't let you take care of all of them."

"Only Hector and Primrose were ridden," she replied, glancing back at the other horses, none with a saddle, following along behind on long reins. "And even our horses didn't work up much of a sweat. Let's give them a quick rub and then you'd better go. I'll feed and water them and turn up at the club about half an hour after you leave. What time will the boar be ready?"

"We planned it for around eight-thirty and it's just past seven," he said. "We have a little time."

After the horses were settled, Bruno took off his shirt to wash himself at the stable sink. As he dried himself off, Pamela came up behind him and wrapped her arms around his waist.

"That was a lovely way to spend an afternoon," she murmured.

"Just the thing to celebrate our tennis partnership, but I don't think we should make a habit of it."

"You're probably right," he said, the regret obvious in his tone. "You usually are."

She turned him around to face her, gave him a deep and very fond kiss and said, "Off you go, dear Bruno. I'll see you in about half an hour."

Back at the club and wearing his uniform to support his explanation that he'd been called away on police business, Bruno headed straight for the fire, where he found Balzac and the Bruce sitting just beyond the heat, almost drooling as they enjoyed the scent of the roasting meat. Bruno's friends were poking skewers into the boar to see if the juice ran clear showing it was done. The skin was crisp and dark brown, burst here and there so that the exposed fat dribbled down the sides, still glistening from the latest application of the basting fluid. He realized that while for Balzac this was a familiar sight it must be the Bruce's first attendance at such an event, an open-air roast of a beast that, however tantalizing, was several times larger than he was.

"Time to take it off and let it rest before we carve it," said Sylvain, the local butcher and acknowledged expert in such matters. Bruno asked them to give him time to change and came out minutes later in the same jeans and denim shirt he'd worn when helping Momu with the lamb. He donned a pair of leather gloves and joined the others in heaving first the lamb, then the boar, off the supports of the spit and onto the carving table.

Their faces glowing red from the heat coming from the firepit, the men gathered at the bar to quench their thirst with glasses of beer. On the nearest court, Fabiola and Gilles were playing the other Spanish couple, and Bruno struggled a moment to recall their names: Iker and Jacinta. The scoreboard showed the Spaniards ahead by one set and leading the second set by five games to four. Jacinta was serving. By now the terrace was thronged with spectators, all cheering for Fabiola and Gilles. They did their best. Gilles slammed back what was probably the best return of serve he'd ever struck. Bruno was sure it would win the point. But Jacinta had somehow read Gilles's mind, moved wide and slammed it back straight at him, a forehand drive with lots of topspin. Gilles moved in from the baseline and spooned the ball up for Iker to take an easy volley. The Spaniards had won.

"So that's who we're playing in the final," said Pamela, who had suddenly appeared at his side. "A tough proposition."

"Play like you did today and we'll eat them alive," he replied.

"That may depend on how much of that roast boar you devour tonight," she said, nudging him just as Bruno's phone vibrated. He pulled it out and glanced at the screen. It was a three-digit message from Isabelle in their private code, asking him to call her burner phone for a conversation she did not want to be known. That meant he could not use his own phone. He went to the baron and borrowed his. Bruno went outside into the woods and called the number of her burner.

"I'm with the big man and he wants a back channel to the Brits," said Isabelle. "Can you get Jack Crimson to call this number tonight?"

"Can I tell him what it's about?"

"Tell him it relates to the woman buried in Moscow at the same time as Kim Philby," she replied, her voice serious.

"Give me a few minutes," he said and closed the phone. The big man had to be General Lannes, a figure little known to the public who seemed to have wide influence over most aspects of French security from his perch in the office of the interior minister. The reference to Philby was baffling. Bruno knew that Philby had been a KGB spy from the 1930s well into the Cold War even when he was in the running to be the next head of British intelligence. And what could that have to do with Spanish snipers and "Song for Catalonia"?

Bruno found Crimson sipping whisky by the fire as men argued whether or not it was time to start carving the boar. He pulled him to one side and out of the hearing of the others to say that Lannes would like a discreet word. Bruno then repeated the mysterious phrase about Philby's grave.

Crimson raised his eyebrows and followed Bruno deeper into the privacy of the woods behind the club, waiting while Bruno dialed Isabelle's burner phone again. When he heard her voice, he passed the phone to Crimson, who liked to be known as a retired diplomat but who had also been secretary of Britain's Joint Intelligence Committee and had long been on friendly terms with General Lannes.

Bruno backed away out of earshot as Crimson spoke. He would be a perfect back channel to the Brits, trusted by both sides, with contacts throughout the intelligence world. If the French needed help in the form of the fabled decryption skills of Britain's Government Communications Headquarters at Cheltenham, Jack Crimson was probably the right man to consult.

But why had Isabelle changed her mind? Over the video link to the *préfecture* earlier that day, it had been Isabelle who cut off Colonel Morillon when he'd suggested asking the Brits or the Americans to help decrypt some phones. Had the situation changed, or was she speaking for the benefit of someone else on that video call who had carefully kept out of the camera's view? That probably meant someone from the president's team of security advisers at the Elysée, who had the reputation of being overly concerned with politics and the president's image.

Bruno saw Crimson end the call, then pull out his own phone, check a number in the memory and use the baron's phone to call it. As he turned to get some light to dial the number, Crimson's voice suddenly became audible, and while Bruno's English was makeshift, he picked up the key words.

"Ah, Dicky," Bruno heard him say. "Sorry to bother you at home but something a bit delicate has come up with our French colleagues and they'd appreciate a chat with our decrypt boffins. To do with our old playmates, the Fancy Bears."

Bruno recalled that "the Fancy Bears" had been one of the terms Colonel Morillon had used to identify the Russian cyber-tricks group.

"I suppose you heard enough of that," said Crimson as he closed the phone and stepped back toward Bruno, who shrugged.

"I know who Philby was, and I assume the Bears are Russian," Bruno said.

"And I imagine you might explain why my old friend Lannes is going through this cloak-and-dagger nonsense over a perfectly routine piece of consultation between allies on decrypting phones being used by a less-than-friendly power."

"Politics," said Bruno. "The president's staff wouldn't want the press to know that we turned to the British for help on such matters."

Crimson nodded. "Yes, our politicians tend to be equally silly. And now, I think, it's time for some roast boar."

"Shall we share a table?"

"Not tonight, I'm afraid," Crimson replied. "The mayor has put me at his table with Fabiola, Gilles and Jacqueline. And the baron has invited Miranda, Yveline and Florence to his table, so I suspect you may be starved of female company."

"I'll just have to make do with those charming young women

from Catalonia," said Bruno as they got back to the clubhouse bar. He bought a glass of wine for Crimson and another for himself before the Englishman was pulled away by the mayor.

He wasn't alone for long.

"A kir for me, please, and here's Florence, so you might get one for her, too," came Pamela's voice as she appeared at Bruno's side and began waving at Florence to join them.

Bruno braced himself for another curt dismissal from Florence, but this time she came and stood in front of him, eyes downcast, looking embarrassed.

"I'm sorry for being so rude earlier," she said, raising her eyes to his. "I was still shocked by the news that Casimir was not just out of prison but nearby."

"I shouldn't have said what I did, so I'm sorry, too," Bruno replied, smiling with relief. "Would you like to join Pamela and me in a glass of kir before we eat?"

He got their drinks, and they went outside, away from the crush around the bar to watch Sylvain sharpening his long knives. He heard the sound of an acoustic guitar and saw Jordi sitting on the steps of his camping van, playing something classical Bruno did not recognize. Iker was sitting cross-legged on the ground beside Jordi and using his left hand and the fingers of his right to tap out a tricky rhythm on a small double drum.

"I know that," Florence exclaimed. "It's *Asturias*. I have a record at home of Isaac Albéniz playing it. The children love to twirl around to it. It's too bad they aren't here to hear this."

Florence's twins were staying the night with Miranda's children, all being babysat by the mother of Félix, Pamela's stable boy. Sitting beside Balzac, one hand on the hound's shoulder while the Bruce clambered over his lap, Félix was staring longingly at Alba, the blonde Spanish girl who was stretched out facedown on a blanket beside the camping van, her head on her clasped hands watching Jordi play. Ah, thought Bruno, so it begins for Félix, as it had for endless generations of young men before him, that spark of attraction that stirs so much of human life.

"Can you tell me exactly where we are with Casimir?" Florence said, interrupting Bruno's thoughts. He turned to see her watching him intently and suggested they go and sit at one of the tables scattered amid the trees.

"Please, I'd like you to come with us," Florence said to Pamela. They found a table that was far enough from the others to be private. Bruno explained that Casimir was under the stewardship of the priests in Bergerac and on probation, required to sleep at the priest's house every night and to wear an electronic tag on his ankle. He added that he was planning to go to Bergerac the next day if his duties allowed, to talk to the priest and recount Florence's understandable fears.

"The rest is up to you, Florence, whether you want to go public and get the media and women's groups involved and launch a noisy campaign," he said quietly. "Only you can judge whether that would be in the best interests of the children, bearing in mind that at some point in the future they are likely to be curious about their father and may even want to meet him. That would only be natural."

"What happens if these legal efforts fail?" she asked.

"If you stay in France, you may have to allow him access to the children under controlled circumstances from time to time, depending on the decision of the family court. It could be once a week or once a month. You wouldn't need to be there and could nominate two friends to sit in on the meetings to reassure you and ensure that the children stay safe. Perhaps you might nominate Yveline and Pamela, or me and Fabiola."

"And if I leave the country?"

"If Casimir gets through his year of probation successfully and the legal system waives the rest of his sentence, you can't stop him from getting a passport and coming to find you. The family court can require you to keep him informed of your location. Immigrating to Canada may not be a way out for you."

"What if I were to marry again?" she asked bluntly. It took him a moment to think about that.

"I don't know. You might want to check with Annette. But Casimir remains their biological father, so if the family court grants him rights of access a new marriage wouldn't change the situation."

"So there's really no way out for me?" Her jaw quivered as she spoke, and Pamela instinctively put a hand on her arm. Florence seemed not to notice.

"There is hope," said Bruno. "We'll challenge the hearing on the grounds of deception. Casimir claimed he could not contact you, and we know that's a lie. I also want to find out why the policemen he attacked and his other victim were not consulted. This isn't over, Florence."

Florence stared fixedly at him, then took a deep breath and suddenly seemed aware of Pamela's hand gripping her arm. She smiled at Pamela, then at Bruno, tossing her head as if girding herself for the fray, and said, "So the fight goes on."

Her last words were almost cut off by the boom of a large brass gong that one of the chefs was holding.

"Line up in two lines, if you please," called out Sylvain, his face red and shining, his floor-length chef's apron smeared with blood and grease. A large carving knife was brandished in each hand. "Wild boar to my right and lamb to my left. Roast potatoes and salads at the kitchen door, wine on the tables and *bon appétit*!"

"Oh good, boar and lamb," said Florence, rising and striding purposefully to the carving table, saying over her shoulder, "I'm starving. I think I'll have both." Bruno and Pamela stared at each other, startled at the shift in Florence's mood, and then quickly followed in her wake.

Chapter 18

There was no sound from Flavie and Joël in the spare room when Bruno awoke the next day and took Balzac and the Bruce out for their morning run. Glancing back, he noted with approval that Balzac stayed behind to help the puppy keep Bruno in sight, if not to match his pace. He turned around when he reached the end of the ridge and then trotted back to rejoin the dogs, slowing his pace to let them keep up on the return. He put on the kettle, turned the radio on softly and then went for his shower. Then, dressed in his summer uniform, he took the bread he had saved from the previous night's feast at the tennis club and began grilling it as he set the outside table for three, fed and watered his chickens and returned with six eggs. Two he boiled at once for himself, the others he left ready for when his guests came down.

He finished eating and was sharing toast with the dogs when his phone vibrated at his waist. It was Hervé, a former soldier now in his sixties whom he knew from a hunting club south of the Dordogne River, near the old hilltop bastide of Belvès. Bruno at once recalled Hervé's splendid *porcelaine,* that classic of French hunting dogs, all white with the body of a greyhound except for long, floppy brown ears.

Bruno greeted Hervé and asked after the *porcelaine*. Hervé replied that after Bruno's emailed alert to all the hunting clubs for the sounds of a heavy gun, he'd been out that morning with Chirac—the *porcelaine* he'd named after the former president—and had heard two shots less than a minute apart.

"Once you've heard it, you never forget the sound of a twelve-point-seven millimeter," Hervé said. "And I reckon the two shots were to calibrate the sights. There was enough time for his spotter to work out where the first round had hit and for the sniper to adjust his sights and fire again to be sure."

"Where was this exactly, Hervé?" Bruno checked his watch. It was just past six-thirty.

"I'm out in the woods south of Ste. Foy de Belvès, near Orliac, and the shots were well to the south of me, down toward St. Cernin, only a few minutes ago."

"Thanks, Hervé. I'd better hang up and call this in. Can you stay there for me to join you as soon as I can?"

"Take the dirt road south from Ste. Foy, and after a couple of kilometers I'll be waiting for you."

Bruno put the dogs in the old Land Rover, unlocked his gun cabinet and took out the Lee-Enfield rifle that was older than he was, the sniper version that had been chambered for the standard 7.62-millimeter NATO round. The ammunition was widely available, unlike that for the original 303 rifle that the British had used through two world wars. He loaded one five-round clip into the magazine and put another into the pocket of his camouflage hunting jacket. Then he slipped on the red vest that hunters used and added an orange baseball cap so that he'd look like just another hunter. He hung his ex-military binoculars around his neck, checked he had the right map for the area and set off, taking the fast road through Le Buisson.

Bruno hated to use the phone while driving, but this was an emergency. J-J was already in his car on the way to his office in Périgueux. When Bruno said this was important, J-J told him to hold on a moment and pulled onto the side of the road to give Bruno his full attention.

"I was going to call you," J-J spoke first. "The fire inspector's report is definite. Two gasoline bombs."

"I can't say I'm surprised," said Bruno. "But something else has come up, and if you don't have a good map, take notes." Bruno then related what he'd just heard from Hervé.

"We'll need roadblocks at Villefranche, Monpazier, St. Laurent la Vallée, maybe St. Pompont. It's mostly woodland, lots of it burned in that forest fire. You might have to call in gendarmes from a neighboring *département,* like the Lot. What reinforcements have you got?"

"Not enough, a couple of squads of *mobiles* and a squad of CRS riot police," said J-J. "We can't put ordinary gendarmes on this job, it's too dangerous. We've been told to expect a Special Forces team, I think from Pau, sometime today with their own chopper. Where are you?"

"I'm driving there, armed, to where my friend heard the shots. I just left home, and Joël, the likely target, is staying there. He's with his girlfriend and decided he'd rather stay here than go to a military base."

"Does Isabelle know his location?" J-J asked.

"Yes, I emailed her yesterday, but I'm going to call her with this latest info as soon as we end this call."

"I'll get on to the gendarme general. And do you have the number of this hunter who called you?"

"His name is Hervé, Hervé Brandenoix. I'll have to text you

his number. I can never work out how to put a call on hold when I look up contacts."

"Right, I have the same problem," J-J said with a chuckle.

"When I get to the site, I'll call you again, so you can get a fix on my phone, and then you can get France Télécom to check which cell towers I'm using. We might get a telephone number for these guys with the gun."

"Thanks, Bruno. We'll talk later."

Bruno then found Isabelle's secure number. She was still at home, drinking coffee, getting ready to leave for work. He explained about a hunter hearing the distinctive shots.

"Can he be sure?" she asked.

"He's a former soldier and recognized the sound," Bruno said. "I'm heading there now, and J-J is trying to get extra roadblocks." He explained the rough location, adding that they'd probably need extra manpower from the Lot.

"I'll get the Elysée to call the prefect, but your Special Forces squad should get to the St. Denis gendarmerie later today. Yveline agreed to have them based there; she told us she had a couple of spare apartments in the barracks. How are your houseguests?"

"They're fine, but before those Special Forces troops come to St. Denis, you might ask J-J if he wants them checking the place where the sniper shots were heard. He has the location. It's up to him, but in their shoes I'd think I'd want to have a full briefing before being dropped into a danger zone by a military chopper."

"I'll warn him, but we'll let him and the officer in charge of the squad make that decision. Are the targets with you? Can they hear this?"

"No, I left them asleep. I'm with Balzac and the Bruce."

"Lucky you. We might do a videoconference with Yveline's

office when the Special Forces guys land. *Bisous,* Bruno." She hung up, and Bruno concentrated on driving. It was close to thirty minutes before he saw Hervé at the side of the road.

"We'd better walk from here," he said when Bruno pulled up, his face breaking into a grin as he saw Balzac followed by the pup. "I heard your basset fathered a fine litter. If that's one of them, don't forget to put me down for a pup from his next one."

It took them just over ten minutes to walk to the spot where Hervé had heard the shots and as long again to get close to the point from which he thought the firing had come. He sent Chirac, the *porcelaine,* casting around for a scent to the left, and Bruno sent Balzac in the other direction, the Bruce following dutifully behind, stopping to sniff just like his father. Bruno checked his phone, saw that he had a signal and called J-J. He was with Yves, his forensics officer, who was already on the special security line to France Télécom.

"Right, we've got you," said Yves. "How long ago might they have been there? J-J thought about forty minutes. We'll check all numbers linked to the towers. Thanks, Bruno, take care."

Hervé looked up. "If he was calibrating his sights, he'd have wanted a long shot, at least five hundred meters, maybe more. There's only one direction that's clear of woodland for that kind of shot." He pointed to the south where the ground fell away into woods before rising again into open space some seven or eight hundred meters away.

Chirac gave a short bark and then a howl. He was standing on a patch of level ground about forty meters away. The two men walked over to him, and Bruno sniffed, but there was no lingering smell of cordite. Hervé kneeled down near his dog, put his nose to the earth and sniffed.

"He fired from here," he said. "Take a sniff."

Bruno did so, and the unmistakable scent of cordite came to him, the gases and minuscule shreds of the charge that had been spat from the muzzle when the bullet left the barrel. He looked up, trying to see if there was anything identifiable on the ground at the far side.

"No sign of a target," he said.

"They might have taken it with them."

Bruno took out his phone and called J-J again. "They've been here, and we've found the firing point. Ask Yves if he wants to come here and take some samples."

"Yves here." J-J must have passed his phone to him. "I can be with you in fifteen minutes. We have the gendarme helicopter, and I know roughly where you are. Is there enough space to land?"

"No problem. I'll mark the spot."

Bruno took two fallen boughs from the nearest patch of woodland, dragged them over and tied a handkerchief to the point where they crossed. He raised his binoculars and scanned the high ground opposite where the woods gave way to scattered trees and shrubs before reaching the bare plateau. One tree looked foreshortened, and he thought he could see the white of freshly exposed timber on the jagged stump. A 12.7 round could do that easily.

"If there's a sniper at work here," said Hervé, "he must have a serious target in mind. Who's he hunting?"

"We don't know for sure, and that's the problem. But please, keep all this to yourself."

"Well, if he's still around I want to take cover. Are you sure you want to bring a chopper in? They're bound to see it."

"It's more than an hour ago now that you heard those shots," said Bruno. "These guys aren't fools. They wouldn't hang around. They stayed just long enough to recalibrate the sights and move on."

He handed Hervé his binoculars, saying, "There's a solitary tree just below the plateau at about two o'clock, looks like it's been blown in half. Could that be the target, do you think?"

Hervé took the binoculars, focused and grunted agreement. His dog sat at his feet, tongue out, watching with interest as the Bruce advanced slowly, almost politely, toward him, lying down for a moment, his eyes on Chirac, before crawling forward again.

"*Putain,* I wouldn't want to be on the wrong end of that bullet," Hervé muttered. "This is big stuff, Bruno. Terrorism, is it?"

"Could be," said Bruno. "I'll take a look at that tree while you wait here for the chopper."

"I think it's best to leave the pup with me."

It was close to eight when Bruno reached the newly shattered stump of tree, and he could already hear Yves's chopper. He turned and watched it land, Hervé pointing to the spot with the two branches. Yves climbed out with his forensic bag, waved at Bruno and took out a phone. Moments later he got a text message from Yves saying Bruno should stay where he was.

There was no trace of the heavy bullet in the tree, but the force of its impact was evident from the splinters and chunks of wood scattered around. Bruno tried to trace a line from the firing point to the tree and beyond, to see if there might be any chance of spotting where the bullet had landed. He used his binoculars for a closer look on the ground ahead, seeing old, long-abandoned rabbit holes, and one spot that looked more freshly turned.

He walked across to the hole where the newly turned earth looked too big for the impact, even of a big bullet, but then Bruno thought it might have been spinning after smashing through the tree. He bent down and used the all-purpose tool on his waist belt to start digging out the hole. By the time he found the bullet, its head squashed but still recognizable, Yves had joined him.

"It still went forty centimeters into the earth even after punching through that tree," Bruno shouted into Yves's ear.

"Right, good work," Yves said, also shouting over the beating of the rotors. "Let's get back. Hervé is heading to where your Land Rover is parked with his dog and your puppy."

Bruno took out his leash for Balzac, who was looking at the helicopter with considerable alarm. Bruno picked Balzac up in his arms and scrambled aboard.

"He's never flown before," Bruno explained, and Yves grinned as the basset hound tunneled his head between Bruno's arm and chest as the rotor noise redoubled and they took off.

Chapter 19

"Bonjour, Bruno," said Flavie on his return. She rose from the terrace to give him the *bise* and pour him a coffee. He could smell her shampoo and soap. "Joël is shaving, but he'll be right down. Were you off somewhere? I heard the Land Rover coming back."

"Some police work came up," he said. "Boiled eggs, toast, croissants?"

"Croissant, please, and maybe some orange juice. I slept like a log after we dined well on your cheese and pâté and salad from your garden." The brightness of her tone seemed forced to Bruno, an impression confirmed when she looked away from him, raised a hand to her neck and asked, "Any news about the fire?"

"It was arson, sure enough. The Police Nationale are handling it with a forensics team." He tried to make a joke of it. "Could be some outraged music critic."

As if he hadn't spoken, Flavie said, "This is real, isn't it? Not some bad dream that will go away."

"You've got a lot of well-trained people committed to keeping you safe, with reinforcements coming," he said. Then he changed the subject. "I'll bring back some more provisions later today. But you might want to join me and some friends at a riding school nearby for dinner. We get together every Monday night. Do you ride?"

"Yes, I love it, and so does Joël, although he's a beginner."

"If we drive over there in my van with you two in the back, that should be safe enough. I'm on duty all day, but with luck I should be back here before six. I'll call your mobile if I'm going to be late."

"That's fine, but there's just one thing, Bruno. We'll need to meet and talk about this, the whole band. The concert can't go ahead unless we all agree, and even if we do, we need to rehearse. Can we bring them here for that or meet them somewhere else?"

"Let me consult people about that, and I'll give you an answer later," he said. "I'd better go. Give my regards to Joël. Is it okay to leave the dogs with you?"

"Yes, please, I'd like that. And we'll take them for a walk, just here in the woods around the house. We know we have to stay out of sight. See you tonight. Oh, and do you have spare riding boots?"

"Yes, of course, it's a riding school," he said, waving goodbye.

At the *mairie,* he told Claire, the secretary, that he'd be out of the office most of the day but could probably be found with the gendarmes that afternoon. At the sound of his voice, the mayor put his head around the door and asked Bruno to come in. He then asked Claire to make two cups of his private brew of coffee, closed the door behind Bruno and handed him copies of the court transcript of Florence's divorce case and of the latest hearing that had granted Casimir parole.

"My Senate friends got me these," the mayor said. "The ex-husband told the parole judge that he had no knowledge of Florence's whereabouts, the lying bastard. And the doctor's account of her injuries in the divorce hearing is truly shocking. The doctor told the court she thought that Casimir was deliberately trying to bring on a miscarriage. I've forwarded copies to Annette."

Bruno wondered whether the Bergerac priests would have been willing to give Casimir shelter if they had known the extent of his violence toward Florence.

"We had a security alert this morning, somebody firing a specialist sniper's weapon over near Belvès," he said. "And we're being assigned a squad of Special Forces to ensure security for the concert. They'll probably arrive this afternoon. In the meantime, I thought I'd call on the priests in Bergerac and see how much they really know about Casimir."

"What purpose do you think that will serve?"

"I'm not sure they're aware of all the facts of the case."

The mayor grunted. "And this fire? Does that mean we should cancel the concert?"

"Not yet. We have four days to decide. We might catch these guys by then."

Claire knocked on the door, bringing two coffees. Bruno drank his quickly and took his leave.

"Keep me informed," said the mayor and returned to his desk before looking up. "Maybe you should withdraw from the tennis tournament with all this security business on your plate. You know what your priority should be."

"I'll think about it," Bruno replied, although he felt abashed. He walked briskly to the gendarmerie, where Yveline told him a helicopter was coming from the Special Forces base at Pau but had to pick up a team of paratroop dragoons at Martignas and would not arrive until noon at the earliest. A videoconference had been arranged with Paris for two that afternoon. Some extra roadblocks had been installed near Monpazier and Belvès. Bruno said he'd be back before two and went to find Father Sentout to invite the priest to accompany him to Bergerac.

"If the choir is going to keep its top soloist, it's as much your mission as mine," Bruno told the priest, insisting that he come along.

"Why is it so awful to allow this husband of hers to see his children?" the priest asked when they set off.

"Have you asked Florence that question?" Bruno countered.

"There's been no opportunity. I only see her at choir practice."

"You haven't made an effort to see her privately?"

"I tried to take her aside yesterday morning after the service, but she said she had to tend to the children. Perhaps I should have tried harder."

"But not if it meant skipping your lunch, Father? Maybe you wouldn't see your congregation shrink every year if you thought less about your stomach and more about your flock. And without Florence making yours the best church choir in the region, you'd lose even more worshippers."

"That's not very kind, Bruno."

"I don't think kindness comes into it, Father. She's been a great asset to St. Denis. Now the return of this man, who killed one person, crippled another and attacked the police who were arresting him for drunken driving, is putting at risk the life she has made among us. I think you and I each have a duty to help her."

"What do you want me to do, other than introduce you to Father Francis?"

"I thought you might say something about Florence's importance to your choir, your flock and our town."

"Yes, but that's unlikely to impress Father Francis. He's a good man but old-fashioned. He'll see Florence as a strayed soul who has broken the wedding vows she made before God and now seeks to block any paternal role for her husband."

"Do you share that view, Father?"

"To a degree, Bruno, since that's largely required of me as a priest. But I also recognize that we are all human, all flawed and with little right to judge others. As Jesus said, 'Let him who is without sin cast the first stone.' But then one can usually find some biblical remark that can be trotted out to justify almost anything. And we know that without forgiveness life would be extremely unpleasant. Still, I'm too old to want to talk theology in the morning or any other time of day. What do you think of our prospects for the coming rugby season?"

For the rest of the journey, they chatted amiably about rugby, until they arrived in the center of Bergerac and parked opposite the presbytery on the rue St. Esprit. It was one of a group of church-owned buildings around the church of St. Jacques, including offices, a school and a homeless shelter.

Bruno was fond of the church, poised above the river and founded in the eleventh century by the monks who went on to develop the great dessert wine of Monbazillac. The church was destroyed by the English in the fourteenth century, rebuilt only to be destroyed again by Protestants during the vicious religious wars of the sixteenth century, finally to be rebuilt once more with a gift from King Louis XIV. That was the Périgord, he thought to himself, repeatedly knocked down, always rebuilt, and producing good wine along the way.

Bruno followed Father Sentout through a long corridor lined on each side with shelves of books. Soon they reached the office of Father Francis, a large, semicircular room filled with light from an enormous bow window. There was ample room for a desk and office chair; a table with six chairs; a chaise longue and a prie-dieu placed before an antique crucifix on the wall.

Father Francis was in his sixties and very thin, and his height was disguised by a cruel stoop that forced him to swivel his head to squint up at Bruno when he was introduced. He then sank down onto the chaise longue, allowing him to lie back with his legs and hips propped up so that he could keep both eyes on Bruno.

After the usual greetings and small talk, Father Francis began: "So you want to know about our new brother, Casimir."

"I think it's the other way around. I think you and your colleagues need to know more about him," Bruno replied. "I'm here as a courtesy to inform you that the mayor and council of St. Denis are today filing a number of lawsuits concerning him, and indirectly concerning the Action Catholique arm of your church, which is acting as supervisor of his parole."

"What are these lawsuits about?"

"The first one seeks to annul the grant of parole, since his former wife was not consulted on her views. This was because Casimir claimed he had no idea where she was, a falsehood, since he was in correspondence with her at the time."

Father Francis glanced at Father Sentout and asked, "Is this true?"

"I believe it is," Father Sentout replied.

"Are there other legal issues?" Father Francis demanded, turning back to Bruno.

"Yes. The second one seeks to forbid him from setting foot in the commune of St. Denis due to his ex-wife's understandable fear that he will repeat the physical attacks he made upon her during their marriage and her pregnancy."

"Attacks?" the priest asked.

"Repeated beatings that left her no option but to flee from him to protect herself and her unborn twins. We support this claim with evidence from the doctor who treated her at the time, who says that the injuries were such that she believed Casimir was seeking to injure his wife so badly that she would abort. That would be a mortal sin, an embarrassment to the image of your church and to your work here."

Father Francis turned again to Father Sentout. "Do you believe this also to be true?"

Father Sentout turned to Bruno in appeal, who held up a hand to silence him, before taking a folder from his shoulder bag.

"Father Francis," he said, "here is a copy of the legal transcript in which the doctor gave this evidence. Perhaps I should warn you that unless we come to an understanding, we can make this evidence available to the media."

Bruno paused to let that sink in and went on: "Given the other embarrassments the church has recently undergone, in France and elsewhere, I think this would be unfortunate. You can imagine the headlines: 'St. Jacques's New Lay Brother—Abortion by Wife Beating.' Then there are other issues: the failure of the parole board to consult the police officers who were the victims of another of Casimir's drunken assaults; whether the church has given due care and attention to the safety of those with whom Casimir will be working, particularly the women, given his record of violence."

"You presume to bargain with the church?" Father Francis almost spat out the words.

"No, Father. It is because we in St. Denis understand and admire the fine motives that persuaded you to offer Casimir this opportunity of a new life outside prison that I hope to dissuade you from making an unfortunate mistake."

"Do you have an alternative proposal?" Father Francis asked.

"Yes, I do, and it's very simple. The terms of his parole require you to guarantee that Casimir sleeps in Bergerac each night. We would like your assurance that he will not be permitted to leave the city precincts unless under competent supervision and on no account is he to visit St. Denis."

Father Francis squinted at Father Sentout and asked, "What is your view?"

"That seems reasonable in the circumstance," Sentout replied.

Father Francis shook his head. "That means he will not be allowed to see his two children, which I understand is the main reason why he sought to come here."

"Perhaps one of several reasons, including freedom from prison and to pursue his new vocation in the church," Bruno replied. "And any question of seeing his children is in the hands of the family court."

"I need some time to reflect on this, to pray for guidance and to consult colleagues. You said the lawsuits have been filed today."

"Since they do not include criminal matters, lawsuits can always be withdrawn, Father." Bruno was not sure that was the case, particularly the one that claimed that Casimir had secured his parole by deception. He'd cross that bridge when he came to it.

"Well, perhaps you will give me until this evening to let you know my decision. I will inform Father Sentout. In the meantime, I must ask for your assurance not to seek out Casimir nor to approach him until my decision is made. Will you give me your word?"

"Yes, I will. Where is Casimir now?"

"He's working at the food bank today, and this evening he'll be helping with the Action Catholique project for alcoholics. We want him to get experience in all the aspects of our charitable work. And now perhaps you would allow me to consult privately with Father Sentout for a moment."

"Very well, and thank you for your time." He added that Father Sentout could find him in the church of St. Jacques.

Bruno paused in the main hallway of the presbytery when he caught sight of a noticeboard with a series of photographs pinned to it. OUR NEW VOLUNTEERS, it said. He drew closer, and the name beneath the last photo was that of Casimir. He saw a man of about thirty, with prematurely balding dark hair, a badly broken nose and an extremely thick neck, the kind that Bruno had only seen before on professional rugby players and weight lifters. The eyes were blue and slightly hooded, the chin pointed, and he was smiling with his lips firmly closed. He wondered if Casimir had looked like that when he'd married Florence, or if the muscled neck had come from the prison gym. He'd seen that look on former prisoners before. He pulled out his mobile and took a close-up of the photo, with its list of Casimir's various assignments, thinking it might come in handy.

"What did you make of Francis?" Father Sentout asked as they left the city, taking the back road through the Pécharmant vineyards to Ste. Alvère and St. Denis.

"Hard to say, since we saw him in circumstances not likely to bring out the best in people. He seemed more an Old Testament type than a follower of the Sermon on the Mount," said Bruno. "I'm not sure he believes that the meek should inherit the earth."

"What a strange way of putting it," said Father Sentout, with a chuckle. "But I know what you mean. He has a kind heart, but he can be rather severe. I think a lot of it is due to his illness. He has Parkinson's disease, and I'm sure that back problem keeps him in constant pain, but he's a very good organizer and fundraiser."

"Did you get any idea of what he's thinking about my suggestion?"

"No, he thinks in compartments, one thing at a time, and he didn't want to discuss Casimir with me. Instead he wanted to know about you, how long I'd known you, if you were a regular at Mass, your background and your role in the town, that sort of thing."

"I hope you gave me a decent report."

"I told him you were a born pagan, hardly a Christian bone in your body, but a natural humanist with a strong sense of justice, devoted to your town, and that I'd always found you trustworthy."

Bruno tried to cover his surprise with a laugh. "So I'm a pagan? What on earth did you mean by that?"

"A pagan is someone who does not believe in the one, all-powerful deity, whether we call him God, Allah or Jehovah. A pagan usually believes in lots of gods, the sun and moon, thunder and lightning, trees and rivers, that sort of thing," Father Sentout said. "I find it's quite common around here among country folk and there may be some ancestral tradition behind it. But it's certainly healthier than believing in the class struggle, or a master race, or the slaughter of the infidels or any of the other extremist lunacies that we humans have dreamed up from time to time."

"I don't think Father Francis would have much time for that analysis," Bruno replied.

"Oh, I don't know. I've always found that Christianity can be a remarkably flexible faith. With God the Father for discipline, God the Son for mercy, God the Holy Ghost for mystery, and Mary as the mother goddess, we are almost spoiled for choice, not counting the great company of saints to whom we can pray for their intercession."

"Do you do that, Father?"

"Pray to the saints? I'm not sure. I have a lot of conversations in my head with any number of people, including some saints and probably some sinners. And sometimes with God or Jesus or Mary, which may be a kind of prayer."

"What do you talk about in those mental prayers?"

"Most of them boil down to me asking, Why? And their answers being many different ways of saying, Because!"

"Because what?" asked Bruno.

"My feeling exactly, which is why I suspect you may be a better pagan than I am a priest. For example, I know intellectually that Florence's divorce puts her in breach of the church's teaching, but I can't help but feel that it's her business rather than mine."

"Good for you." Bruno took his eyes off the road for a moment, just enough to glance at the priest in an attempt to interpret his expression. "Does that mean you sometimes regret having become a priest?"

"It is far too late in my life for regrets, Bruno, and the church has given me an interesting life. I have been a teacher, a scholar, a bishop's office boy and a village curé. I have spent a year in Rome, explored the Vatican Library and met the Holy Father. And now I get a great deal of satisfaction in being a simple country priest, spending my days in a region and a town I have become extremely fond of. And perhaps I have been of some use."

"How do you mean?"

"I know you're friendly with Dr. Gelletreau, as am I. He told me the other day that he thought simply by hearing confessions and giving absolution I had done more for the mental health of St. Denis than he and all the town's other doctors combined. It was a kind thought."

"Listening to all those confessions over the past few years probably means you know more about the secret lives of St. Denis than I do," Bruno said with a grin.

"I've been here in St. Denis for eighteen years, and given the shortage of priests I expect to die in office. They don't want us retiring these days, not so long as we can still celebrate Mass. You know that more than one in ten of our priests is now foreign, mostly from poor African countries that probably need priests praying for God's help even more than we do."

Bruno pulled up at the gate that led into the large garden of Father Sentout's house, children's toys on the grass and two young women lying on towels and sunbathing while a third breastfed her baby. Once the place had housed the local priest and two or three young curates who served outlying parishes, and a housekeeper, cook and maids to care for them. When it had been reduced to just Father Sentout and a housekeeper who was older than he was, he had decided to open the house to young families in need of low-income housing.

Along with the priest's passion for the local rugby team, this opening of his home was one of the reasons that Bruno had a soft spot for Father Sentout. While he never broke the secrecy of the confessional, Father Sentout had various ways of discreetly drawing Bruno's attention to circumstances that might need his attention.

"Before you go, Father, do you think we're doing the right thing here, trying to keep Casimir away from Florence and the children?"

"Well, through no fault of her own, Florence has been doing a fine job of raising those children alone while also being a real asset to our town. Above all, I don't think Casimir is in any position suddenly to burst into her life and demand that he be allowed to assume a parental role. Not, at least, until he has demonstrated to Florence's satisfaction—not just to that of Father Francis—that he has become worthy of her trust, which is not going to be won in just a few days or weeks. That's what I think, and it's what I told Francis after you stepped out of his study."

"Thank you, Father. I enjoyed our talk."

"So did I, Bruno. May God be with you."

Chapter 20

It was well past noon when Bruno climbed the stairs of the *mairie* and sat down to go through the mail and the emails that had accumulated. There was nothing too urgent, and he called Yveline to ask if there were any developments and whether the Special Forces team and their helicopter were still expected that day.

"I was told to expect them around midafternoon, whenever that is. Sergeant Jules can look after them, since you and I have that videoconference with Paris at two," she said. "It's just a matter of showing them the vacant apartments in the barracks and giving them the keys. We were told they take care of themselves for rations, but we provide transport."

"I'll probably come a little earlier, tell you where we are with Florence's problem," he said. "And how's the ankle?"

"Still a bit stiff, but it's healing. A bit of good news: the forensics people at the fire got some decent tire tracks, Michelin Agilis, very distinctive but not uncommon. Most campers use diesel, so we've got gendarmes checking security cameras at filling stations for any camper that bought regular gasoline. We might get lucky. Come and join me for some soup and salad if you have no plans for lunch."

"Sounds good on both counts, lunch and the campers, thank you," Bruno replied. "I just have to brief the mayor, so give me half an hour. Can I bring anything?"

"No, you're always feeding me."

Bruno was not looking forward to the meeting with the mayor to explain the possible deal he had reached with Father Francis, and even less to present it to Florence. But unless the appeal to reverse Casimir's parole succeeded, he thought it was probably the best that could be done. He was about to call Annette when there was the ping of an incoming email from her on his desktop computer. He read it, began to smile and printed it out before going in to see the mayor.

"You know you've always told me that an amicable agreement is better than the gamble of a lawsuit," he began, once installed in his customary hard-backed chair facing the mayor's desk.

"I know what you're going to say," the mayor interrupted him. "Father Sentout just called me and explained. On the whole, I approve. But it's not me you have to convince; it's Florence. I gather you said we would drop our lawsuits in return. Are you sure we can do that?"

"Yes, we can drop the exclusion order to keep him out of St. Denis. The other matter of Casimir's deception of the parole board is not in our hands."

Bruno handed him a copy of Annette's email, which explained that she had called the lawyer for the police union in Amiens to ask if the officers Casimir had attacked had been consulted on the parole decision. They had not, so the police were now filing their own complaint, which would almost certainly mean a new hearing, to which Florence could now be called to give evidence.

"So we will keep the letter of our agreement with Father Francis, if not the spirit. Our hands, however, would not be entirely clean," the mayor said.

"The grubby hands are those of the dishonest ex-husband and the prison officials who tried to mislead the parole board by neglecting to consult the interested parties—Florence, the wheelchair-bound widow and the police," Bruno replied as he stood up. "Now I have to go to Yveline's office for a videoconference with Paris on the security issue, then I'll show the Special Forces troops the neighborhood."

A little later in the commandant's apartment in the barracks block where Yveline lived, Bruno cleared away and washed up the soup and salad bowls in Yveline's kitchen. She made coffee in some gleaming black box of modern technology with dials and controls that had Bruno baffled. It was, however, extremely good coffee.

"What do you expect from this video call?" she asked as they sipped.

"Normally I would expect approval for the concert to go ahead with precautions, searchlights and screens, all likely sniper sites patrolled, that sort of thing," Bruno said. "But the fire may change that. In any case we need to hear the rules of engagement and the expected political fallout afterward if things go wrong. I don't mean Joël getting shot, but some civilian in the audience or one of the Spaniards getting killed by accident."

"What would you do?"

"We might try using a heavy-duty dart gun of the kind designed for big wildlife. They use them on hippos and walrus, so it would certainly knock out a man. The Turks used them in Syria to get high-value targets they wanted to interrogate."

"And then what do we do with them? Put them on trial?"

"That's beyond our pay grade. If it were up to me, I'd hand

the sniper and his spotter back discreetly to the Spaniards to deal with, even if we could convict them of arson. Anyway, it's nearly two, we'd better go down to your office."

The big screen on the wall showed a test pattern as Bruno and Yveline took their seats at her desk. Then the screen cleared, and a prompt appeared, asking if encryption had been enabled. Yveline used a control handset to confirm that. General Lannes then appeared on-screen in civilian clothes. He adjusted his own handset, and the camera pulled back and Isabelle appeared beside him.

"I take it the Special Forces group has been delayed," Lannes said without any introduction.

"Yes, sir, we're told another hour or so," Yveline replied.

"Right. I'll be brief. I plan to come down to join you Friday morning with a Spanish colleague to check on the arrangements. I'm hoping by then we'll have the two targets rounded up. If not, we'll have to make decisions on the spot. What about this test-firing this morning, Bruno? Was your hunter friend certain it was the weapon?"

"Yes, he was, and we found the tree they used for target practice and dug out the bullet. It was a twelve-point-seven, the sniper weapon. This was south of Siorac, and J-J is trying to track their phones from the cell towers."

"I see," said Lannes. "And I recall from the incident with the Basque terrorists there were a lot of Spanish connections in your region. Are you pursuing those, Bruno?"

"Yes, sir, but they were mostly refugees from Franco's fascism eighty years ago, so I don't see them helping these Novios, who see themselves as Franco's heirs."

"If I may interrupt," came J-J's voice, and his florid features suddenly appeared on a small window in the screen. "We are pursuing the Spanish connection, since quite a few Spaniards come here to pick fruit and grapes, often at farms or vineyards owned by families of Spanish origin, so we're visiting them all. France Télécom traced all the phones using the cell towers Bruno mentioned. We have two phones using prepaid SIM cards bought at a supermarket in Bayonne. We could not monitor the calls because they were using WhatsApp, which is end to end encrypted. Maybe Colonel Morillon's team could help with that. We have an alert for any similar SIM cards in the region, but nothing yet. You have the fire inspector's report, and my forensics experts have come up with tire tracks, so we are checking on that."

"But we missed our chance this morning," Lannes said. "We must do better."

"Excuse me, sir," Bruno said. "If we had spotted the sniper, what were we supposed to do? We have no rules of engagement."

"Rules of engagement are currently being negotiated with the Spanish government," Lannes replied. "You'll be informed as soon as they are agreed to. In the meantime, you shoot only when your life or that of other civilians is in danger."

"Chief of Police Courrèges and I were discussing this earlier," Yveline interrupted. "Has consideration been given to our being issued heavy-duty dart guns of the kind used to tranquilize big game? The Gendarmes Mobiles are routinely issued them during hostage situations."

"Good idea, you'll have some tomorrow. And perhaps I should now introduce Colonel Gerardo Manzaredo of Spain's Centro Nacional de Inteligencia, who sits on the European security coordinating committee. He will be flying down to join you, along with his colleague on that committee, our own Commissaire Perrault, who is known to you all."

The display on the screen widened to reveal the Spanish intelligence officer. He looked to be in his late forties, maybe older, balding, but with sharp eyes and a pronounced chin.

"A question for Colonel Manzaredo," said Bruno. "Would it be possible to obtain quickly some items of clothing from the homes of these suspects in Spain? We have sniffer dogs available to patrol the possible sniper locations."

"A good suggestion. I'll see to it right away," Manzaredo said in excellent French. "Madame of the Gendarmes, I also agree with your idea of tranquilizer guns. And if there are any problems with fire insurance for the loss of the recording studio, my government will compensate the owners if our ex-soldiers were responsible."

"That's very generous," said Lannes. "Bruno, once again you've been seconded to my staff and your mayor has been informed," Lannes said. "I want you to drop everything else and focus on this operation. I understand that the main target, Joël Martin, along with his singer, is lodged somewhere safe until the planned concert."

"Yes," said Bruno, intrigued that Lannes had not mentioned that Joël and Flavie were staying at Bruno's home. Maybe he didn't quite trust Colonel Manzaredo?

"Colonel," Bruno went on. "If we come across Spanish citizens or people of Spanish descent who may be of interest, should I communicate those names to General Lannes's office in the usual way, or to you directly?"

"To my office as usual, Bruno," Lannes intervened. "We are coordinating this affair, and Colonel Manzaredo will be in our own operations center for the duration. And Commandante Grenache," he addressed Yveline, "you should know that the deputy chief of the Operations Directorate of the Gendarmerie Nationale is now in Issy-les-Moulineaux in our ops center, so you're under his command while being part of this team. Is that clear?"

"Yes, sir," Yveline replied. "Does that leave the Gendarmes Mobiles who are being assigned here under his command or mine?"

"Under yours, for all matters pertaining to this operation, and I'm authorized to inform you that, as of today, you have been promoted to the rank of *capitaine.* My congratulations."

Bruno tried to conceal his surprise. Yveline was evidently being prepared for a grander career than running the gendarmerie of St. Denis.

"Chief of Police Courrèges will remain in local command until Commissaire Perrault arrives," Lannes went on. "If there are no questions, we will hold another videoconference at the same time tomorrow, including Lieutenant Duvalier of the Parachute Dragoon Regiment, who commands the Special Forces team. I regret that logistical issues have delayed their arrival until later today. Thank you, everybody."

"Sir, I have a question, perhaps two," said Bruno. "Will the Special Forces team be in uniform, which will certainly excite public speculation, or can we dress them as civilian hunters who will fit into the landscape?"

"Good idea, do that," said Lannes. "And you had another question."

"If they don't have civilian clothes already, I will need a contingency fund to buy some," Bruno said. "And I would rather not have a military chopper with a heavily armed group of men in uniform landing in the middle of St. Denis, so perhaps the pilot could be asked to put them down at the field in front of my house, four kilometers due north. I can be there in five minutes and lay down a couple of sheets to show him where to land."

"That makes sense. I'll ensure the pilot is briefed. And, Capitaine Grenache, you are authorized to use gendarme funds. Thank you, everybody."

The screen went blank.

"Congratulations on the promotion," said Bruno, shaking Yveline's hand.

"Thanks, Bruno. Right now I'm coming with you, first, to meet the soldiers and, second, to get the sizes for the civilian clothes. And since my car is parked outside, we'll take that."

In Yveline's Twingo, Bruno said, "I'm happy for your promotion, but sad that I don't see you remaining long in St. Denis with your exalted new rank."

"You might not be rid of me just yet," she said, glancing from the road to grin at him. "You know they're building us a new gendarmerie on the road to Campagne? It's going to be a lot bigger, and we'll be responsible for the Dordogne and Vézère Valleys, and south all the way to Belvès. It looks as though I'll be running it."

"Excellent news," Bruno said. "It also means that Sergeant Jules will be staying here, just as he always wanted."

"I couldn't do without the old devil," she said. "And you remember Sabine, from Metz, who was with us on that Stasi business? I've asked for her to be assigned here just as soon as she graduates from the officers' course."

"Better still," said Bruno with a laugh. "Nothing more useful for a village policeman like me than to be on first-name terms with gendarme officers."

"As of now, though, I'm under your command," she said, "so tell me what you want me to do to help Florence."

"If Father Francis agrees with my request that he keep the ex-husband out of St. Denis, and the police request for a new parole hearing goes ahead, we may not have to do anything. But at some point he's going to be released, and under current law I'm not sure that any family court would deny him the right to visit his children."

"So eventually Florence may have to learn to live with that?"

"I'd be surprised if when they are older the twins aren't curious about their father. I think that Florence's friends should help make her feel secure enough to deal with that reality. At the moment, she's in complete denial."

"So what would you be doing if you were not under orders to spend your whole time on this Spanish business?" she asked, turning onto the road that led to Bruno's home.

"I'd try to meet the ex-husband, Casimir, and get a sense of whether he has genuinely undergone a transformation. Alcoholics can do that sometimes, when they stop drinking. Maybe he really has developed a religious vocation. On the other hand, he may just be doing whatever it takes to get out of prison."

She parked in front of the house, and Bruno went inside, shouting a greeting to Joël and Flavie, who came out to be introduced to Yveline. Bruno had picked up two white sheets, one of which he handed to Yveline, and a dishcloth. They were followed by Joël and Flavie, who watched curiously as they took the sheets into the field where Bruno allowed a neighbor to graze his cows in winter. At this time of year, there was enough pasture on the farmer's own land. They spread out the sheets on the ground, Bruno standing in the gap between them holding the dishcloth. They each listened for the sound of an approaching helicopter.

"Why the dishcloth?" Yveline asked.

"The pilot needs us to show him the wind direction," Bruno replied, holding it aloft. "And don't forget to hang on to your hat when he comes in to land."

Chapter 21

Lieutenant Duvalier was short, even shorter than Yveline, with broad shoulders and big hands. The sergeant with him was the opposite, tall and willowy. The other six members of the team represented every variety of soldier, plump and skinny, solemn and cheerful, bright eyed or jaded. Had he not known they were Special Forces paratroopers who had undergone the toughest training the French military could provide, Bruno would have deemed them very like his own infantry squad in Bosnia.

The difference was in the weapons. Bruno's squad had each carried the standard French equipment of the day, the FAMAS assault rifle with the plastic cheek guards that tended to break. Worse still had been the magazines, designed to be disposable, but the troops had to use them again and again because of budget constraints, so they often jammed. The officer and sergeant of the Special Forces had American M16s with the grenade thrower beneath the barrel. Four of them carried the Heckler & Koch 416 assault rifle that was becoming the standard French infantry weapon. Another had a Mossberg pump-action shotgun and the last one carried the FR F2 sniper rifle, bolt operated, with a laser range finder and thermal sight to track warm bodies in the dark.

"Bonjour and welcome to St. Denis. You're loaded for bear, I see," Bruno said, shaking hands first with the lieutenant and sergeant and then with each man in turn. He looked back to see the lieutenant standing at attention and saluting.

"Chief of Police Courrèges, Lieutenant Duvalier reporting for duty, sir."

Bruno gaped at him in surprise. "You needn't salute me, I'm a civilian."

"We always salute winners of the Croix de Guerre, sir. We were briefed on your military background."

"That was a long time ago, and from now on please call me Bruno, all of you. This is Captain Yveline Grenache of the gendarmes, who played hockey for France in the Olympics. We're honored to have you here in the Périgord. I suggest you unload your gear, and then we'll take you to your quarters. We'll meet for a briefing at fifteen-thirty before I show you the terrain, and you tell me what we can do for you. What about your chopper, does it stay here?"

"No, it stays on standby at Bergerac airport for as long as we're here."

"We have funds to buy you civilian clothing, but do you have some with you?" Bruno asked. "Men in uniform will get people asking questions, so it's better if you look like hunters. I suggest jeans and civilian jackets for at least half of you, but I don't want you all looking the same."

They all had jeans in their kit bags, a couple had casual jackets or sweaters, and the sergeant had a civilian baseball cap. Yveline checked for sizes and made a note of what to buy while

Bruno inspected the weapons. He nodded at the shotgun and the sniper's rifle, but no hunter Bruno knew used an assault weapon. The M16s and the Heckler & Koch weapons would have to be replaced with something more credible.

He took them up to his home, where they received a warm welcome from the dogs. Bruno explained that Balzac was the sniffer dog. He left the troops clustered around the animals and went indoors. Joël and Flavie had disappeared, but Favie's hand-bag was in the living room, and from the spare room upstairs he could hear music being played very softly. Probably not a good time to disturb them, he thought.

He unlocked his weapons cabinet, took all his guns out to the table on the terrace and asked the soldiers to gather round. He handed Duvalier the priceless Purdey shotgun he had inherited from a wartime pilot who had gone on to make a fortune in the aviation industry. Bruno had saved his family from a nasty scandal. He handed the sergeant his MAS-36 bolt-action rifle that had been standard French army issue through World War II into the 1960s and was still widely used by hunters. With it he handed over a box of the seven-millimeter cartridges it took. The last weapon in Bruno's collection was his favorite: his first hunting gun, a secondhand St. Etienne shotgun made by Manufrance and sold in the tens of thousands to hunters.

"I'll borrow some more weapons from friends in the hunting club," he said. "I know you'll take care of them. You can store your own in the gendarmerie's arsenal. It's locked and secure. If we haven't caught this sniper team by Friday midday, you can have your own weapons back. We think they intend to kill their target at a concert Friday evening, and at that point all bets will be off. I was told we'll get rules of engagement later today. When Yveline gets back with your clothes, we'll all pile into my Land Rover and her Twingo and go to the gendarmerie, where you have quarters in their barracks. We'll drop off your gear, and then I'll brief you before taking you out to the key terrain."

He led them into his living room and spread out on the dining table a map of St. Denis and its surroundings that was issued by the local tourist office. He pointed to the main square and *mairie,* the gendarmerie and the church with its landmark spire. Finally, he marked with a small cross his own home and the concert site.

"If I were the sniper, I'd hole up somewhere along this wooded ridge, where I'd have a pretty clear shot at a distance of between one and two kilometers. I'll take you up there on foot so you can familiarize yourselves while your sniper looks around for other possible sniper sites. Have you had anything to eat since breakfast?"

"No, Bruno," said Duvalier. "But we have combat rations."

"Is it still the same old chili con carne, crackers and that salmon and pasta salad?" Bruno asked. He was answered by a chorus of groans and nodding of heads. "And the muesli with chocolate bits? The best stuff, as I remember, were the canned rillettes of duck."

"We always eat that first," said the sergeant, grinning at him, and Bruno knew that a rapport had been established. "We also have this," the sergeant went on, and brought out a large *pain.* Wordlessly, the sniper and the soldier with the shotgun each brought out another.

"I can cook you a big omelette from my own hens while we wait for Yveline to get back," he suggested, which proved to be a popular idea. He sent three of the troops to the chicken run and told them to bring back all the eggs they could find and asked another to pick four of the fat beefsteak tomatoes from his *potager.* He put his two biggest pans on the stove and began melting duck fat. He asked Duvalier and his sergeant to peel cloves of garlic and the sniper to set the table, pointing out where to find the utensils. He took the other soldiers out to the barn to gather a five-liter box of red wine from the town vineyard, two jars of his venison pâté and one of pickled cornichons. Back in the kitchen Bruno opened the jars and began grating a log of Stéphane's aged goat cheese.

Six beaten eggs and a splash of cream went into each pan with three crushed cloves of garlic. He sprinkled salt and pepper, swirled the pans, nudging the egg mixture gently with the spatula. He asked them to slice the bread and open the jars of pâté and cornichons and asked Duvalier to slice the tomatoes. He darted outside to pick some fresh basil and parsley and came back in time to sprinkle the grated cheese before folding the omelettes and topping each one with hand-shredded parsley before taking them out to the table. He returned to the kitchen to pour olive oil and apple cider vinegar over the tomatoes before tearing up the basil leaves and tossing them on top.

The soldiers had awaited his return before helping themselves, and his glass of red wine was already poured.

"Welcome, and *bon appétit,*" he said, and began slicing and serving the omelettes and telling them to help themselves to the pâté. It all disappeared with remarkable speed, and Bruno realized he'd forgotten how quickly soldiers could eat.

"That was magic," said the sergeant.

"You don't get eggs like that at the base," added the sniper. "And that venison pâté was great."

When the last of the wine from the box was poured, Bruno suggested they should all visit the town vineyard before they left. By the time Yveline arrived, the plates had been cleared away and washed.

Yveline brought from the car eight sleeveless nylon vests in bright reds and orange, the usual French hunters' garb, and told each man to dirty his by rubbing it on the earth of Bruno's flower beds and then roughing it on the driveway. She had also found half a dozen baseball caps, two of them advertising *Sud Ouest* and others for Lespinasse's garage, the town rugby club and the Lascaux cave.

"Now they'll look like the real thing, along with the hunters' traditional greasy faces," she said. "I assume you fed them."

"Napoléon said an army marches on its stomach," Bruno replied solemnly. "And I assume you've never had to live on combat rations."

"No, thank heavens."

"Funny thing, in Bosnia the British troops preferred ours, and we swapped ours for theirs whenever we could. It was just as bad but in a different way," he said. "They had lots of curries and a thick soup they called Scotch broth. Made for a change."

"Was that where you won your Croix de Guerre?" one of the soldiers asked.

Bruno nodded. "They called it peacekeeping."

"You can't say the army doesn't have a sense of humor," the soldier said, grinning.

At that point, Flavie made her entrance, looking dramatic in tight black jeans, an even tighter black T-shirt and a flamboyant orange scarf draped loosely around her neck that matched her belt. Joël followed discreetly behind, looking nervously at the gathering of armed men. In jeans and a polo shirt, he could have been one of the soldiers. Bruno introduced them as friends who were staying and explained to them that the troops were on a security exercise.

"Any of you heard this new hit number, 'Song for Catalonia'?"

he asked. Two guys looked blank, the others nodded with varying degrees of enthusiasm, while keeping their eyes on Flavie.

"She's the singer, Flavie, and he's the songwriter, Joël. We have a couple of Spanish political extremists who have gone to ground around here, and we think Joël and Flavie are their targets. They are a two-man sniper team, ex–Special Forces, and we know they are carrying a twelve-point-seven. Our job is to stop them, preferably by arrest, before the concert on Friday."

"How long since these Spaniards were operational?" asked the sergeant.

"At least ten years, but the sniper's skills are still excellent," Bruno said. "After a hunter near Belvès heard gunshots soon after dawn, I went to the spot and found a small tree that he'd demolished, presumably when he was calibrating his sights. The range was about eight hundred meters, maybe more. We found the bullet, a twelve-point-seven."

"Oh, *mon Dieu,*" said Flavie, turning to sink into Joël's arms. His face looked ashen, as though he had finally understood just how much danger they were in.

"These Spaniards are looking to kill them over a song?" said Lieutenant Duvalier, almost in disbelief.

"Are you sure these guys don't know that these two are staying here with you?" asked the sergeant. "No offense, Bruno, but I think we'd better have a couple of our guys on patrol here, just in case."

"Balzac will see to it that nobody gets near this place without my knowing," said Bruno. "But you're right, that's a good idea. Now we'd better go and scout out the locations."

"Two men will stay here on guard while the rest of us come with you, Bruno," said the lieutenant. "I want to get all the men familiar with the immediate terrain around your place. Sergeant, perhaps you'd make a patrol schedule."

Two soldiers stayed behind while four piled into the Land Rover with Bruno and two more into Yveline's Twingo. Each man had to carry his rucksack and weapons on his lap, since the cargo space at the back was packed with bags and two cases that Bruno was told contained drones. While Sergeant Jules showed them to their quarters in the barracks, Bruno collected maps from the tourist office. He gave one to each soldier and told them to make their own way to meet him at the concert site.

They arrived from different directions. The river was behind them with the bulk of the town rising to the high ground to the north around Boutenègre. To the right was the medical center. To the left and ahead was open ground leading to the rugby field with the tennis courts behind them. Woodland began to the left about two hundred meters from where they stood. Almost as one, their eyes looked for the high ground. To the right, on the far side of the river, was the long, wooded ridge Bruno had mentioned. To the left was another, lower ridge that led up to the hilltop village of Audrix.

"The stage will be here, the crowd on the open ground in front," said Bruno. "We'll have the sides and rear of the stage screened with trucks. So I think the main threat will come from that ridge ahead to the right, and then possibly that second ridge to the left, but that's a tricky angle." He turned to the sniper. "What do you think?"

"If he's got a twelve-point-seven, up to two thousand meters distance should be no problem, so I'd be on that ridge ahead. If I had a second shooter, I'd have him on the other ridge, but you think it's just one?"

"One with a spotter."

"Have you got a name?" asked the sergeant. "I met some Spaniards in Eurocorps, good guys. If you give me a name I can ask, unofficially, how good this guy is."

Bruno opened his notebook. "Sergeant Luis Eduardo Jaudenes, the sniper. And Major Jose-Maria Garay, both ex-Legion, and members of the Nineteenth Special Operations Group that was also called Maderal Oleaga."

The sergeant took out a notebook of his own and scribbled down the names and then walked a few steps away, pulled out a mobile phone and called up his contacts list.

"I suggest we all find our way up that ridge ahead separately and scout it thoroughly," said the lieutenant. He then turned to Bruno. "Is there any convenient meeting place up there, a hut or something?"

"You'll find a hunters' cabin just over the top of the ridge, a wooden shack with a green roof," Bruno said. "There's a footpath to it along the crown of the ridge."

"How often is this cabin used?" the lieutenant asked.

"Not much, and I'll make sure the local hunt club knows to stay away for the next few days."

"So I could post two men there, or nearby? We have the new, silent drones with an infrared camera, and we can use them to scout each ridge. Even if the drones don't spot the snipers visually, they should pick up their body heat."

"That's up to you and your men," said Bruno. "One more thing: I'm hoping to get some clothing from these two targets delivered here, since the Spanish authorities are being very cooperative. Once I get that, my dog, Balzac, will check the entire ridge. I'd imagine the two of them may already have been scouting this place out."

There was a discreet cough from behind him. It was the sergeant, putting his phone away.

"Just spoke to a good friend of mine, Spanish Special Forces. We did some training together in the Sahara. He says that Sergeant Jaudenas used to be the best sniper in the Spanish army, when he was sober, which apparently was not very often."

Chapter 22

Flavie rode well. Joël hung on gamely, knuckles white on the reins, his knees squeezing the patient old horse he'd been given. Bruno, who recalled his own novice days, reined in Hector to let Joël catch up and then they rode side by side, chatting about Joël's history and Occitan websites until he was sufficiently distracted to relax and they could build their pace to a gentle canter and catch up with the others. They had stopped to enjoy the view over the Vézère Valley as the river flowed on to join with the stronger current of the Dordogne at Limeuil.

As they returned, Hector decided it was his turn to run, and he gave a little jump and then set off, quickly reaching the gallop he wanted and taking the lead until Bruno stopped him above the spring of fresh water where the trail led to the riding school. On the way down from the ridge to the stables, Bruno brought his horse alongside Joël again to resume their conversation.

"Until I visited your website, I had no idea that we owed so much to the Muslims in Spain," Bruno said. "What was the name of that man, Avero or something, who reintroduced Aristotle to twelfth-century Europe?"

"Averroës, or Ibn-Rushd, the chief jurist in Córdoba and also the court physician," said Joël. "He was the first medical man to describe the symptoms of what we call Parkinson's disease, and the first to analyze the role of the retina in our eyesight. His commentaries on Aristotle were translated into Hebrew and Latin just as the new universities at Paris and Oxford were emerging. People talk now of a twelfth-century renaissance, with the building of the great cathedrals and the flood of translations of ancient Greek and Roman texts that emerged from Islamic scholars in Spain. But I'm also interested in the way that Duke William of Aquitaine, Eleanor's grandfather, brought Arab music and poetry back from his Crusades in Spain. He was one of the first troubadours and a very good one. And of course Occitan was his native tongue."

"You said Arab music? Do you mean chants?"

"No, I mean the instruments," Joël said. The medieval lute was a copy of the Arab *oud* and the long-necked version was the Arab *buzuq,* he explained. The rebec, the early fiddle which became the violin, came to Europe as the Arab *rabab,* and the zither came from the Arab *qanun,* which over the centuries developed into the dulcimer and then into the modern piano.

"As well as the instruments, it was the people, the Arab minstrels, from a tradition that is older than Islam," Joël said. "Have you heard of Ziryab, a ninth-century Iraqi minstrel who is said to have mastered more than ten thousand songs? He came to Córdoba and brought with him the *oud,* and you can still hear his music today in flamenco. He's also supposed to have invented a toothpaste flavored with mint."

They reached the stables, dismounted and hitched the horses before removing the saddles and leading the animals inside to the stalls. Joël seemed to have little idea about feeding them, turning the straw or checking their legs, so Bruno showed him the routine and then resumed the conversation as he brushed Hector down.

"I had no idea that the minstrels and the music arrived like that," said Bruno. "From Iraq to Spain to Aquitaine and then on to a wider Europe."

"In my view, the crucial transition points were Andalusia, where the caliphates were established for seven centuries, and from them through Catalonia and the Occitan world," Joël replied. "And since the Celts had their bards and the Anglo-Saxons had their scops, the music and songs of our Occitan jongleurs, or minstrels, could be transmitted easily across Europe. Musicians are always borrowing from each other, and every culture needs its songs and poets. And once Eleanor was married to King Henry, Occitan culture spread to England and to his lands in Normandy. Of course, there were other contact points, Sicily, for example, ruled by Normans and probably the most civilized place in Europe at that time."

"See you back at the house, Bruno, and you, Joël," Pamela called. Bruno waved back at her, realizing to his surprise that the others had already finished, leaving him and Joël alone in the stables.

"You must have been a fine teacher at the lycée," Bruno said. "Did you miss teaching when you married and moved to Barcelona?"

"Yes, but I realized that social media gave us other ways to teach, and to a wider audience than one classroom at a time, constrained by one fixed curriculum. Sure, I missed the interaction with the kids. The ideal would be somehow to combine the two, the reach of social media with the personal contact with the students, so that I could see how they responded to this argument or that line of thought. What I loved about teaching was seeing how I might get them engaged and interested, even excited, by what they were learning. You can't get that on YouTube."

"But you must be aware of the impact 'Song for Catalonia' has had," Bruno said.

"Becoming a target for assassination was not in my mind when I wrote it," Joël said with a short bark of laughter. "The news of the fire at the recording studio and seeing those soldiers today brought it home to me. I hadn't really taken the thought of danger seriously until then. If I wasn't now so scared, I might almost find it funny. But it must be much worse for Flavie. It isn't even her cause."

"Maybe she's decided that you are," Bruno replied.

"You think women are more concerned with people than with causes?" Joël asked, almost bridling.

From his few interactions with Joël, Bruno already knew that he had a short fuse, quick to take offense where none was meant. But Bruno reminded himself that the prospect of being hunted by a sniper would put anyone on edge.

"I'm not sure I'd put it like that," he replied equably. "I've become wary of generalizing about people. As a village policeman, I meet so many different types. So I imagine there's as much variation among women as there is among men. I wasn't talking about women in general, but about Flavie."

"Is she any of your business, Bruno?"

"No more than you are, Joël. And no less. My job is to keep you both safe. Come on, let's go and have some supper. I'll save my other questions about Avero of Córdoba for another time."

"Averroës," Joël corrected.

It was Pamela's turn to cook for their friends on this Monday evening, but in these summer months when the riding school was busy with families and their children on vacation and with the *gîtes* all filled with tourists, Pamela and Miranda were so busy that they shared their turn at cooking. Bruno had suggested that for the two weeks of the tennis tournament they might all go to the club supper table instead. Pamela wouldn't hear of it, insisting that the children enjoyed the Monday dinners too much to break the ritual. Salads and barbecues, she argued, were easily prepared in summer.

Those who had not been riding—the baron, Florence, Miranda and her father, Jack Crimson—were chatting with Flavie and the others as the baron poured a splash of crème de cassis into their glasses of white wine. Miranda's and Florence's children played with the dogs, paying much more attention to the new puppy than to the familiar Balzac and Pamela's sheepdogs.

Joël's arrival was greeted with such enthusiasm that he looked embarrassed, smoothing down his red hair, still wet from rinsing himself in the stable sink, as he responded to their eager questions about downloads and Facebook likes and record deals for Flavie. No, he hadn't counted the latest downloads, nor had he had time to look at Facebook nor to count how many people were following him. And he'd heard nothing from Catalonia for a couple of days. "Nothing since this madness started," he said, and the strain on his face was plain for all to see.

"Thank you for letting me ride," he said to Pamela. "I know I'm not very good, but I enjoyed having my mind taken off everything except trying to stay on the horse's back."

"You're welcome and Bess is very forgiving," she replied, handing him a glass of kir. "Now come and meet everybody. You don't have to remember all their names, as long as you don't forget mine. We're very pleased to have you and Flavie with us tonight. Flavie's concerts on the riverbank are a highlight of the year in St. Denis, so we all think we know her. And we're thrilled at the success she and Les Troubadours are enjoying with your song."

Pamela was good at this, Bruno thought as he watched her

steer Joël around the room, giving him not just the names but a detail he was likely to remember: so it was Florence the science teacher, mother of the twins and countess of computers; the baron, whose ancestors fought in every war France had waged, including his own in Algeria; Miranda, the business partner and mother of the two older children; her father, a retired diplomat who'd become an expert on the wines of Bergerac and selected what they would be drinking tonight; young Félix, who managed the stables and was determined to pass all his exams to become a vet; Gilles, the journalist who had once interviewed Joël for *Paris Match,* and his partner, Fabiola, our star doctor.

"Countess of computers," Joël said, shaking Florence's hand. "Why that title?"

"I started a computer club at the *collège* here where I teach, and it's become popular with the students," she said. "I'm impressed with the teaching material you put online about Occitan culture. Several of our pupils have become engrossed in it all. I wish my colleagues who teach history had some of your imagination."

"Thank you, I'm sure your computer skills could make my online posts much better," he said, and went on around the group, taking up Pamela's skillful cues to have a polite word with each one. Bruno suddenly understood that this must be how presidents, premiers and monarchs faced the world, meeting endless strangers but with an aide at a shoulder murmuring just enough detail about each new face to smooth the social path.

"And what will we be drinking tonight," Joël asked Jack Crimson.

"In the kir is a white wine from Château des Eyssards, made by a gentle giant of a man who plays the tuba in a brass band formed by local winemakers called In Vino Veritas," said Jack. "Then we're having a very special chicken dish from Pamela, so

I've picked a lovely white Montravel from Domaine de Perreau, where a charming young woman called Gaëlle is doing wonders with sauvignon *gris,* which as you might know can be a very difficult grape. She has balanced it just right, but then she's the fifth-generation winemaker in her family. There's a Pécharmant from Château de Tiregand if you prefer red, and then for dessert I've picked a Saussignac from Château le Payral."

"He only buys wine when he's been to the vineyard and has gotten to know the winemakers and tasted the wines on the premises," said Miranda, looking at her father fondly. "It's his new hobby."

"I want to thank you, Joël, for what you have done for our Occitan tradition," said the baron. "A friend told me about your websites, and I've been enjoying them. I'd never really understood the significance of *pretz* and *paratge* before."

"What are those, Joël?" Pamela asked.

"They are two of the key aspects of Occitan culture," he replied. "*Pretz* is the concept of the intrinsic worth of an individual, without regard to their birth or sex or even their religion and, by extension, their race. The poorest plowman or maidservant was worthy of the respect of the Duke of Aquitaine if he or she had *pretz*. And *paratge* was the word used to describe a range of moral qualities to which the whole community should aspire—generosity and kindness, honesty and sincerity, courage and tolerance. *Paratge* was a central concept in Occitania. In the 'Canzo de Crozada' it is mentioned at least fifty times."

"'Canzo de Crozada'—'Song of Crusade'?" said Pamela, her tone of voice making it into a question. "Was that about the wars against the Moors in Spain?"

"No, Pamela, it's about the Crusade waged against the people of this region in the first decades of the thirteenth century," Joël said. "It was a war of loot and conquest justified in the name of religion, with the Catholic church sharing in the spoils by claiming that the Cathars were heretics. The song is in two parts, the first viciously anti-Cathar, and the second very much more sympathetic to them, written by another hand, and suggesting it was really a war against the south by the men of the north."

His voice, calm and explanatory, rose in volume as he warmed to his theme.

"Once the pope declared a Crusade, with the lands of the heretics to be forfeited, the northern barons swept down to grab all that they could," he went on. "The king of France dispossessed the dukes of Toulouse of most of their lands. The church took its share, as revenge for the way the Cathars had criticized the wealth and corruption of the Catholic Church, much as the Protestants were to do three centuries later."

"But they were heretics, weren't they?" Gilles asked. "The Cathars believed in a good deity, the merciful God-is-love of the New Testament, and against him they set a bad deity, Satan. And they denied the Holy Trinity and also denied the Eucharist, the essence of the Mass, as the wine and bread are turned into the Blood and Body of Christ."

"Yes, and in that they prefigured some of the thinking of the later Protestants. So the church reacted in the same way, inventing the Inquisition to crush the Cathars and burn them at the stake. There is an extraordinary letter to the pope written by the spiritual leader of the Crusade, Arnaud-Amaury, the abbot of Cîteaux. He reported that his troops had taken the town of Béziers, adding, 'Today, Your Holiness, twenty thousand heretics were put to the sword, regardless of rank, age or sex.' He was also famous for replying, when asked how to tell a Cathar from a Catholic: 'Kill them all, God will know his own.'"

"Oh dear, how dreadful," said Pamela. "But then history is so full of tragedies. I often think how fortunate we are to be born in this generation when we Europeans have learned something of the dangers of the dreadful old ways. On that note, I think it's time we all sat down to dinner."

"Great," said Bruno. "And what are we eating tonight?"

"A modern classic, a dish that was invented for the British queen when she ascended the throne, so it is called coronation chicken. It's very simple to prepare, very delicious, a chicken salad for a warm summer evening such as this."

"It's one of my favorites," said Crimson. "And don't look at me like that, Bruno. You know you've come to appreciate Pamela's cooking."

"My admiration for the culinary daring of our British friends knows no bounds," Bruno replied with a smile. "What are the ingredients?"

"Cold chicken, cooked shallots, apricots, tomato purée and a secret ingredient, folded into cream and mayonnaise, sprinkled with watercress and served on a bed of lettuce," Pamela replied with mock solemnity. "And if you can't identify the secret ingredient, Bruno, no wine for you. Or perhaps none of the fruit tarts I made for dessert."

"I can't think which is the worse fate," he replied. "But I'll bear the deprivation with *pretz* and *paratge*."

"Well said," said the baron. "And if Bruno fails the test, I'll follow in his footsteps for the honor of the Périgord."

"And if the baron also fails the test, I will step forward as the third victim," said Joël.

"I suspect Bruno knows enough of Pamela's culinary wiles by now," said Fabiola. "But I'm tempted to bet on this. A bottle of Château de Tiregand says Bruno identifies it."

"Done," said Crimson. "I say he can't. The bet is on."

As they took their places around the big table, Pamela declared, "No wine for Bruno until he's made his guess."

"Guess?" he protested. "Never. My answer will come from my taste buds and from my sense of your psychology. Also—if it's not cheating—my knowledge of that shelf in your kitchen of extraordinary British flavors: the bottles of thick and thin brown sauces, the green sauce and the red and yellow."

Once they were all seated, the salad was served. Bruno took a forkful, sniffed at it and then popped it into his mouth and chewed carefully, rolling his eyes a little and making a performance for the children.

"I seem to see in my mind's eye those bottles of British sauces," he said. "So I might consider your tomato ketchup, but no, that's American and there is more of a bite here. Maybe the children can guess? My taste buds tell me that the secret ingredient is something beginning with *C*."

"Chutney!" declared Miranda's elder.

"No, but an excellent suggestion," said Bruno. "What else begins with *C* and comes from India?"

"Curry," said the younger child.

"Right. Curry it is. Am I right?" he asked, looking at Pamela.

"Yes, it's a curry paste mixed with tomato purée," she said, and the table erupted in applause. "Fabiola wins her bet."

"And now my glass of wine, if you don't mind," Bruno said, and Jack poured out a generous glass of the Domaine de Perreau.

"Be honest, Bruno, was that a guess?" asked Florence.

"No, not a guess, but perhaps a gamble. I remembered the combat rations the British soldiers shared with us in Bosnia, which always seemed to have curry in them. It seems to have become a national dish, alongside fish-and-chips and steak-and-kidney pie."

"And pizza," announced Miranda's children, both at once.

"You see how cosmopolitan we've become?" said Crimson as the children used chunks of baguette to wipe their plates clean.

"That is Occitania for you," said Joël as Pamela brought apple and black-currant tarts to the table. "Everyone has been here, Neanderthals, Cro-Magnons, Celts, Gauls, Romans, Visigoths, Franks, Arabs, English and even the French."

"And don't forget the Scots," said Pamela. "Flavie, could I make a special request of you? Because everybody is talking about your song and the children are too young to stay up for the concert on Friday, I'd hate to deprive them of the chance to hear it in person. Could you sing 'Song for Catalonia' for us all after dinner, please?"

"With pleasure. I need the rehearsal. And that reminds me, Bruno, would you mind if we bring the other band members to your place, or somewhere else that is secure, to have a rehearsal tomorrow night?"

"We'll work something out," said Bruno, turning away to check an incoming text message on his phone. It was from Father Sentout. Father Francis had agreed to instruct Casimir that he was on no account to visit St. Denis.

Chapter 23

Tuesday was market day in St. Denis, so, after an exhilarating ride on Hector, Bruno was making his usual early morning patrol as the clock of the *mairie* struck eight. He strolled the length of the rue de Paris to the old parade ground, Balzac and the Bruce trotting at his heels. This being the peak tourist season, every available spot was taken, with stalls selling clothing, souvenirs, secondhand books, knives and newfangled kitchen tools almost elbowing out the usual food stalls. Some latecomers were still setting up their stalls and unloading the delivery vans that were supposed to be out of the street, emptied or not, by eight. Bruno greeted most of the stallholders by name before heading into the *mairie* to check his emails.

Nothing seemed urgent so he googled "University of Lleida, sports," then clicked on "tennis" and saw it was headed by a photograph of the four young players at his club, smiling in their tennis whites as they stood before the net on a clay court. So, he thought, they were genuine. But then his eye caught a reference to Alba, named as the university champion for women. That seemed odd, since Jacinta had been by far the stronger player in the St. Denis tournament. He made a mental note.

Then he searched for something else that nagged at him, the connection with Kim Philby buried at the Kuntsevo Cemetery in Moscow. He found only a bunch of Russian names, some American defectors and Ramón Mercader, the assassin of Trotsky. Could this be what Isabelle had meant? He skimmed down the page and came to a link to a new name, Africa de las Heras, a Spanish woman who joined the Communist Party during the Spanish Civil War and fled to Moscow before Franco's victory to be trained as a Soviet intelligence agent. She was indeed buried at a separate Moscow cemetery but at the same time as Philby, a name and a time no member of British intelligence would ever forget. And reference to her had instantly excited the interest of Jack Crimson. But what was her background, and what would she have to do with Joël Martin?

He found a Spanish Wikipedia entry for her and tried to puzzle it out, thinking Spanish was not too far from French. Then he gave up, copied the text into a translating app and read the account carefully. It explained that she had won two medals for valor while serving as a radio operator for partisan units behind the German lines during World War II. He kept searching and came across a much-longer entry on a Spanish historical site. There he found that she had also been awarded the Order of Lenin, the highest civil decoration of the Soviet Union. She had been given an honored burial in 1988. On her gravestone it was revealed that she had been awarded the rank of colonel.

On another Spanish-language website he found more about her and used the Google Translate system to turn it into French. Born in 1909 to a prominent Catholic family in Ceuta, a Spanish enclave in Morocco, Africa de Las Heras was named for her birthplace. Her father was a lawyer and later mayor and her uncle a general, but she was a militant Communist in Barcelona by the time the civil war began in 1936. She was recruited for Soviet intelligence and trained in Moscow by Caridad Mercader, the mother of Leon Trotsky's assassin, and young Africa was sent to Norway to infiltrate the group around the exiled Trotsky, Stalin's political rival and archenemy. Africa had become one of his secretaries, and accompanied Trotsky to Mexico, where she helped set up the assassination. Later, based in Uruguay, she was ordered by Moscow to marry the KGB chief for Latin America and became his liaison officer, building networks in Argentina, Chile, Mexico and the Caribbean. She was credited with alerting Moscow and the Cubans to the disastrous invasion at the Bay of Pigs in 1961 by American-backed Cuban exiles who sought to overthrow Fidel Castro. On returning to Moscow, after her husband had died in mysterious circumstances, quite possibly murdered by Africa, who had denounced him as a supporter of Tito, Africa became head of the Hispanic training section of the KGB.

Mon Dieu, thought Bruno, slightly surprised that he'd never heard of her. What an extraordinary life she'd led, but she'd been dead for nearly thirty years. There might be a Spanish connection to the threat to Joël, but Bruno could not see any link to this woman named Africa. Bruno felt he was flailing in the dark, unable to make the various parts fit together. He shook his head and went to see the mayor, leaving the dogs in his office.

"Ah, Bruno, bonjour. I have a familiar fax from General Lannes requisitioning you to his staff yet again. How goes the investigation?"

"We still haven't found the two snipers, which is worrying, since we know they were testing their weapon yesterday. The general asked me to make some inquiries among our local people of

Spanish descent, just to be sure they aren't hiding among them. I was about to go and see Joe, who knows everybody's family background." Joe had been Bruno's predecessor for thirty years.

"Good idea, he's just the right man. What does General Lannes think you'll find among our Spanish families? Since they were all refugees from Franco, anarchists and communists and the like, I don't imagine you'll find many right-wing sympathizers."

Bruno nodded. He'd read enough of the local history of World War II to know that the Spanish refugees had been an important part of the French Resistance. Those who had worked as miners and quarrymen at Veyrines, near Domme, had taught the local Resistance volunteers how to use dynamite, and the "forest Spaniards" who made charcoal had taught the French townsmen how to live and fight in the woods. The first unit to reach the Hôtel de Ville on the day Paris was liberated in August 1944 had been the all-Spanish Ninth Company of the only Free French armored unit, the Deuxième Division Blindée.

"I agree, it's unlikely, but those are my orders."

Now close to eighty, Joe still kept one of the best *potagers* in St. Denis, and Bruno found him at work, sprinkling crumpled eggshells between rows of lettuces to keep the slugs away. Joe's elderly hunting dog, dozing in the early morning sun, opened a bleary eye to stare at the two bassets, recognized Balzac as a friend and went back to sleep. Bruno explained why he had come and was invited into the kitchen for coffee and a little *pousse-café* of eau-de-vie to chase it down.

"I told you all about the Spaniards the last time you asked me, with that Basque business," said Joe. "The wartime generation has gone now, God rest their souls. Their children are all getting on and the rest of them are as French as you and me. I presume this has to do with those two faces in the paper the other day?

I remember thinking at the time it was strange—'Wanted for questioning, armed and dangerous,' but nothing about what they were wanted for."

"They are nationalist fanatics armed with a heavy sniper's rifle and we think they're hunting Catalan refugees."

"*Merde*, here in the Périgord? They have a nerve. A lot of our Spaniards came from Catalonia, so they wouldn't give these snipers the time of day. You might want to talk to Puig, who has that big nursery down beyond Limeuil. He brings in Spaniards for the strawberry picking but not many of them are Catalans. Puig recruits in the poorer areas. And Ferreira, up by Vergt, brings in mainly Portuguese but he might have some Spaniards, too. I'll give them a call, if you like. Then there's Oriol, with the big vineyard near Lalinde; he's a Catalan. I can have a word with him, too, but it might be too early to have brought people in to pick the grapes."

"I'll leave it with you, Joe, and thanks. Can you give me a call later today if there's anything I need to follow up on?"

Bruno then went to the town vineyard to see if Julien, the manager, had started hiring pickers yet, and if he knew of any Spaniards looking for work. No and no came the answers. It was too early.

He went to Puig's place and showed him the two mug shots. Puig shook his abundant jowls but pointed him to a clearing where he found a dozen caravans and camping cars, mostly empty, with the people at work in the sweltering atmosphere beneath the huge plastic tents. In a way that had worked with strangers before, he used Balzac to make friends before showing around the mug shots. The pup made it even easier. But despite the smiles for the dogs, he got only shaken heads from the two elderly women and the children there. When he returned to the main house, Puig showed him the registers he had to keep of each of the temporary workers, with names and ID card numbers. Bruno used his phone to take a picture of each of the two pages and sent them to General Lannes.

Next he drove to the tennis club and found Jacinta, Jordi and Iker warming up, Iker against the other two. They were the only players. Since it was a weekday, the tournament wouldn't resume until later in the afternoon. The club secretary wasn't there and the clubhouse was closed. Nor was there any sign of their camper.

"Just wanted to check if you'd seen either of these guys anywhere," he said, showing the two mug shots. He left the dogs in the van.

"What are they wanted for?" asked Jacinta.

"Not sure. It's a European arrest warrant from Spain. Where's Alba?"

The two young men looked at Jacinta, who said, "She hasn't been feeling well, which is why she played so badly against you. She's usually better than that, better than me. She'll be fine in a day or so."

"So where's your vehicle?" he asked. "If she's taken it, she must be well enough to drive."

"She says it takes her mind off the cramps; she went for a drive to explore the region."

He nodded, smiling reassuringly. "And you haven't seen either of these guys?"

The three of them shrugged and shook their heads. "When it says they're armed and dangerous, that means what, exactly?" Iker asked.

"That's above my pay grade," said Bruno. "But usually in France it means they have previous convictions for using weapons and are believed to be carrying them again. If you see them, please let me know. I'm sorry for interrupting you, and I hope Alba gets better soon."

"Why not stay and hit some balls with us?" Jacinta asked.

"Nothing I'd like more, but I'm on duty."

As he opened the van door, the dogs tumbled out eagerly and at once went to greet the three tennis players, who bent down, delighted to see them.

"He's adorable," exclaimed Jacinta, picking up the Bruce to let him nuzzle her neck. "Such a shame Alba isn't here to see him. She was talking about your dogs this morning, saying they made her feel better about herself."

"I can't look at a basset hound without smiling," said Bruno. "Any basset hound, they look so unique and friendly. When I take Balzac to the old people's home, they all cheer up and want to pet him and give him treats."

"I'm not surprised," Jacinta said. "You know, Bruno, it's been a bad time for Alba—she lost a very serious boyfriend."

"Too bad, but these things happen," said Bruno. "Couples break up."

"Not lost like that," Jacinta replied. "I mean as in killed, or at least missing, presumed killed. Kiril had been studying with us on some scholarship. He went back home at the end of last term to spend the summer doing his military service. He's Ukrainian and the skirmishing around Donbas has never really stopped. She got a phone call from Kiril's mother."

"That's terrible," Bruno said. "But I thought there was a cease-fire?"

"Apparently it gets broken quite a lot," said Iker. "One dead here, two wounded there. It hardly ever makes the news anymore."

Bruno shook his head sadly, loaded up the dogs and drove back to the *mairie* with something nagging at him, some subconscious irritant that he couldn't identify. He parked and stayed in the car, trying to work out what it might be. Was there some line of inquiry he'd forgotten or something he'd neglected to do?

He ran back through the inquiries he'd made, the videoconference with General Lannes and the one at the prefect's house in Périgueux. Then it came to him: it was the way Isabelle had cut off that cyberexpert, Colonel Morillon, just after he'd mentioned the fascinating detail of the forty-seven names they'd found among the staff at the Russian cyberwarfare center. Why had she done that? Did it suggest a degree of cooperation between American and French cyberwarriors that was too sensitive for others' ears?

Putain, he thought, frustrated at being left in the dark. And now there was a back channel being arranged between Morillon and Jack Crimson. It seemed too important to leave it there. He climbed out of the car, took the dogs up to his office and thought about how to reach Morillon. It was probably not a good idea to call the cybercommand switchboard and ask for him. Instead, Bruno phoned a friend at army records who had been helpful before and asked if he had any contact details for Colonel Morillon. He was given the number of Morillon's office, called it and as soon as the phone was picked up he heard a familiar voice.

"This is Chief of Police Bruno Courrèges. We were on that video call together with Commissaire Perrault and the prefect in Périgueux."

"I remember," said Morillon. "You were the one with the Croix de Guerre ribbon. That's rare enough these days, so I looked you up. What can I do for you?"

"You were cut off when talking about the forty-seven names of people at Unit 74455. Do you have them?"

"Yes, but I'm not sure I can share them," Morillon said. "You'd better explain."

"I'm looking for a Spanish connection, perhaps from a family that fled Franco's Spain after the civil war."

"Have you found one?" Morillon asked, his voice neutral, giving nothing away.

"Possibly," Bruno replied. "I'm interested in a woman who has been dead for thirty years, Africa de Las Heras, awarded the Order of Lenin and buried at the same time as Kim Philby."

"She interests me, too. But perhaps you don't know of her French connection," Morillon went on. "In 1946 she was based in Paris, claiming to be a refugee from Franco. But we don't know what she was really doing. Her cover job was as a dressmaker. While in Paris she met a Uruguayan writer named Felisberto Hernández and married him, moved to Uruguay and had a daughter, also called Africa. In 1975, this young woman, who was living in Moscow, had a daughter of her own, who was also named Africa."

"And I presume that is the connection to Unit 74455 and the Fancy Bears," said Bruno, trying to make two and two add up to five or six.

"It's more complex than that. The Fancy Bears are Unit 26165, linked to the GRU, Russian military intelligence, and the Americans call it APT28. The other one I mentioned in that videoconference was APT29, Unit 74455, which we believe is run by the SVR, the Russian Foreign Intelligence Service. It uses somewhat different cybersystems, and they are known in the cybercommunity as the Cozy Bears."

"You're losing me," said Bruno.

"Don't worry, what you need to know is that young Africa, the granddaughter, is a Cozy Bear, Russian foreign intelligence," Morillon said. "Africa Nikolayeva Pashkova is her full name, having married a former KGB man called Pashkov, now a very prosperous businessman. He in turn seems to be related to another interesting figure, Vladimir Igorevich Pashkov, who was Moscow's choice to become prime minister of the breakaway Donbas region of the Ukraine. Our Africa seems to be doing well, since the car registered to her in Moscow is a BMW, but maybe her husband bought it for her. Is that the kind of connection you were looking for?"

"Maybe, but why 'our' Africa? Do you know what she does at this Unit 74455?"

"Not exactly, but I wish we did. I say 'our' Africa because she's here in France. We caught her on facial-recognition software coming through Gare du Nord on a train from Brussels. One of our commercial diplomats happened to meet her last year through her husband, at a reception at the Moscow Country Club. He said she spoke excellent French, which is interesting. We'd like to know more about her."

"Another thing," Bruno said. "We've been tracking the cellphone towers trying to trace some phones that have a connection to the sniper duo we're looking for. The Police Nationale say they can't break the encryption. But I understand you're now in touch with our neighbors across the Channel."

"No comment."

"I don't want details, just your prospect of breaking into the two Spaniards' communications."

"We're working on it, and we're hopeful, yes. If you can get hold of one of the phones used by the sniper or his partner, that would help. Good luck, Bruno. Call this number anytime. There's a duty officer here if I'm not, and I see you're on the secure network, so I can call you."

The call ended and Bruno sat back, thinking through the various connections until his musings were interrupted by a phone call from Lieutenant Duvalier. The chopper was on its way, bringing old clothes from the homes of the two Spaniards, courtesy of Colonel Manzaredo. It was time for Balzac and his nose to earn their keep.

Chapter 24

As before, the chopper landed in front of Bruno's place and took off at once after delivering two plastic bags full of clothes. He loaded the dogs into his van and drove back into town, past the fire station and up to the parking area for the local Bara-Bahau cave with its prehistoric engravings. It led to a ridge, a likely place for a sniper to choose, where Lieutenant Duvalier and his team were patrolling. Bruno took off his uniform jacket, put on a red vest he kept in his car and his orange baseball cap, grabbed the plastic bags and set off on foot with Balzac trotting ahead, the Bruce behind him, up a narrow path that led to the hunters' cabin. He had called Duvalier to say he was on his way.

Ten minutes later they reached the cabin, where Duvalier was waiting. Bruno opened one of the plastic bags and took out what appeared to be an old T-shirt. He gave it to Balzac to sniff and said, "*Cherche,* Balzac, *cherche,*" since this was the command he used when he wanted Balzac to find truffles.

Balzac nuzzled around it for a few moments, and then stepped back for the Bruce to do the same. Balzac raised his head, sniffed the air and looked around, then put his nose to the earth and began circling. After a moment he stopped, trotted into the cabin and put a paw on the ground below a small log that looked as if it might be a makeshift seat. Then, nose to the ground, he trotted out, the Bruce at his heels, and followed the footpath up the ridge. He followed it for thirty meters or so and then moved left, over the peak of the ridge and into the undergrowth. Bruno and Duvalier followed him into a small space, less than a clearing, and saw Balzac was standing with his nose and paw to the ground. Bruno looked north where there was a gap in the foliage and St. Denis stretched out before him, with the open space before the river where the concert would be held in full view.

"Merde," said Duvalier. "This is a perfect firing point."

The sniper on Duvalier's squad had his rifle tucked into his shoulder and began adjusting the long sight that was mounted above the barrel.

"One four three zero meters," he said. "Laser range finder. It's an easy shot. Your dog is good, very good."

Bruno broke a dog biscuit in half, handed Balzac the larger portion and the Bruce the smaller, bent down to caress the two dogs and said, "Balzac, you're the best."

"We found a couple of other possible firing points, but there are so many trees, so much foliage, we found very few places for a clear shot," said Duvalier. "Do you think your dog can tell us if our targets have been there?"

"Yes, I think he probably can if the scent holds; since there's been no rain, it should. We have to attend a videoconference back at the gendarmerie in a few minutes. Let's go."

It was crowded in Yveline's office with Duvalier, his sergeant and his sniper. The screen opened to Isabelle and Manzaredo sitting side by side. Isabelle first spelled out that the rules of engagement were unchanged; the troops and all police officers could shoot to kill if their own lives or those of members of the public were in immediate danger. She then asked if they had any news. Bruno thanked Manzaredo for the delivery of the Legionnaires' clothes, described the success of Balzac as a sniffer dog and said the patrols would continue.

"I have a question," he went on. "On Sunday we heard from the cyberexperts that a great deal of the apparent success of Joël Martin's 'Song for Catalonia' and his other writings was being driven not by the general public but by automatic bots, believed to be Russian. So is this all a false-flag operation we are dealing with here, not so much a project of extreme Spanish nationalists and more a Russian operation using Spanish tools and designed to drive a wedge between France and Spain?"

"That's a suspicion that hasn't been confirmed yet," Isabelle replied. "Both our governments are very much aware of the possibility, and if that was the purpose, then the Russians have failed, as exemplified by the unprecedented degree of cooperation between us and our Spanish friends, as embodied by the Spanish officer at my side."

Putain, Bruno thought to himself. She's even learned to speak like a politician.

"Are there other measures being taken regarding that possible Russian operation?" he asked.

"You may assume so, and France Télécom is still tracking the cell towers and burner phones. J-J's team is monitoring that," she replied. "In the meantime, the search for these two Spanish men is to continue. They must be hiding out somewhere near you. You said the sniffer dog had tracked them. Did he then lose the scent?"

"Balzac tracked them to what we believe are the most likely sniper positions, but the trail then went cold at the bottom of a path that led to a parking lot. Whether they then used a car or bicycles, we don't know. We'll continue the search, looking for the less obvious sniper positions."

"We can bring in some more dogs tomorrow from Suippes," she said, referring to the 132nd Régiment d'Infanterie Cynotechnique, the specialist dog-training and canine-operations center which had recently been awarded a Croix de Guerre for its operations in Afghanistan.

"Please make sure they dress like civilians," Bruno said, "unless you want the media full of stories about military operations around St. Denis. And since there's no more room here, you might want to find other locations for them to stay. The St. Cyprien gendarmerie may have space."

"Good point, thank you. You remain in overall command on the ground until Colonel Manzaredo and I relieve you, probably tomorrow evening. Can you book us rooms at a local hotel with good internet, please, Bruno? And now, any questions?"

"Please let me know the arrival times for the new dog teams and your plans for their accommodation," said Bruno. "We may need to hire some civilian transport to take them back and forth, so can you also confirm use of contingency funds?"

"I confirm it. Captain Grenache, you are hereby authorized to use your official credit card for such purchases. Right, I think that's everything. See you all late tomorrow, I hope."

Bruno used his Land Rover and Yveline's personal car to take the dogs and the French troops to the possible alternative sniper positions to the south. But after two hours of scouting on the rising ground that led to the hilltop village of Audrix, Balzac found no scent. They returned to St. Denis, since it was time for the troops to eat, and to change the guard of the two French soldiers left watching Joël and Flavie at his home.

En route, Annette called to say that she'd heard from a lawyer that the TV news program of France 2 had arranged to interview the elderly woman whom Casimir had widowed, and they would probably air it the following day. Two senators had now filed formal questions as to whether the justice minister would review the decision on Casimir's release.

"We still don't know whether the minister will require Casimir to go back to prison at once or whether he can remain free until the minister reviews the initial grant of parole," Annette added. "But that review of the decision will now take place, so even if Casimir remains free, that's the first battle won."

"When is Casimir likely to hear about this?" Bruno asked.

"I don't know. But the prison officials and the judge who chaired the hearing may have learned already about the TV interest. I presume France 2 will be asking them for comment. Casimir may have to explain why he said he couldn't contact Florence when in fact he'd written to her. Of course, the prison governor will know as soon as the minister's office asks for his explanation. He might pass the word to Casimir, or perhaps to the Bergerac priests."

"Thank you, Annette, you did a great job. Will you let Florence know?"

"Yes, I will. By the way, Bruno, I'm told your mayor's Senate contacts played a big role in this. I imagine Florence will want to thank him."

Bruno waited until the line was clear and at once called Amélie. As soon as she answered, he said, "I'm calling to thank you because I suspect you deserve it. We just heard that the justice minister wants to review this case about Florence's ex-husband."

"No thanks needed," she responded cheerfully. "I just had a

word with one of her aides to make sure the minister wasn't going to be embarrassed by this, and reminded her that the mayor was an ex-senator, so official questions were likely to be raised."

"I presume you know about the TV side of this, France 2 news?" he asked.

"No, I was just focused on the Senate. What's that about?"

"Remember that before he attacked the cops, Florence's ex-husband killed an elderly man and badly injured his wife in a supermarket parking lot?" Bruno asked. "They're going to inter-view the old lady in her wheelchair while she says what she thinks of the justice ministry releasing the drunk who killed her husband."

"*Putain de merde,* you're kidding me."

"No, ask Annette. She got it from the lawyer for the police union because they want the cops he attacked to be interviewed, too."

When he finished briefing Amélie, Bruno checked his watch and saw that the school day should have ended at the *collège.* He drove there and trotted up the steps to Florence's maisonette, a small two-bedroom apartment that was offered at a subsidized rent to attract teachers to rural schools. Florence answered the door wearing an apron, Dora and Daniel darting forward to greet Bruno and ask why he hadn't brought Balzac and the puppy.

"Because I have to talk about something grown-up with *maman,*" he said, and they trooped sadly back to the kitchen. Bruno steered Florence outside to her small balcony and explained what he'd heard from Annette.

"There will have to be a review of the hearing at which you, the old woman and the police will all be able to register your objections to Casimir's early release," Bruno summed up. "What's more, you can accuse him of deliberate deception in concealing his knowledge of your whereabouts, something that will give the prison authorities the chance to blame it all on Casimir."

"So he's going back to prison?" she asked, sounding hopeful.

"Probably, but not necessarily for the full sentence. He may be out again in a year or two and then we're back where we started. He has a right of access to his children, and you might want to ask Annette how best to manage that. You'll want to set out a strategy that lets you control the frequency and timing of those sessions, whether you should be there or leave it to nominees like Annette or me to be there instead."

"If the law won't let me keep him from my children, I'll disappear," she said, her face hard.

"You can't," Bruno replied patiently. "If you leave France without telling the family court where you're going, you'd be breaking the law. You can't go to Canada or anywhere else without taking your and the twins' medical records. Then there are financial records, flight and shipping and passport records, social media and employment records. You can't duck this, Florence. You have to start planning how to manage it, and that means making sure you keep the legal high ground. Write to the family court, suggesting the twins are too young and you are still too traumatized to see him yet, but that you'll review matters in the future. Draft a letter to Casimir explaining why it's too soon for him to meet the twins but perhaps in the future . . . Play for time."

Florence shook her head stubbornly. "Why is it me who always has to be reasonable?" she demanded.

"Think about it, please," Bruno said. "You're winning this round. Make sure you set the terms for the next round, because as the twins grow up there will be several next rounds. Eventually, I'm prepared to bet, there will be one where they start being curious about this mysterious father of theirs. Better that you let that happen under conditions where you can set some rules and make sure they understand the context."

He put his hands on her shoulders and gave Florence a brief hug. Her body was stiff and her face set like stone. As he turned and went down the steps, she ducked back into her home without a word or gesture. Bruno sighed and went back to the *mairie* to tell the mayor that his old colleagues in the Senate had done well.

"Good," said the mayor. "Right now, I'm more concerned about this concert. Where are these Special Forces?"

"They're here, and they've already checked out the possible sniper positions and worked out their own patrol routes. You haven't noticed them because they're dressed like hunters. We also have various arms of French intelligence working on this because it looks as though these Spanish nationalists are being manipulated by the Russians as a way to undermine Europe."

"I suppose that's why General Lannes is involved?"

"Yes, and he may even be here for the concert, along with Isabelle and a colleague from Spanish security."

Chapter 25

Back at his house, Bruno found Flavie sunbathing decorously on the grass, wearing shorts and a T-shirt. This was unlike her. Flavie was proud of her figure and like many Frenchwomen usually went topless at swimming parties at the riverside beach near Limeuil, where Bruno had shared barbecues with the band.

"She decided it was not a good idea to distract the soldiers," said Joël, smiling as Balzac and the Bruce galloped to greet Flavie and nuzzle at her neck. She must have been dozing because she sat up with a start before hugging the two dogs. Joël laughed out loud at the sight. He was sitting in the shade and working on his phone. Looking up at Bruno, he said, "Replying to Twitter and Facebook and stuff is a full-time job these days. Any news, Bruno?"

"We have more reinforcements and specialist dog teams coming tomorrow, and we have some old clothes of the guys we're looking for so the dogs will have a scent to follow." He turned to Flavie, who was fondling the Bruce. "Are you still planning to rehearse tonight?"

"Yes, once we've decided whether to go ahead with the concert. That's still uncertain after the gasoline bomb attack," Flavie said. "The guys will be here soon, and they said they're bringing stacks of pizza, wine, ice cream and what Arnaut called a surprise. I thought we'd rehearse in the back, by your barn. Is that okay?"

"I look forward to it. I'd better see to the changing of the guard." He gestured to the two soldiers behind him. "These two new ones are Jérôme and Philippe. I'll drive the current two back to town and make sure your musicians aren't being followed here."

Bruno was back within twenty minutes. He went indoors to shower and change, and then checked his weapons cabinet. When he'd handed out his own hunting weapons to the French Special Forces, they had left him a Heckler & Koch 416, which used the 5.56-millimeter NATO round. He would use it to take the place of the two soldiers on watch, one at a time, so they could get some pizza. Before locking the cabinet again, he loaded the two twenty-round magazines from the box of ammunition they'd left him, inserted one into the weapon and put the other close by. If he was going to need it, speed would be crucial.

He heard cheers and went outside to see the three musicians clambering out of their van as Flavie and Joël applauded their arrival. But to Bruno's alarmed surprise, they were not alone. Alba was with them, laughing and showing no sign of the discomfort her friends at the tennis club had described. Arnaut's arm was around her shoulders, and he was proudly introducing her to Flavie and Joël as a new Catalan friend and fan of their group.

They looked like Beauty and the Beast, the slender, blonde Alba, taller than the squat and tubby Arnaut, whose five o'clock shadow suggested he hadn't shaved for a couple of days. His sleeves were rolled up, and his forearms and hands were covered in dense, dark hair. Bruno saw Arnaut toss a triumphant glance at Flavie as he and Alba advanced. It was not the contrast in their looks, however, that concerned Bruno.

Alba looked abashed as Bruno advanced upon them, his face set and cold.

"Are you crazy, Arnaut?" he began. "This is a security zone where we're trying to keep Joël and Flavie safe, and you're bringing in a stranger without giving us any notice."

"Alba's not a stranger," Arnaut protested. "She knows you from the tennis club."

"You realize we have armed guards posted around here for your protection, and I'm sure Joël told you why they are necessary. Not to mention the fire." Bruno turned to Alba. "You were supposed to be ill. Am I supposed to believe you made a miraculous recovery? And how did you just happen to run across Arnaut?"

The raised voices had brought Philippe, in uniform and body armor with his weapon at the ready, to the side of the house to see what was happening.

"I was looking around Sarlat and saw a CD of their music on sale so I bought it. Arnaut's address was on the packaging," Alba said, pouting prettily, but she was also defensive. "I went there and met Arnaut, we started chatting, went for a coffee, and he invited me to the rehearsal. I didn't mean any harm, Bruno. I'm sorry."

Bruno pondered this while thinking about her supposed illness, about the way her tennis game in St. Denis had hardly lived up to her status as a university champion and about her "missing, presumed killed" Ukrainian boyfriend, Kiril. He took a deep breath.

"Well, since you're here, you might as well stay, but I'm going to have to take your phone. I don't want the rest of your tennis team turning up as well. Or have you called them already?"

He held out his hand, waiting.

"I haven't called anybody," she said, giving him her phone, a large model that looked new. He didn't recognize the make.

"Do they know where you are?" he demanded.

"No, I just left the camper at the tennis club because they were playing. I shouted that I was going off with some friends but would be back later. Then I came here in Arnaut's van."

Bruno stared at her until she dropped her head, and he turned to Philippe and asked him to make sure nobody came up the approach road. Then he asked the others to gather around, suggesting politely to Alba that she should go into the house, out of earshot.

"Sorry, but we have to take this threat seriously," he said when she'd gone. "I've been tramping the hills half the day with sniffer dogs and soldiers checking out possible sniper sites. Joël and Flavie know there's a sniper team out there with a rifle that can kill people at two kilometers. Believe me, they're here somewhere. I found where they tested it and calibrated the sights. That's why I'm serious about this."

"Hey, cool it, Bruno," said Joël. "She looks like a nice kid."

"I know she does, but I'm responsible for keeping you two alive," Bruno snapped. "She can stay for the rehearsal, but immediately after that I'm moving you and Flavie to another secure location where nobody else will know where to find you. Please go and pack now before the rehearsal because, as soon as it ends, I'm moving you."

Bruno looked grimly around the members of the band, Joël and Flavie seeming abashed, Vincent and Dominic looking startled and alarmed and Arnaut staring at him defiantly from beneath his black brows.

"As for you, Arnaut," Bruno said. "Did you tell Alba where Joël was staying?"

"No, I'm sure I didn't." His features were distorted with dismay, anger, guilt, whatever barrage of emotions was bombarding him.

Bruno turned to Flavie. "You told me that you'd explained the security issue to the rest of the band. Did you make it clear how serious this could be?"

"I said just what you said, that it was a precaution to leave home and that you were providing security but that the rehearsal and concert could go ahead," Flavie replied. "After the fire, we all know how serious this is."

Bruno turned away and went back into his house, where he found Alba in the kitchen, looking out of the window at his garden.

"Thank you for understanding the security issue here," he said. "Please, feel free to go back to the band."

Once she had gone, Bruno went to the laundry room that held his gun cabinet to check that it was still locked. He opened Alba's unfamiliar phone, and the screen saver was a good-looking young man in his twenties, dark haired and with blue eyes, blowing a kiss. There was no security system demanding that he insert a code or give a fingerprint. The usual array of symbols greeted him. He thumbed through, stopping at the page with a WhatsApp logo, and tapped it. It opened, but this time a small window asked him to punch in a code. Behind the window he could see a series of times, perhaps each one signifying a different call. He couldn't tell.

He put her phone into a pocket, opened his own and in the search box he wrote "Ukraine + casualties + Kiril," and almost at once an Agence France-Presse news story from May appeared. It was titled "Skirmish in Donbas." Two Ukrainian soldiers had been reported missing, presumed killed, after a firefight at the disputed border: Bohdan Adriyvic Boyko and Kiril Pavlovic Oslyenkov. He then put Kiril's name into the search box along with "Lleida University," and a photograph appeared, recognizably the same young man as the one on Alba's phone.

He stood for a moment by his gun cabinet, thinking this coincidence was too powerful to ignore. Could Kiril have been taken prisoner, interrogated and forced to contact Alba for help at the behest of whatever Russian organization might profit from this? He drafted an email to Isabelle, spelling out his suspicions. He attached the news clip and added a note saying he would try to contact Morillon about Alba's phone.

What should he do about Joël and Flavie now that his own home was no longer secure? The St. Denis gendarmerie was full. Pamela's *gîtes* were occupied, and he didn't like the idea of putting her, Miranda and her children at risk. He could ask Gilles and Fabiola, but he could imagine Isabelle's reaction once she learned that Joël was staying with a journalist who wrote for *Paris Match*. What about Jack Crimson, a friend of General Lannes? Possibly, but was it wise to make a former head of Britain's Joint Intelligence Committee part of this particular problem? That left one obvious alternative. He punched in the familiar number on his phone.

"Baron," he said when his friend answered. "I need a favor. Joël, the Occitan specialist whom you met yesterday evening—do you have a spare room where he and Flavie can stay for a couple of days? My own place has been compromised and is no longer secure."

"I'd be delighted," the baron replied. "I very much enjoyed meeting him, and this place is a fortress, anyway."

"Thank you. I'll bring them over later."

He checked the assault rifle, slung it over his shoulder and put the spare magazine in his pocket. He relocked the cabinet and went back outside, where everyone was standing around the table on the terrace, talking while eating pizza and drinking wine. He grabbed one of the last slices and wolfed it down with a glass of wine, saying nothing but staring solemnly at Arnaut and Alba. Then he went down the lane to stand guard, Balzac and the Bruce at his heels, sending Philippe back up to the house to eat. After a while the music of Les Troubadours began, and he called Morillon. The phone rang a long time before it was answered.

"Hello, Bruno," said Morillon.

"Still in the office?" Bruno asked.

"No, at home. A call to that office line transfers here automatically. What can I do for you?"

"I've obtained a phone using WhatsApp that may be involved in this case. Can you come here, or should I send it to you?"

"That depends on whose it is and what's on it."

Bruno explained about Joël and Flavie hiding out at his place, the arrival of the band for a rehearsal and the unexpected appearance of the Spanish girl Alba with her phone.

"She's been mourning her Ukrainian boyfriend she met at university in Catalonia. He was called back to do military service and was reported missing and presumed killed in late May. That's one too many coincidences for me."

"So this Ukrainian boy is now a prisoner, possibly wounded. It looks like he and his girlfriend have been forced to cooperate. Which suggests that the Russians are not only running the bots to boost this 'Song for Catalonia' but are running this operation."

"Exactly," Bruno replied. "Particularly when you add a Russian intelligence operative of Spanish origin who's involved in this cyberwarfare center you told us about. If you could send me one of the photos you have for this Africa woman, I'll see if the Catalan girl recognizes her."

"I'm sending you a photo of Africa. Do you still have a chopper at your disposal?"

"Yes, based at Bergerac airport."

"If you hand the phone to them by eight tomorrow morning, I'll have it here in Rennes at ten. We have our own landing site here, and I'll text you the coordinates. You'll have to fix the paperwork with whoever can assign the chopper, General Lannes or the police."

"Right," said Bruno. Immediately, he called Prunier in Périgueux to ask if the gendarme helicopter was still available. Yes, he was told, but only within the *département*.

Bruno then contacted General Lannes. He reached a duty officer, and his call was forwarded to Lannes. He explained the situation all over again.

"Who authorized you to contact Colonel Morillon, Bruno," Lannes asked. "Or is this just you following one of your hunches?"

"You always expect me to show initiative, sir," Bruno replied. "And perhaps you should ask Morillon about the Russian woman called Africa, who seems to be one of his counterparts at the Ulitsa Kirova Building in Moscow. The Catalan girl has an encrypted WhatsApp facility on her phone that Morillon thinks he can get into. As you know, we have these WhatsApp phone messages on phones we can't trace on the cell-phone towers where we know the sniper team was active."

"Very well, Bruno. The chopper that brought the Special Forces team will be at your disposal at Bergerac airport at eight tomorrow," Lannes said. "Did Morillon give you coordinates for his headquarters? Don't bother. I'll call him myself."

He ended the call, and Bruno saw that he had an incoming message from Morillon, with an attachment. He opened it and saw a black-and-white photograph of a handsome woman in her forties, maybe a little older. She was closing the driver's door of a BMW that carried Cyrillic license plates. Whoever had snapped the photo must have been in a car or a building on the far side of the street because the woman's full face was clear. She was attractive with streaked hair and lively, dark eyes that made Bruno wonder if this suggested her Spanish heritage. She seemed well dressed and self-assured.

"Africa," he said to himself as the opening notes of Joël's song came from his barn. He looked across just as he felt a pressure on his foot, Balzac laying his paw on Bruno's shoe as if asking what troubled his master. He bent down to reassure his dog and then strolled back to the barn to enjoy the music. The band members were all standing. Joël and Alba were sitting on a pair of garden chairs watching. Bruno pulled out another chair and took it so he could sit beside Alba, who gave him a worried look.

When the song ended, he opened his own phone and called up the university photo of Kiril, held it where Alba could see it, and in a friendly, almost-casual tone he asked, "Have you heard from Kiril lately?"

"*Madre de Dios,*" she exclaimed, her hand going to her mouth, her eyes wide with surprise. "You know," she said dully. Then she looked at him. "Do you really know?"

"Not everything, Alba, but I think Kiril is alive, if not well, and some very unpleasant people are using him and you," Bruno replied quietly. He closed the image of Kiril and brought up the photo of Africa.

"How about this woman, the Russian. Do you recognize her?"

Alba looked even more stunned. "Why do you say Russian? She's Spanish, and she's with an NGO, an ecumenical group in Brussels working with the Russian Orthodox Church to arrange prisoner exchanges. She arranged for me to talk to Kiril on the phone."

"And I suppose she told you she would arrange to bring Kiril back if you could help her keep track of Joël and Les Troubadours?" Bruno said. "Look at the photo again, the Cyrillic license plate. That was taken in Moscow. She's a professional intelligence agent, and she has very cleverly used you to get to Joël."

Alba's mouth fell open in something that was worse than surprise, perhaps a recognition that she had been a gullible pawn in someone else's game.

"Am I right in thinking that Arnaut knows nothing of Kiril?"

She shook her head and then gazed at him with eyes that looked suddenly bruised as tears welled up and the music began again.

"Not that it matters," he went on, aware of how cruel he was being with this innocent and foolish young woman. "Are you really prepared to put all these people at risk in the vague hope that Russian intelligence might someday let you see Kiril again?"

When the rehearsal ended and the others had left, Bruno drove Flavie and Joël to the baron's house.

Chapter 26

Shortly after eight the next day, Bruno stood on the tarmac watching the military helicopter lift off from Bergerac airport with Alba's phone, heading for Morillon's landing pad in Rennes. His gaze followed it as the pilot turned to the north and his eye was caught by the proud spire of the Bergerac church, the tallest building to be seen. His thoughts turned to that hard-faced but decent man Father Francis, who bore his pain and illness with such fortitude.

The priest deserved to be warned of what was coming. Bruno drove across the bridge, parked on the quayside and walked up to the building he'd visited before with Father Sentout. It was locked. He headed back into the church of St. Jacques and found Father Francis celebrating Mass with one altar boy. Bruno had expected only a few elderly people in the pews, but the front half of the nave was filled with worshippers, men and women, young and old. He took a seat at the back of the church, prepared to wait, and then noticed that many of those in attendance were wearing blue overalls that looked like a kind of uniform. As they rose to sing, he saw that the uniforms carried the words ACTION CATHOLIQUE scrolled across the back.

Bruno took off his uniform jacket so his profession would not be so obvious and slid along his pew into the shadows, wondering whether he'd see Casimir when the congregation left the church. He remembered the photo of Casimir's face on the noticeboard and took out his phone to look at it again. It wasn't the face, however, that struck him when Casimir joined the others to file out of the church; it was his size. He was at least a hand's width taller than Bruno but must have weighed half as much again, all muscle. Bruno recalled the massive neck from the photo, and now he saw that Casimir had shoulders to match. He had the build of a heavyweight wrestler or boxer, or a professional rugby player. He strode out of the church alone, the others seeming to keep their distance. Even a gentle tap from fists like those could have broken the ribs of a slim young woman like Florence.

"I came to thank you, Father," Bruno said, once he was alone in the church with the priest. "Also, I thought I should warn you that events have moved on. It wasn't my doing, but the media has become involved in Casimir's situation. There will be a news item on TV today, an interview with the woman who lost her legs and her husband in a supermarket parking lot when Casimir drunkenly drove into them. I believe the policemen he attacked will also be interviewed. It seems that politics may play a role, perhaps to embarrass a justice minister who's accused of being too lenient, since questions about Casimir's early release are being raised in the Senate. You might want to prepare yourself for some controversy."

"If I were worried about dealing with sinners, I'd never have become a priest," said Father Francis, squinting up at Bruno from his hunched and twisted stance. "It's our mission to bring sinners to the Lord in a spirit of forgiveness and redemption. I'll never apologize for that and never regret it. But thank you for coming to Mass, Bruno. We may make a Christian of you yet."

Bruno had silenced his phone while in church. Back in his car he found he'd missed a call from J-J. The message he'd left was blunt: Did Bruno have any idea what was going on? J-J had heard nothing from Isabelle nor anyone else since the last videoconference with General Lannes. The prefect was pressing Prunier for news, and Prunier was pressing J-J. Bruno called him back, said he was in Bergerac and offered to come directly to the Périgueux headquarters to share what little he knew.

"Paris isn't telling me any more than they're telling you," Bruno said as he and J-J sat over coffee in Prunier's office, with its view over the rooftops to the almost Byzantine domes of the cathedral of St. Front. "It's the usual problem—politics. Remember that first videoconference at the prefect's house when Isabelle cut off Colonel Morillon when he suggested they bring in the Brits and Americans to help crack the Russian encryption? That was because the Elysée had someone watching who doesn't want us to involve outsiders. Isabelle and Lannes thought this was crazy and opened a back channel to the Brits through Jack Crimson. And now they have one of the Russian phones to work on. That's why I was in Bergerac airport, sending it to Morillon. It may even be with him by now."

"Who is this Africa woman whose photo you sent me overnight?" J-J asked.

"She's the key to all this." Bruno explained her role in Russian intelligence, her current cover in the NGO in Brussels and the use Africa was making of Alba and her love for Kiril, the young Ukrainian.

"This is a Moscow-backed operation to drive a wedge between France and Spain, all part of a broader strategy to divide and weaken Europe," Bruno concluded. "Joël Martin and Catalonia and these Spanish snipers are just tools, and Alba and Kiril are collateral damage.

"Remember, J-J, how you said at the prefect's house that the crashed car and the sniper bullet and all the rest looked a bit too convenient?" Bruno went on. "That's because they wanted us to start looking for a Spanish sniper. It seems to me they have set this up so they win either way. If they kill Joël, they have their political sensation. If we find the sniper and arrest him, we'd have to put him on trial. Then the story becomes how right-wing Spanish extremists tried to kill a French songwriter who wants freedom for Catalonia. That's the headline they want."

"Last time we spoke you said they wanted to distract us. From what?" J-J asked.

"They made us think the problem was a sniper so we brought in Special Forces and mounted searches, but I think they may be planning something different," Bruno replied. "We need to find out what that might be. At least we have a way in through Alba, and a possible target in this Russian woman Africa. She's in the Périgord somewhere. Alba recognized the photo of Africa that Colonel Morillon sent me, a picture that was taken on a Moscow street. I'm pinning my hopes on what Morillon might find on Alba's phone. We might get lucky."

"But you think their target is still Joël?" asked Prunier.

"Joël, his song and the band, the cultural symbol of Catalonia that the Russians have built up in order to destroy it in the most dramatic way they can. When it was snipers, I was pretty sure we could patrol and search and stop them. Now I worry the sniper might be a distraction. I'm honestly not sure what they're planning. Maybe we should think again about canceling the concert."

"We have time," said Prunier. "It's only Wednesday. We have a couple of days before the concert. If we have to, we can always cancel at the last minute."

"I think they want a spectacle, something very public, maybe a bomb, maybe some nerve agent like they used in Britain," said Bruno. "They need something outrageous that will put France and Spain at odds. The Russians have spent a lot of time trying to undermine NATO, and now they're doing the same with Europe."

"Why are you so sure it's the Russians?" asked J-J.

"How many precedents do you want?" Bruno asked. "Estonia, Georgia, Ukraine, radiation poisoning in London, nerve gas in Salisbury, political interference with funding and cyberattacks on Brexit, the American elections and then the attack on our own president's election campaign."

"What happens if we cancel the concert?" Prunier asked.

"They'll try to find another way of reaching their objective. So long as Joël is killed by what looks like a Spanish conspiracy, they win. If we cancel the concert, we buy time to track them down through Alba's phone and Morillon's cyberexperts before they can devise something else."

"Why not arrest this Alba woman?" J-J asked.

Bruno shook his head. "On what charge? Possession of a photo of her boyfriend?"

"Accessory to terrorism," J-J replied. "At least we'll have her in custody if and when Morillon gets something more solid from her phone."

"That makes sense," said Prunier. "The Spaniards will go along with it. They're as worried as we are."

"Let's see what Morillon comes up with," said Bruno. "I think we'd rather have Alba as a willing witness than hostile and defensive. And we might get lucky with the photo of Africa at the roadblocks or with the hotels, campsites and *gîte* owners I sent her photo to or by tracking the vehicle that was used at the fire. Is there anything new on that?"

"Nothing yet," said J-J.

"Isabelle is supposed to be coming down later today with that Spanish colonel," said J-J. "I hope she knows more than we do."

"She usually does," said Bruno.

Once at home, Bruno switched from his police van to his Land Rover. He picked up the dogs from the riding school, where he'd left them early that morning, before driving to the baron's *chartreuse* to see Joël and Flavie. He found the three of them sitting in the baron's small, walled garden, hidden from view, the remains of salad and cheese on a table.

"Ah, Bruno, and how are you, Balzac? It's such a pleasure to see you with your splendid puppy," said the baron, bending down to fondle the dogs.

"Thanks for bringing us here, Bruno," Flavie said, raising her head for the *bise*. "Your place was great, but this château is magical. We even have a four-poster bed. And the baron's stories are fabulous."

"It almost makes up for being somebody's target," said Joël, with a faint smile.

"I just wanted to check in and see that all is well and you were happy with last night's rehearsal," said Bruno. "So the concert goes ahead?"

"We agreed that we should do it. Dominic was so angry at the firebombs that he was damned if he'd be stopped by a bunch of thugs," said Joël. "That sort of set the tone for the rest of us."

"The rehearsal was kind of ragged so the concert should be great," said Flavie. "Unless Arnaut's heart gets broken by that pretty little Spanish blonde and he jumps off a cliff."

"Arnaut's heart is always getting broken," said Joël, shrugging. "The poor guy is used to it, and he hasn't jumped off any cliffs yet."

Bruno rose to go. "When is your final for the over-sixties?" he asked the baron.

"Saturday, and I'll be playing the mayor. He beat Horst yesterday and he should win. He's nine years younger than me and a cunning old devil on the court."

"That makes two of you," Bruno said. "I'll see you all before that. I'm proud of Les Troubadours, deciding to go ahead."

He waved as he walked back to the Land Rover, the dogs trotting behind him. He stopped at the office to check emails and see whether there'd been any response to the photo of Africa he'd circulated. Nothing so far. The only interesting item was from Amélie, who said the TV interview with the woman Casimir had widowed was confirmed for the evening news show. To get in front of the interview, the minister would announce at six o'clock that Casimir's parole had been revoked and a new hearing scheduled. Amélie had added that she would be coming down for the concert and the rest of the weekend. She had been invited to stay at Château Rock as Rod's guest and spend time with him in the recording studio.

He called Florence, got no reply and left a message for her to phone him urgently. Then he went in to tell the mayor, whose instant reaction was to ask if Florence yet knew. Bruno explained that he'd tried to contact her.

"It's odd," he added, starting to feel a touch of concern. "Like most young mothers, she's normally reachable, even when she's teaching."

He reached Pamela at the riding school and then Fabiola at the clinic, but neither one had heard from Florence. Then he tried one of the youngsters who worked with her at the computer club, but the club was not meeting that day. He contacted the nursery school. Dora and Daniel were still there, and Florence was expected to pick them up within the hour. Leaving Balzac and the Bruce on the balcony outside his office, Bruno headed to ask for Yveline's help. On an impulse, as he was about to pass the church, Bruno paused, looked in and saw a familiar figure sitting in the small side chapel dedicated to the Madonna. Florence was immobile, staring up at a small stained-glass window depicting a bland-faced woman in a blue robe and white shawl, an infant Jesus in her arms.

Bruno walked in quietly and sat down beside her.

"There's news," he said. "The justice minister has withdrawn Casimir's parole. He's going back to prison pending a new hearing at which you will testify."

She took a deep breath and turned her head to look at him, then up once more to the Madonna and then again at Bruno.

"So my prayer has been answered, even though I'm not sure I'm a believer anymore."

"Have you been here all afternoon?"

"No, maybe thirty, forty minutes. I was trying to calm down after a difficult meeting with that damn reporter Philippe Delaron before picking the twins up from the *maternelle*."

Bruno felt a sense of foreboding. "What was difficult about it."

"I wanted him to add to the voices of that poor woman whose life Casimir ruined and the policemen he injured, to have him write that the ex-wife had also been beaten by this man when she was pregnant. I wanted him not to use my name, but he kept insisting that he had to and that he would need photos of the children. I said he had to keep the children out of it. Too late, he said, and anyway he had photos of the twins on file from the Christmas party at the *maternelle*."

Tears were spilling down her cheeks, and she whispered, almost to herself, "What have I done?"

"Don't worry about it," he said. "Leave Philippe to me. You go pick up the children and take them home. I'll see you later."

He strode quickly along the rue de Paris to the old camera shop that had belonged to Philippe's parents and was now his home and office. The door was open and he saw Philippe tapping away at his laptop. Bruno went in, turned the key in the lock behind him and held up a hand to silence Philippe's surprised protest.

"You will kill that story about Florence and her twins or you'll never get another story from me again, nor from the mayor, nor from Sergeant Jules and the gendarmes, nor from J-J and the Police Nationale."

"What the hell . . . ," Philippe spluttered. "Bruno, what is this?"

"You heard me. You'll also miss the best story of international espionage and assassination to come out of France in years. I will give it instead to your biggest rival, and explain in great detail to your editor in Bordeaux exactly why."

"Espionage? Assassination? Here in the Périgord?"

"If there is one word or image about Florence and her twins in the paper over the next few days, I won't tell you a word about this and I'll give the full story to Gilles for *Paris Match*."

"*Putain*, Bruno, you can't . . . "

"Don't tell me what I can and can't do. I've made myself perfectly clear, Philippe. If you want to take advantage of an over-stressed young woman at the end of her tether in trying to protect her children, for the sake of a story that's already out of date, you'll have to face the consequences."

"How do you mean, already out of date?"

"At six this evening the justice minister will announce that Florence's former husband, Casimir, is going back to jail because he lied to the court that released him. The minister is protecting herself against the criticism she will face after France 2 this evening interviews Casimir's other victims. Tell your editor that and kill the story about Florence."

Bruno unlocked the door, let himself out and walked back to the *mairie*. To his surprise, Bruno found preparations underway for some kind of celebration, furniture pushed back and bottles lined up on the long table in the council chamber.

"What's this about?" he asked Claire.

"It's for the TV show tonight, about Florence's ex-husband."

Bruno took a deep breath and went in to see the mayor, who looked up, beaming. "Ah, Bruno, can we count on you to bring Florence in a few minutes before the show starts at eight? That's not too late to have the children there, too, is it?"

"She won't come," Bruno said. "She's devastated and feels deeply ashamed that all this history that she tried to keep private is now becoming public knowledge. She dreads what that could mean for her children as they grow up with all the town knowing about their father. She doesn't even want to watch the program."

"Oh," said the mayor, looking disappointed.

"I know you meant well," said Bruno. "But—"

"Yes, of course," the mayor interrupted, looking a little shame-faced. "I didn't realize she might react that way. Silly of me."

Florence did not watch the TV that night, nor did Bruno, Pamela or Jack Crimson. Florence brought the twins to Pamela's kitchen and Miranda brought her children. Fabiola and Gilles joined them with a kilo of fresh strawberries and two liters of vanilla ice cream. Bruno drove home to get a bag of the bouillon he had frozen from boiling down a duck carcass, along with some homemade venison sausages. With onions and garlic from

Pamela's garden and cans of tomato pulp from her larder he made a sauce for the spaghetti that Fabiola was putting on to boil in two large saucepans. Gilles made a big salad, Jack grated cheese, the children chased the dogs around the stable yard, and for the first time in a week Florence seemed to relax and laugh and pile her plate high with comfort food.

Chapter 27

Bruno woke at seven, feeling fully refreshed after a long sleep. He'd gotten home before ten, silenced his phone and gone straight to bed. After his usual morning routine, Bruno checked his phone and saw four messages he'd missed the previous evening. Isabelle and Colonel Manzaredo would arrive at Bergerac airport on the morning flight soon after eight. They proposed to take the helicopter for a meeting at the St. Denis gendarmerie at nine. In a message sent just before midnight, Colonel Morillon reported that he had broken the encryption on Alba's phone but without elaborating. He asked that Isabelle call him when she arrived in St. Denis. The third was from Dougal, who ran the Delightful Dordogne agency for vacation rentals. Could Bruno drop by in the morning? He'd be there from eight. The fourth was from Rod Macrae to say he'd be on the afternoon flight back from London, was looking forward to the concert and asking where he should pick up the Bruce, whom he'd greatly missed. Bruno sent back a brief text saying the puppy was in great form and would be staying with the baron.

Bruno drove back into town after dropping off the dogs with

the baron, parking outside Dougal's office just before eight. He found Dougal refilling the little pods for his coffee machine.

"My daughter insisted I stop buying the ready-made pods and use these ones we can recycle," Dougal explained. Then he turned on the screen of his security camera and inserted a disc marked SATURDAY and fast-forwarded it to a point where the on-screen clock said 11:00 a.m.

"That photo you sent around of the woman," he said. "I'm not sure but I might have a match. My daughter remembered her. She came in last weekend, a Belgian, Flemish speaker. I wasn't here, but she took a three-bedroom villa for a week and paid cash. It was the last one we had available. We got her credit card for the deposit, a Visa card issued by a bank in Brussels. I've made you a photocopy. Here she is."

The images were in black and white, the figure foreshortened by the position of the camera high on the wall. A fashionably dressed woman with a helmet of curly fair hair and large sunglasses entered the office and began talking to Dougal's daughter, who was sitting at the desk. She was handed a large scrapbook of the villas the agency handled, already opened to a page. She barely glanced at it, nodded, spoke and after a couple of minutes she took a purse from her shoulder bag and then removed her glasses to count out some banknotes. Her head was lowered, but from what he could see of her face, it might have been Africa wearing a wig.

"Can you freeze that frame?" he asked. Dougal did so, and Bruno examined it closely. He wasn't certain, but it was a passable likeness. "And can you print out the image?"

He took the printout and the address of the villa from Dougal, thanked him and left, planning to round up some of the Special Forces to visit the rented home. With any luck the occupants might still be asleep. But as he opened the door to his van, he heard the sound of shouting, high-pitched voices and then screams from the far end of the rue de la République just beyond the church. There was a pedestrian crossing there from the nursery school to the post office. Bruno ran toward the sound of the disturbance, unusual in St. Denis at any time of day but very strange so early in the morning.

He saw two firemen running across from the fire station. The focus of the trouble seemed to be close to the *maternelle*. He began to sprint as he realized the high-pitched voices were those of the mothers, interspersed with shrieks from the children. He pulled out his phone as he ran, touched the autocall number for the gendarmerie and as soon as it was answered he shouted, "This is Bruno. Urgent support needed at the *maternelle* in St. Denis."

He was almost there now. A large bunch of women with strollers were shouting angrily at a big man who was standing with his back to the post office, holding up his hands as if trying to pacify the angry crowd. Then Bruno realized that he was trying to protect himself from the women, some of them hurling half bricks at him from the stacks by the wall that was being rebuilt beside the post office.

Suddenly Bruno understood that the man was Casimir, tracks of blood on his face from a woman's nails. One of the firemen piled in to pull the women away, and the other one charged at Casimir, who turned and unleashed a powerful punch that stopped the fireman in his tracks and sent him crumpling to the ground.

"Stop!" Bruno roared, trying to push his way through the women. "Stop, all of you, Annalise, Francette, Marie-Dominique . . . "

"Get the wife-beating bastard!" shouted the usually placid Amandine.

"Leave this piece of shit to us, Bruno," called another female voice as Bruno suddenly saw coming at him that same mighty fist that had felled the fireman.

He just had time to sway to one side to avoid the punch, but Casimir's arm knocked off Bruno's képi on the follow-through. Then his hand clamped powerfully on the back of Bruno's neck and pulled.

Automatically, too fast for rational thought, Bruno did not resist but went with the pressure, using the extra momentum to slam his fist as hard as he could just below Casimir's breastbone. He was now so close that he could bring his knee up powerfully into the man's groin and slammed his forehead into Casimir's nose with a crunch that Bruno could hear above the tumult.

Casimir's eyes rolled up so only the whites could be seen as blood spurted from his nose. His knees buckled and, gasping for breath, he sank down to his knees and toppled facedown onto the ground. As he sprawled, Bruno landed with all his weight on Casimir's back, slamming his knees deliberately into the man's kidneys. Casimir grunted in pain, twisted his head to one side to breathe and then whimpered as blood continued to gush from his shattered nose.

Bruno pulled out a set of the plastic ties that he used as hand-cuffs to lock first the man's hands and then his ankles together while trying to stop the infuriated women from kicking at Casimir as he lay on the ground. Suddenly came the sound of an approaching siren. The women's cries stilled, two more firemen joined him and then Sergeant Jules arrived with a couple of gendarmes.

"What the hell happened here?" Sergeant Jules asked as the mothers began moving triumphantly away, finding their astonished children and taking them by the hand to lead them across the street and into the nursery school. After a few moments the only woman still there was Florence, her blouse ripped to the waist and her lip bleeding, her usually tidy hair a mess. She was kneeling down, holding a weeping twin tightly in each arm.

"The other women were protecting us from him, me and the twins," she said, gulping as if fighting for breath and gasping her words. "Casimir was standing there—in the doorway of the post office—waiting for me to bring the children to school. He came out and grabbed my shoulder, said they were his kids, too. I screamed and scratched his face," she panted. "The other mothers all went for him—a swarm of bees."

"He's Florence's ex-husband, just out of jail and in violation of his parole, and now he's going back behind bars," Bruno told Sergeant Jules, loudly enough that the others could hear. He picked up his battered képi and saw that one of the women's heels had made a hole in the cap. He shrugged, put it back on his head and rose to nod his thanks to Sergeant Jules before bending down to the stricken fireman, still lying on the ground out cold, blood seeping from his nose.

"Please call an ambulance and get this *pompier* to the clinic," Bruno said. "The prisoner is called Casimir. I'm charging him with assault on a fireman, on Florence and on me. You might want to take some statements from the mothers once they've finished dropping off their children."

He turned to Florence. "How about you? Are you hurt? You know your face is bleeding? Should we take you to the clinic?"

"I'll be all right," she said, still breathing hard, pulling together her torn blouse. "He grabbed me and slapped me in the face. I'll have a thick lip. Can I bring charges for that?"

"Yes, you can," said Sergeant Jules. "I'll take your statement. Meanwhile we'll put this bastard in jail where he belongs. Who needs to be informed about him?"

"Father Sentout. He can contact the priests in Bergerac who

were supposed to be watching this guy," said Bruno. "I have to get back to the gendarmerie on security business. Can I leave the rest of this to you? And can you take Florence and her kids home? Then find out how the hell this guy got here from Bergerac. Train, bike, stolen car? Maybe he walked all night."

Jules nodded. "Leave it to me."

Bruno kneeled down and put one hand on Dora's shoulder and the other on Daniel. "It's all right, it's over. You have to help your *maman* now, get her to clean up that lip once Sergeant Jules takes you home, and I'll come by as soon as I can, okay?"

The two children nodded bravely. Bruno gave each of them a kiss on the forehead and headed back to the gendarmerie. Bruno took out his phone as he walked and contacted Annette to tell her of the latest development with Casimir. The assault charges, one on a policeman, another on a fireman and the third on his ex-wife, would mean even more time in prison, she assured him.

It was just past eight-thirty when he entered the gendarmerie. He greeted Yveline and pulled from his pocket the paper with the address of the villa which Africa may have rented. There was no way he could head out there and still make the meeting with Isabelle and the Spanish colonel. He found Lieutenant Duvalier, showed him the photo of Africa that Morillon had sent and gave him the printout from Dougal's security camera. He made sure Duvalier had a copy of the wanted photo with the pictures of the two Spaniards, briefed him on what he might find at the villa and warned him to be very cautious.

"Just watch the place and report back," Bruno said. "Don't move in until we can get J-J to send a forensics team to search the place if it's empty. Take my Land Rover so you'll look like hunters." Bruno gave him the keys and turned to Yveline. "Could you get a gendarme to guide Duvalier and his squad to the villa? Do you have tear gas if we need it? And a loudspeaker?"

"We have tear gas, but you know the rules of engagement," she said. "There may be innocent vacationers in there."

"I know," Bruno replied. He turned to Duvalier. "What do you think?"

"I'll go now, set up a surveillance perimeter," Duvalier replied. "Can you get us a floor plan of this villa?"

"Check with Dougal and see if he has one?" Bruno asked Yveline.

"We have to be in this videoconference," Yveline replied. "I'll ask Sergeant Jules. And you need to clean yourself up, Bruno. You look as though you've been in a fight."

"Sergeant Jules came along in time to save me from the worst. You'll have Florence's ex-husband in your jail very shortly. His name is Casimir and he's enormous, and strong as an ox from workouts in the prison gym. But he was no match for the women of St. Denis, who were defending Florence. When he's cooled down in the back of the gendarme van, they will bring him to you."

"I'll be surprised if he doesn't happen to have a nasty fall on the way down the stairs to the cells," Yveline replied, handing Bruno a clothes brush. "How did he get here from Bergerac?"

"I don't know. I told Sergeant Jules that he should call Father Sentout," Bruno said. Then he went to the bathroom to wash his hands and face, comb his hair and brush his dusty shirt and trousers. He glanced in the mirror. His forehead was swelling. He still looked disheveled, but that would have to do. As he climbed back upstairs, he saw that Isabelle and the Spanish colonel had arrived and were being greeted by Yveline.

Bruno paused, looking at Isabelle, but neither she nor Manzaredo were yet aware of his presence. She looked cool, professional, a woman of authority, but then her face widened into a welcoming grin as Sergeant Jules arrived. Isabelle seemed about to give him a friendly hug, but then two more gendarmes came in, half leading and half carrying their stumbling prisoner. Casimir was demanding that he be seen by a doctor, although the blood from his nose had stopped. His mouth, neck and shirt were covered in it. He was swiftly booked, fingerprinted and taken down to a cell, protesting loudly, as Yveline led the others into her office. Bruno brought up the rear.

"St. Denis used to be such a quiet, law-abiding town," said Isabelle, cocking an eyebrow at Bruno. "Don't tell me you're losing your touch."

"All right, I won't," he said flatly, still irritated at the time that had been lost by Isabelle's abrupt ending of Morillon's explanation of the Russian role during the videoconference at the prefect's home. She seemed ever more ready to defer to the Elysée and the politicians. "Have you heard yet from Colonel Morillon? He said he wanted to talk as soon as you arrived."

"He can wait," she said. "We have a videoconference with him and Paris at nine-fifteen. In the meantime, say hello to Colonel Manzaredo, who has something for you."

Bruno shook hands, and the Spanish colonel handed him a large gun bag. "Here's your tranquilizer gun with ketamine darts. The substance acts quickly and is rarely fatal, but it does not act at once, so even when hit, a sniper may still have time to shoot. The range is less than thirty meters and if they are wearing body armor it won't penetrate. Frankly, I'd recommend getting our own snipers to fire a disabling shot. We'd rather take these men alive."

Bruno stared at him coolly. "Thank you, but I'm sure you'll

agree that it could be difficult to ask for a disabling shot in combat conditions, Colonel. But I'll give this to Lieutenant Duvalier and let him decide how to use it."

"You could always use it to shut up that prisoner howling away downstairs," said Isabelle, looking up from her stroking of Balzac. "Any other developments?"

"Yes, Lieutenant Duvalier and our Special Forces team are scouting a villa rented by a woman who may be associated with our sniper," said Bruno. "She looks very like this Russian woman Colonel Morillon is interested in."

Isabelle nodded. "I know your own place became insecure for Joël Martin," she said, ignoring his remark about the rented villa. "Where is he now?"

"Joël and Flavie, that's the lead singer of Les Troubadours, are staying with the baron, along with Balzac and his pup."

"And where is this young Spanish woman with the Ukrainian boyfriend?"

"In a camper at the tennis club. The big question is whether we still go ahead with the concert."

"We don't have to make that decision until tomorrow, when General Lannes will be here," Isabelle said. "I'm sure that the Special Forces can keep all viable sniper sites under close observation. What of the other steps we discussed, searchlights and strobes, artificial smoke?"

"They are coming tomorrow when we set up the stage. Yveline and our public works people are taking care of that," Bruno said.

"Right, it's time for our video call," she replied. "Let's see what Morillon has to say."

Chapter 28

They crowded into Yveline's office. She set up the screen, and after a moment the face of General Lannes appeared.

"Any developments?" he began after a brief greeting.

Bruno explained the fresh news about the villa and the possible sighting of the woman, Africa, as the screen split into two and Colonel Morillon's face appeared. Bruno was about to explain about the Belgian bank account when Morillon spoke.

"Bonjour, everyone," said Morillon. "And thank you, Bruno, for the phone. Should I give my report?"

"One moment, Colonel," said General Lannes. "We may have something new for you."

Bruno showed the photograph from Dougal's security camera, explained about the villa rental and read out the number of the credit card the woman had used and the name on it, Adalheid Van Diest. Isabelle at once turned away and began texting on her phone, saying that she was getting her Belgian counterpart to check on the name and account number.

"Can you get that camera tape to me today?" Morillon asked. "We can enhance it, check that it's Africa."

"If there's a chopper to get it to you, yes," said Bruno.

"Not a problem," said Lannes. "Go ahead with your report, Colonel."

"We managed to get into the phone belonging to the young woman, Alba," Morillon said. "It's the latest Russian-made Sistronics model, not yet available to the public. It has a Russian-made operating system. She had three highly emotional contacts with a young man whom she called Kiril, who was in a prison located in what we established is the city of Donetsk, in Russian-occupied Ukraine."

After each brief session, Morillon went on, Alba spoke to a Russian female and agreed to do whatever was asked of her in return for the safety of the young man. The Russian woman was believed to be the operative known as Africa. Alba asked for Kiril to be returned to his university in Spain, and Africa replied that his fate would depend on how useful Alba could be.

Alba had two further conversations with Africa in the last four days, which took place while Africa was in the Périgord region, in two separate locations. The first was in the vicinity of the Château des Vigiers, with its famous golf course; the second had been on Tuesday afternoon.

"That was a few hours before Bruno confiscated the phone," Morillon said. "When Alba was in Sarlat, she called Africa to say she would have a location for what she called 'the songwriter' later that day. From the cell-phone towers we know that Africa was then in a car driving from Belvès toward Bergerac. We can track the movements of her phone but not the messages, so we're now trying to break a further degree of encryption on Africa's phone. But I can confirm she has made more than sixteen phone calls since then."

"And those sixteen calls were to whom?" Lannes asked.

Morillon looked down at a list on his desk and read out that there had been six calls to a burner phone with a temporary SIM card that was in the Périgord region, four to Moscow, two to Brussels, one to Madrid and three to Donetsk.

"We're now trying to trace all those numbers, and I'm emailing you a list," he said. "The Brussels number is listed for an ecumenical liaison office."

"Africa told Alba that she was with an ecumenical group, working with the Russian Orthodox Church on prisoner exchanges," Bruno said.

"What's the French SIM card number?" asked Isabelle, opening a notebook. When Morillon read it out, she said, "It's the SIM card J-J's people got from the cell towers where they tested the gun on that tree. This is really coming together."

"What are the chances of you breaking that extra level of encryption on Africa's phone?" Lannes asked.

"We're working on it, but it's very tough," Morillon replied. "And while we were working on Alba's phone, we got two calls coming in from Africa's number. We sent back signals that the battery was dead, but I doubt that will have fooled anybody. Then we received another call to Alba that was routed through a virtual network that we tracked through Serbia, which probably means Russia. We're trying to peel that open, but I imagine it was Africa again, trying a more secure way to contact Alba."

"Call me if you get anywhere further or if your photo people confirm that the woman on the security camera is indeed Africa. We'll get that tape on its way to you within the hour," Lannes said. "Good job, Colonel. I'm impressed. Please get back to work."

"Yes, sir, but there's one last thing," said Morillon. "In each of her calls to Africa in the last week, Alba has referred to Bruno, as a local policeman, by name. That makes him a target. I'd get him out of there to somewhere safe, if I were you."

"That is an operational decision, Colonel Morillon, but thank you for your input," Lannes said, and closed Morillon's image.

"Bruno, what do you think?" Lannes asked.

"We should think again about J-J's remark that the various indications of a sniper threat were all a little too convenient, especially since we know the car crash was faked. We were meant to find that special bullet," Bruno said. "What's more, Lieutenant Duvalier and our own snipers agree that the possible sniper locations around St. Denis are not good, too much foliage and not enough options for evasion. It may all be a distraction. I have also learned that Sergeant Jaudenes may once have been a great sniper, but he's better known these days as a heavy drinker. Still, whoever tested the weapon on that tree was certainly a good shot."

"So what are you suggesting, Bruno?" Lannes asked.

"We've been looking for two snipers from a larger group of Novios extremists who may have other potential ways to attack the concert. They could plant a bomb or even use mortars, which is what I'd do if I didn't care about causing many more casualties. And since I'd be firing a mortar from much farther away, my prospects of escape would be that much better. Perhaps Colonel Manzaredo can tell us if other members of this Novios group are missing, if they also have military expertise and, if so, what specific skills."

"We keep a general eye on the whole group," Manzaredo said. "But of course lately we've been focusing more on Major Garay and Sergeant Jaudenes and their immediate associates. I'll get Madrid to make some urgent checks as soon as this video call is over."

"It might be useful to let it be known among the Novios that this appears increasingly like a false-flag operation by the Russians," said Isabelle. "I can't see Spanish nationalists being happy with that. It certainly seems as though the Russians are hoping to set up the Novios and ensure they get the blame."

"Who is watching this villa you mentioned, Bruno?" Lannes asked.

"Lieutenant Duvalier and his Special Forces team, along with a gendarme guide," Bruno replied, at the same time tapping out a quick text to Duvalier asking for an update. "His orders so far are to watch and observe. Other than that, he'll act on his own initiative, if people leave the house, for example."

"We have enough to detain them, even without the anti-terrorist provisions. Faking the car crash, firing at that tree with a weapon that would never get a civilian license," Isabelle broke in. "I think we should be ready to go in hard if they try to leave, and in the meantime try to insert audio surveillance. The chopper that brought us from the airport is still here if you want the tape of the woman we think is Africa."

"Right, that makes sense, do it," said Lannes. "Then you and Bruno should check out this villa and report back. Do you have audio surveillance equipment on hand?"

"Not here, but we can get it from the gendarme base in Périgueux," Yveline broke in. "I can arrange that, and the Special Forces have a drone unit in case we have to monitor and follow a vehicle. But what do you want us to do? Blockade them, follow them or arrest them? And do we shoot if they resist?"

"Blockade them inside the building, but if you believe your lives are in danger, shoot," said Lannes.

"Lieutenant Duvalier reports that all is quiet at the villa. It appears empty, no vehicles," said Bruno, looking up from the screen of his phone where Duvalier's message had just appeared. "I'll head there as soon as we're done here."

"Go now. We can talk later," said Lannes. And Bruno set off while Isabelle arranged to get the videotape from Dougal and deliver it to Morillon.

The villa was nestled into a hollow on the bumpy plateau behind the northern ridge over the River Vézère, on the way to the hamlet of Petit Paris. It had been an isolated barn, but sometime in the 1970s the barn had been turned into a garage and a new house erected in an unconvincing version of the traditional local style. The stones were a thin façade, too evenly cut to be genuine, and the roof lacked the distinctive pitch like a witch's hat. It was L-shaped with a second-storey turret room where the two wings came together. There was a stone terrace with a wooden table and chairs, a lawn and a small swimming pool that needed cleaning. This far from town, they would depend on a septic tank and propane gas.

Bruno left his police van between trees so that it blocked the single-lane road and advanced slowly on foot until Jean-Pierre, one of the French soldiers, beckoned him forward to where Lieutenant Duvalier was stretched out on the ground behind a tree, binoculars to his eyes. Bruno could see one of the soldiers in the shadow of the barn and another behind the small structure that seemed to hold the swimming pool pump.

"What are our orders?" Duvalier asked in a whisper.

"Blockade, follow, shoot if shot at," Bruno replied quietly, his mouth almost touching the lieutenant's ear. "I've blocked the road from the east with my van. Can you do the same to the west, put a guy there to blow out their tires? It's not a busy road, very rural, more tractors than cars."

Duvalier passed the order on to his sergeant, and Bruno handed him the key to the police van.

"I'm almost certain the place is empty, but not quite," Duvalier went on. "No lights, no sound of running water or flushing, no voices we can pick up. Two rooms have closed curtains. I assume they are bedrooms from the floor plan you gave me. I sent the sergeant up to put his ear to the windows, and there was no sound of snoring or breathing."

"Nothing in the barn?" Bruno asked.

"Wide tire tracks for something larger than a family car, maybe a camper, two sacks of rubbish, one yellow for recyclables, the other black. Mainly instant-meal packs, water and wine bottles, empty packs of Ducados cigarettes. And several bottles of cheap brandy I wouldn't use to clean my boots."

"Somebody may have gone to buy bread and croissants. That means they'll come from town. Swap around the vehicles, so if they come that way they'll see an anonymous hunter's Land Rover rather than a police van," said Bruno. "We'll give them thirty minutes, and if nobody comes back with breakfast, then make a discreet entry from the back and wait for their return."

"You must know somebody nearby with a tractor," said Duvalier. "Why not take your police van, leave it at his farm and then come back dressed like a farmer with the tractor. What could look more natural?"

"Good thinking," said Bruno. "Give me a few minutes."

Ten minutes later he was sitting on a tractor wearing the farmer's *bleu de travail* jacket and an old flat cap, heading for the point where his own Land Rover was parked, apparently carelessly, half on and half off the narrow road. He slowed as he felt his phone vibrate. He checked the screen. It was Isabelle. He stopped, put the gear shift into neutral and set the foot brake.

"The credit card, it's on the account of the ecumenical liaison office of the Eastern Orthodox Church in Brussels, nominally run by the Antioch church but with a Russian Orthodox component," she said. "I'm sure it's the cover for the Africa woman. What's happening at the villa?"

"Quiet. Maybe too quiet," he said, and then added, "Hold on," as a Mobylette, a small and underpowered scooter of the kind beloved by adolescents, puttered up the gentle slope toward him. The driver was an elderly man whom Bruno did not know, white bearded with locks of gray hair spilling out from under a dirty beret.

Bruno waved a greeting, released the brake and put the tractor into reverse to give the scooter room to pass before he saw the man reach into his jacket. Instinct kicked in, and Bruno slammed the gear shift into first, hit the accelerator and ducked behind the engine as he headed directly for the scooter, hearing one shot hit the tractor in front of him, then another, and then a quick burst of two or three more from a heavier-caliber weapon.

"Unknown shooter is down," shouted a high-pitched voice.

Bruno stopped the tractor inches before hitting the toppled scooter and its fallen rider as Jean-Pierre emerged from the woods at the side of the road. His assault rifle was still pointed at a sprawled, twitching figure, facedown with ominous red blotches on the back of his jacket. Bruno dismounted, went to the stricken man, still leaking dark blood from his belly and a frothy, brighter red from his mouth. Bruno turned him over to stop the blood from the old man's lungs from choking him.

The smell of fresh alcohol was suddenly fierce, and Bruno saw a smashed bottle of something still leaking from the man's jacket. The hair came off with the beret, and the false beard was now askew. Bruno removed it to see the ashen face of Sergeant

Jaudenes as he heard Jean-Pierre shouting for the lieutenant to call for an ambulance.

"He fired at you first," Jean-Pierre said nervously. "I had him covered."

"You did the right thing," said Bruno, and used a handkerchief to pull the top of the broken bottle from the jacket. A cheap brandy. "Thank you."

Jaudenes was alive, just, his eyes fluttering. Blood bubbling from his mouth confirmed that he'd been shot in the lung. The whole of the front of his shirt was soaked with blood, and Bruno ripped it open to see a big exit wound in his belly. He used his handkerchief to stem the flow of blood and then turned Jaudenes's head to its side so the blood could drip from his mouth. He asked Jean-Pierre to take his phone from his pocket and hold it to his ear. He could hear Isabelle's voice nervously calling his name.

"I'm fine, Isabelle, but we need an ambulance right away for Jaudenes, the Spanish sniper," he said, aware that his voice was pitched an octave higher than normal. "He tried to shoot me, and one of the soldiers got him first. Tell them we're on the road between Petit Paris and St. Cirq, and the casualty has a lung shot and a belly wound. Please call J-J and tell him we need a forensics team here as soon as he can arrange it. And put out an alert for every Belgian registered camper to be stopped and held."

"*Merde,*" said Jean-Pierre. "When you went down I thought he'd shot you."

Behind them, the tractor engine gave an exasperated cough, then another, and then died with a long sigh. Bruno turned and saw oil dripping profusely from the engine as shouts of "Clear" in different voices came from the villa, and a final "All clear, secure weapons."

Bruno took his sodden handkerchief from the belly wound,

replaced it with Jaudenes's beret, and then put his handkerchief over the leaking hole in the Spaniard's right lung. Suddenly Duvalier was there. "The villa's empty," he said. "Who's this poor bastard?"

"This is the Spanish sniper we've been looking for, Sergeant Jaudenes," said Bruno. "But I have a feeling this isn't over."

Chapter 29

The shooting by a French soldier of a foreign civilian from a friendly country was a delicate matter that activated several layers of bureaucracy, each trying to establish that somebody else was responsible. Bruno had the uncomfortable feeling that it would end up being him. Diplomats were involved, then intelligence officials, then the French military, finally the politicians who would inevitably at some point leak it to the press. Isabelle, who was evidently now a skilled navigator in such turbulent political waters, ensured that her narrative of events would prevail.

Isabelle had arrived promptly, following the ambulance. Before the stretcher had been taken from the back of the vehicle, she had sealed the weapon of Sergeant Jaudenes, a nine-millimeter Glock, in an evidence bag. While Fabiola was still opening her medical bag to treat the wounded man, Isabelle had fingerprinted him. As his stretcher was slid into the back of the ambulance, Isabelle used her phone to record her statement that she was formally arresting Jaudenes on a charge of the attempted murder of a French policeman. She also charged him with the possession of an unauthorized firearm.

"Will he live?" Isabelle asked Fabiola as the doctor clambered into the ambulance after stabilizing Jaudenes.

"Probably, and if he does, it will be thanks to Bruno," said Fabiola as the doors closed and the ambulance moved off. "He managed to stanch the bleeding."

Isabelle dictated a statement to her phone that she had just been informed by the emergency doctor that the chief of police of St. Denis had saved the life of the man who had tried to shoot him. She sent this as a text to General Lannes, to Colonel Manzaredo and to Bruno. She then led the search of the villa, where the sniper weapon, a Russian-made OSV-96, was found in the messier of the two bedrooms, where two empty brandy bottles were also found. She fingerprinted the bottles and the weapon, sent the images by phone along with an image of Jaudenes's prints, demanding that they be compared as a top priority. She then used her phone to photograph tire marks in the yard and sent them to J-J for comparison with those left at the scene of the fire.

Within thirty minutes of Isabelle's arrival she had taken control of the official version of events. Colonel Manzaredo was persuaded to call the Spanish ambassador in Paris, sadly confirming that the evidence of the drunken Spanish sergeant's attempt to kill a French chief of police was overwhelming, even without the presence of the sniper weapon. At this point, the competing Spanish and French bureaucracies were able to rally around this version of events. Isabelle then helped Jean-Pierre and Bruno each to draft and record his own statement. Bruno wisely said that the prompt action of the French soldier had almost certainly saved his own life.

The mayor of St. Denis was at the same time persuaded by Isabelle to send a swift email to France's defense minister, formally commending Jean-Pierre's timely action for saving the life of the chief of police of St. Denis, a decorated war hero. A copy of this email mysteriously found its way to Philippe Delaron of *Sud Ouest,* and less than an hour after the incident the young reporter was live on air with France Bleu Périgord recounting Isabelle's version of the tragic events at Petit Paris, including the sensational finding of a Russian sniper weapon.

"You are very good at this," Bruno told Isabelle as they sat in Yveline's office, drinking coffee, sharing their biscuits with Balzac and listening to the radio news.

"In the information age, you have to be," she replied.

"Wait," said Bruno as Delaron's excited voice on the radio went on: "We can now exclusively report that the fingerprints of the Spaniard who tried to kill Chief of Police Courrèges were also found on the Russian-made sniper rifle. A former member of Spain's Special Forces, Sergeant Jaudenes was also known as a member of the far-right Spanish nationalist party, Vox, and is suspected of planning an assassination attempt against a prominent Catalan official now in exile in France."

"Where the hell did Philippe get that from?" Bruno asked.

"Not me," said Isabelle.

"Not me, either," said Yveline. "I suppose it must have been the mayor."

"Even more striking," Delaron's voice went on, "we have learned that the chief of police of St. Denis then gave emergency treatment that saved the life of Sergeant Jaudenes. When Dr. Fabiola Stern arrived at the scene, she said his prompt action had saved the life of the man who had tried to kill him."

"That was me," said Isabelle. "But she really said it. So you'll come out of this smelling like roses, Bruno. You'll probably get a medal."

"If we can't track down Major Garay and this Russian woman, I don't think I'd deserve one," he said. "Africa doesn't strike me as a woman who would let the entire scheme depend on a drunk, so I'm starting to worry that she has an alternative plan."

"With what?" demanded Yveline. "They lost their gun and they lost their sniper. They'll be running, probably separately. And by the way, Bruno, we found out how Casimir got to St. Denis. He stole the car of some priest in Bergerac and has now been charged with stealing the car, three separate assaults and breaking his parole.

"I called the priest in Bergerac and he's washed his hands of Casimir, says he ought to be back in prison," Yveline added. "Apparently it was his car that was stolen. Florence says she wants to throw a party for the mothers at the *maternelle* who came to her aid."

"I can't help but feel a bit sorry for the guy," said Bruno. "He just wanted to see his kids."

"I wouldn't say that to Florence if I were you," Yveline replied. "Right now, you're her hero, but that won't last if you start defending her ex."

"It's not that," Bruno said, shaking his head. "I just think we could have found a reasonable way to let Casimir see his children under supervision."

"You don't change, Bruno," said Isabelle, smiling as she got to her feet.

"Thank you for what you did, managing the fallout," said Bruno.

"It's the least I could do for you," she said, still smiling at him. "Now I have to brief Lannes and then help coordinate the search for the Spanish major and the Russian woman. The Belgian police visited the ecumenical office and found the woman with the credit card had been a regular presence there, in and out for the past three years, setting up and running their computer system. So now both the EU and NATO security guys in Brussels are trying to work out if she was using her cyberskills against them."

"Are you heading back to Paris?"

"That's up to General Lannes. I imagine he'll want me here helping to coordinate the search for the Belgian camper or whatever other vehicle they might have," Isabelle replied. "We've already circulated Africa's photos from the rental agency among all the car rental agencies and used-car lots. The Belgians are trying to track down where she got hold of the camper."

"What if they aren't going anywhere but staying here to finish the job?" Bruno asked.

Isabelle shook her head. "No sniper, no gun, so what are they going to do? Lieutenant Duvalier has already been ordered to prepare to leave with his troops. You, Yveline and J-J can take it from here."

"What about the Spanish girl, Alba?"

"That's up to Manzaredo. But what could we charge her with? Seeing a woman from a church group who was trying to arrange a prisoner exchange to free her boyfriend?"

"In that case," said Bruno, "I might yet get back to play in our tennis tournament." The moment he said it, he had a feeling that he was tempting fate. And as Isabelle left to talk to Lannes, Bruno accepted another cup of coffee and learned from Yveline that Casimir was still in a cell awaiting transfer back to the Bergerac police. The fireman he had knocked unconscious had been diagnosed with a concussion, released from the clinic and sent home.

Casimir had been treated by Dr. Gelletreau and reported to be fit enough to travel, so Bruno asked Sergeant Jules if he might see how Casimir was recovering. Jules led the way with his keys and first slid open the viewing hatch in the steel door and let Bruno take a look. Casimir was sitting back on the ledge with its thin mattress, looking up at the sound of the opening hatch, but all he could see of Bruno would be his eyes. He was still handcuffed, but his face had been cleaned of blood and there was a strip of bandage over his nose.

"Do you want to open the cell?" Jules asked in a whisper. Bruno shook his head. He had nothing to say to the man, except perhaps that one day he would be out of prison again, and he should think long and hard about ways to build some kind of relationship with his children. But this was no time to say that as Casmir sat there, in handcuffs and after being humiliated in front of his ex-wife and children. He was just a couple of years older than Florence, maybe not even thirty yet, with most of his life ahead of him even after he spent another two years or more in prison. Bruno closed the viewing slot thinking Casimir was bound to come looking for his kids and could yet be Bruno's problem again once he was released. He'd have to think about this.

Upstairs, the gendarmerie seemed full, with the French soldiers piling up their equipment and talking of coming back to see the prehistoric caves and castles. Bruno found the sight oddly moving. He'd forgotten how young and eager soldiers tended to be.

"We're heading out," said Duvalier, shaking hands and pointing to Bruno's hunting guns—piled onto a table—which they were now returning. "I hope we meet up again. I'll certainly remember that omelette you made us when we arrived."

"We have a very old and proud culinary reputation to maintain here in the Périgord," said Bruno. "Come back and see us again with time to enjoy the place. Are you going back by chopper?"

"Are you kidding? You know the army. There's a truck coming to take us to the station for a train to Agen and then another truck back to base."

"And then?"

"Nothing official yet, but the word is we'll be heading for Mali."

"Good luck." He shook hands with each of the men, and offered a special word of thanks to Jean-Pierre, who may have saved his life that morning. Then he helped them load their gear into the truck and scramble aboard.

Bruno stood waving the troops goodbye until a sudden shout of his name from Yveline called him back into the gendarmerie.

"We just had a security alert, an explosion at Périgueux station in the parking lot," she said, her eyes fixed on the computer that was connected to the special gendarme network. "A white camper blew up, two passersby slightly injured. One of the station guys said he thought it had a Belgian registration. It had been there a couple of hours or more."

"So get them to check every train that left the station in the last two hours and have them met by armed gendarmes," he said, thinking that with the connection to the fast train network at Libourne or Souillac they could almost be in Paris by now, or Bordeaux, or any one of dozens of other stations. Or maybe that was what Africa wanted them to think, and she had another vehicle waiting. "And see if there's anything left of the tires, maybe you can get a match with the scene of the fire."

"Where's Isabelle?" he asked Yveline.

"She went to lunch with Colonel Manzaredo at Ivan's," she replied.

As he walked along the rue Gambetta to the restaurant, Bruno called the number for General Lannes and informed the duty officer of the explosion and his suspicion that Africa was still on the loose. Isabelle and the Spanish colonel were sitting side by side at a table for four, the mayor facing them. Bruno nodded to Ivan and some other friends in the room and was at once invited by Manzaredo to join them, saying they were all guests of Spain for this lunch.

"Your dog is included in the invitation," Manzaredo added as Balzac padded around the table, greeting the mayor and then jumping to rest his front paws on Isabelle's thigh to nuzzle at her neck.

"J-J says the photos of the tire marks I took at the *gîte* match those found at the fire scene," said Isabelle.

"I'm not sure I'll have time to stay," Bruno said, perching on the edge of his chair and noting that they were all eating the *plat du jour,* rabbit in mustard sauce with *pommes de terre sarladaises.* The aromas made him suddenly hungry. "There's news." He lowered his voice and explained about the camper at Périgueux station, that Lannes had been informed and the gendarmes were checking the possible rail connections.

"The camper had been parked for a couple of hours at least, so the bomb may have been on a timer, and whoever set it may still be in the area and using another vehicle," he said. "It's possible that they're planning to attack the concert by other means. And they may not be alone." He turned to Manzaredo. "What have you heard from Madrid about other Novios?"

"Nothing yet," he answered. "But please, join us. Eat."

"In this place, I don't think Ivan will give me any choice," said Bruno as Ivan presented a plate of the rabbit along with a bottle of one of Bruno's favorite white wines, the Cuvée Quercus from La Vieille Bergerie.

"On the house," said Ivan, opening the bottle with a flourish of his corkscrew, pouring a glass for Bruno and leaving the bottle on the table beside the almost empty carafe of house wine the others had been drinking. "We heard about you putting that bastard down at the *maternelle* this morning. And getting shot at again. So enjoy it while you can, Bruno."

"I'm delighted to see you're still alive and well," said the mayor. "And with our friends in the media trumpeting your exploits, you have evidently been through quite a busy morning, so *bon appétit.*"

"Thank you, all of you, for establishing the correct version of his morning's drama before the bureaucrats had me and that young soldier hauled up for unreasonable force," Bruno said. He savored the first mouthful of rabbit and its slightly piquant sauce, and then raised the glass of wine to his nose and then to his lips in a happy moment of simple self-indulgence. He filled the glasses of his companions and raised his own to them.

"Thanks again and I trust you're not racing back to Paris before enjoying tomorrow's concert, unless that would be politically embarrassing, Colonel," he said to Manzaredo.

"Not at all," said the Spaniard. "And this wine is delicious. But Madrid says this success offers the perfect moment for me to return to Paris to consolidate our excellent relations with our French counterparts."

"I'm also under orders to return and report to a full meeting of all my European colleagues on this excellent example of productive collaboration between member states," said Isabelle, a hint of mockery in her tone as she met Bruno's eyes and gave him a private wink before returning to work on her phone.

"We can get the evening train from Libourne just after seven and be in Paris by nine," she said to her Spanish colleague. "That gives you time to get word from Madrid about other Novios.

Perhaps you should make it clear this is urgent. I've learned to respect Bruno's hunches."

"It's more than a hunch," said Bruno, swallowing a mouthful of the *pommes de terre sarladaises* he'd been savoring. "J-J was probably right all along when he suggested that the sniper was a distraction from something else. Jaudenes may have been a great sniper a decade ago, but these days he's a drunk."

"Two of them aren't enough to operate a mortar," said Manzaredo. "You have sniffer dogs to check the concert for explosives. What else can they do?"

"I wish I knew," said Bruno. "But the Spanish major and the Russian woman are still on the loose. That's why I'd like to hear from Madrid about the whereabouts of other members of this Novios group. Have they been told of the Russian involvement in this, that they're being used as patsies for the Kremlin?"

Manzaredo shrugged, saying nothing. He glanced at Isabelle, as if for help.

"Then why don't we tell them?" Bruno replied. "That's what the media is for. Let's make Madame Africa famous." He stared fixedly at Manzaredo. "Unless you think that extreme-right Spanish nationalists whose grandfathers fought Stalin's Red Army on the eastern front have no qualms these days about being in bed with the Kremlin?"

"Who is Madame Africa," the mayor asked as Bruno felt Isabelle kick his leg under the table. Startled, Bruno looked across at her and saw her glance around the room and shake her head. He sighed and accepted that this was not the place to explain about Unit 74455 and the heritage of the three generations of women named Africa. So he took a sip of wine, told the mayor he would explain later and continued enjoying his lunch.

Chapter 30

"Are you mad?" Isabelle almost spat at him when they were back at the gendarmerie and Manzaredo had gone into another room to talk to Madrid. "You can't go spouting off about that in an open restaurant with your very well-connected mayor sitting there taking in every word."

"Why not?" he replied calmly, leaning back against the desk while Balzac glanced uncertainly from Isabelle to Bruno, troubled by the tension in the room. "It's a serious question. Unless perhaps you're pulling off some coup and turning Africa to work for us, or for Spain or for the Americans. Does that mean any poor singer and songwriter can get killed so Africa can keep her cover? Are they just collateral damage?"

Isabelle raised her eyes toward the ceiling. "It's not that. You don't turn a veteran spook like her, not with her connections. She was born into the *nomenklatura* party elite in Soviet days, and she's still there, one of the winners in Putin's new aristocracy."

"So you want to keep Africa running while you watch her?" Bruno demanded. "While NATO tries to run down whatever cracks she's opened in their computer systems? While Joël Martin goes in fear of his life for writing a song?"

"Calm down, Bruno," she said. "The big fact to remember here is that the Russian operation failed. They wanted to build up the 'Song for Catalonia' so that Joël would be a tempting target for the Spanish extremists, that they would then assassinate him publicly on French soil, make him a martyr, revive the Catalan cause, throw a massive wedge between Madrid and Paris and weaken Europe. That's it, the Russian master plan, divide and rule, set us at odds against the Americans and against one another. And it failed. This time we caught them at it. Madrid and Paris and NATO are working together on this. We unraveled their use of the Orthodox church as cover, we're getting into Africa's financial records and into her phone and into their computer systems. It's a big win. We don't need to turn Africa to work for us. She's busted. And we're picking up the pieces."

"I suppose you're right," he replied. "If this is such a big win, why aren't you going public with it already? Why not bring it into the open and use the media to tell all? Embarrass them with the truth."

"Because nobody trusts the media these days, Bruno. It's all fake news. It's we say this and they say that. That's their big win. Nobody knows what the truth is anymore. It's Moscow's revenge for the Cold War. We were the free world, remember, with the free media. And they were stuck with *Pravda*. Moscow's propaganda was so rancid that even the Russians didn't believe it. And now they've turned that upside down so we in the West don't trust our own media anymore."

"Speak for yourself," he replied. But his heart wasn't in it. He recognized the dismaying amount of truth in what she was saying. All the torrents of social media were spreading like a virus, wide open to disinformation or to the paranoid fantasies of sad people. He nodded at her, smiling as he thought of all the ways he'd looked at her, with passion and admiration, with trust and the fondness of deep-rooted friendship, with the sheer gratitude that chance had brought this extraordinary woman into his life. He knew there was no hope of a future for them, not in the face of Isabelle's consuming ambition, but there would always be a special place for her in his heart.

"You're probably right about that," he said. "It reminds me of something I read once, that once people stopped believing in God the problem was not that they believed in nothing but that they were wide open to believe in absolutely anything."

She grinned at him and opened her arms for a hug, then nestled into his arms, saying, "That's one of the things I miss most about you, dear Bruno, unusual quotations, strange reading habits, unexpected turns in conversation. I never come across anything quite so unpredictable in Paris."

"It was you who got me reading poetry," he said, kissing her hair. "That collection of Jacques Prévert you sent me, remember?"

"Yes, and I remember being so deeply, childishly happy when I saw how well thumbed the book was the next time I came to see you." She gave him a squeeze and then stepped back. "What are you going to do now?"

"I'll worry about what Africa might be doing, what backup plan she has, maybe that she has some other agents in reserve. I just feel this isn't over, and I know you well enough to think you agree."

"You could be right, Bruno, but we're part of a team, and a team has to follow the captain's orders even though we worry that this victory parade Paris wants could be premature. The best I can do is to keep in touch with Morillon until I have to get the train back. Maybe he'll come up with something on Madame Africa."

"I'd better take my guns home and lock them up. Then I have

to meet Rod Macrae at the baron's place where his basset hound puppy has been staying while I've been tied up on the sniper hunt. Come along. You know you like seeing Balzac's puppies."

"Not today, I should carry on working. But the next time you're going to mate him, let me know," she said, bending down to stroke the dog. "I loved that weekend we had the last time, at the kennels with Claire, when Balzac was with Diane de Poitiers. I still remember when I brought him to you as a puppy, and now he's a father." She swallowed hard and shook her head. "*Merde,* how time flies. Maybe I can come down again."

She hugged him fiercely, and he kissed her brow and left for the armory, where the Special Forces troops had left his guns that they had borrowed. He put them into a bag, walked to his van and drove first home, to secure them in his gun cabinet, and then to the tennis club to ask if he could still play in the mixed-doubles final.

"Sorry, Bruno, but it can't be done, not after you asked to be withdrawn earlier in the week," said Bernard, who was in charge of the schedule. "You forfeited the match, so we already awarded the prize to the Spanish couple you'd have been playing."

Twenty minutes later, Bruno pulled in beside the baron's vintage Citroën DS, noting there was no sign of Rod Macrae's car, but Bruno now saw that he'd sent a text from Stansted Airport to say his flight was on time. As Bruno opened his car door, his phone vibrated. He looked at the screen, seeing with a sense of guilt that it was Amélie. He'd entirely forgotten that she was supposed to be arriving today for the concert. He answered, with a warm welcome.

"Hi, Bruno, I'm on the train, due into Le Buisson just after six. Can you pick me up? I'm looking forward to tasting your cooking again."

"I'll be at the station," he said, thinking a little desperately of what he might cook, what was in his garden, in his larder. "It will be great to see you."

"I'm glad you're okay," she said. "I heard the story on France Inter's lunchtime news by that aggressive young reporter we met, Philippe something, about somebody trying to shoot you. It sounded pretty wild. Anyway, it's good to hear your voice. See you soon."

He closed the phone thinking he had tomatoes, and fresh peaches on the tree. It was too warm today for anything heavy. So a cold soup of fresh tomatoes and then maybe a special kind of *salade composée,* light but filling. He had some bottles of Chardonnay from Château de la Jaubertie in his cellar, a new wine, since Chardonnay had never been one of the permitted grapes in the Bergerac appellation. In the right hands it was glorious. Maybe some kir to begin, along with sparkling wine from Château Lestevénie. That would work.

In the baron's garden, he found Flavie in her leotard, ignoring him as she focused on her yoga poses on a pale blue mat, even though Balzac trotted up to say hello and the Bruce darted out like a little rocket from beneath the table to greet his father and bring him back to see Joël and the baron. They were sitting and chatting at a table in the shade, a bottle of wine between them and empty lunch plates on a trolley behind. They turned at Balzac's arrival and saw Bruno approaching, the Bruce now racing toward him. Bruno scooped him up, tucked him onto his shoulder.

"Glad you're okay, Bruno," said Joël, rising to shake hands. "We heard the news on the radio about the shooting and the car bomb at Périgueux station. Is the concert still going ahead as planned?"

"Yes, it is," Bruno replied, deciding not to mention anything about Africa still being on the loose. "That sniper we were worried about has been arrested, and he's in the hospital. And Rod Macrae is on his way from the airport to pick up his puppy. I'm hoping he'll join us for dinner tonight along with one of the baron's favorite people, another singer, Amélie."

"Ah, the young Josephine Baker, the one who tells me I'm a naughty man," said the baron, smiling. "At my age, that counts as flattery. She's coming down from Paris?"

"Arriving at six; she wants to hear Les Troubadours in concert, so I thought all three of you might join us for dinner at my place."

"Sounds like a great idea, thanks," said Joël. "I'll check with Flavie when she's through with her yoga, but I'm sure she'll agree."

Bruno glanced across to where Flavie was looking like a triangle, hands and feet on the ground almost a meter apart, her rump in the air. The dogs found it irresistible. They darted backward and forward through the triangle she formed until Flavie could no longer control her laughter and crumpled to the mat, hugging the two dogs to her. At that moment a car horn gave a double beep, and Rod parked, unstretched his rangy limbs from the car, donned his battered leather Stetson and strolled into the courtyard to reunite with the Bruce.

"I hope he's been no trouble," Rod said, tipping his hat to Flavie and nodding a greeting to the others as he dropped to one knee to greet the Bruce.

"None at all," said Bruno. "Can you join us for dinner this evening at my place? Amélie is coming and would love to see you. About sevenish?"

"Wouldn't miss it," Rod said, heaving himself upright. "Good to see you, Baron, and you, Flavie, and I guess you must be Joël, the 'Song for Catalonia' man. I have a British record deal for you if you want it."

"I'd better go and take care of dinner before picking up Amélie," Bruno said, rising to his feet.

"Why not let me pick her up and bring her to your place?" said Rod. "I need to talk to her anyway."

Bruno agreed gratefully, rounded up Balzac and headed to Oudinot's farm, where Odile raised not only ducks and chickens but also the much-rarer capons, a cockerel that had been castrated in youth and grew plump and delicious. A capon was larger than a chicken and without the rooster's distinctive gamy flavor, a taste the classic dish *coq au vin* was invented to produce. Odile fed her capons on a homemade milky porridge of her own devising that grew the bird to four kilos and more. She skinned and jointed one for him, waving away his attempt to pay. This was a ritual that Bruno knew well. He explained that he'd be unable to attend church that Sunday, pressed a ten-euro note into Odile's hand and asked her to drop it into the collection box for him. Honor thus satisfied on both sides, he kissed her farewell and went to the farmers' co-op shop to buy cream, honey and Greek-style yogurt. He bought a fat, round *tourte* of bread from the Moulin bakery and drove home.

First he went into his garden to gather the vegetables he would need. Then he sliced the capon breasts and put them, the wings and legs into a plastic freezer bag with three generous tablespoons of olive oil, a handful of fresh tarragon leaves, the zest and juice from a lemon, half a head of broccoli broken into florets, three chopped cloves of garlic and a teaspoon of *piment d'Espelette,* the pepper from the Basque region that counted as almost local. He closed the bag and then squeezed and massaged the contents, rubbing them together so the flavors melded into the capon, and left it to marinate.

He set his oven to two hundred degrees centigrade. He cut lengthways the kilo of fresh tomatoes he had just picked, took out the seeds and laid the tomatoes, skin side down, in a big roasting tray. He sprinkled a generous wineglass of olive oil over them, put the pan in the oven and set his timer for thirty-five minutes. He cleaned the sitting room, swept the outside terrace and set the table before taking a quick shower and changing out of uniform.

The timer pinged. He took out the tomatoes and left them to cool, replacing them with another roasting tray into which he put the capon and herbs from the freezer bag, this time setting the timer at forty minutes. He would have preferred to leave them to marinate longer, overnight ideally, but he was short of time. Then he went to feed his own geese and chickens. He put water on to boil, and from the peach trees at the back of his house he took the six ripest fruits, put them into a large bowl and poured boiling water over them, leaving the peaches for a minute before peeling them, halving them and removing the pits.

Now for the tomato soup. He put the roast tomatoes into his blender along with a wineglass of his homemade chicken stock and blitzed them together with salt and pepper. He added another half glass of stock to get the consistency of cream and then pressed the result through a sieve to remove any unprocessed seeds or skin. He poured the result into a jug and put it into his fridge to cool. Then he took the three fat tomatoes he had left, blanched them to remove the skins and scooped out the seeds. He diced the flesh of the tomatoes and put them aside. Next, he rinsed his sieve, lined it with a paper towel and poured in the Greek yogurt so the whey could drip slowly out over the next hour.

Bruno checked his watch: almost five-thirty. He was in good time, so he took Balzac for a stroll through the woods and was back in time to hear the radio news at six. He had deliberately avoided answering Philippe Delaron's phone calls, but Philippe had evidently reached J-J.

"As you know, we have all week displayed wanted posters and made media appeals about two armed and dangerous men, one of them a trained sniper, retired for several years from the Spanish army," J-J said. "Thanks to excellent detective work by Chief of Police Bruno Courrèges we tracked down the sniper this morning to a rented villa near St. Denis. The sniper fired several shots in an attempt to kill the chief of police, who was unarmed. Fortunately, the man was immobilized by another member of the security team. A Russian-made specialist sniper rifle, capable of killing at a range of two kilometers, was found at the villa. The second man, who was not at the villa, is currently the subject of a nationwide manhunt."

"A sniper rifle suggests an assassination," said Philippe. "Who was the target?"

"That's not clear, but the arrested man, who is now in the hospital under guard, was a member of an extreme right-wing nationalist group in Spain, known for its militant opposition to the Catalan independence movement. I'd like to pay tribute to the excellent support we have had from the Spanish authorities in this operation."

It was decent of J-J to give him some credit, thought Bruno, and politically wise to praise the Spaniards, but it was disturbing that Major Garay and Africa were still on the loose.

The yogurt was well drained, so he decanted it into a bowl, chopped up some chives and basil leaves from the garden and beat them in to make a herb mousse. It was still too soon to fold in the beaten white of an egg. He'd do that just before serving. Now he put a quarter kilo of white beans and the broccoli on to boil and began slicing four spring onions and two celery stalks very finely. Once that was done, he took the beans off the boil, blanched them by putting them into a bowl of ice water to keep them al dente and then went to his cellar for the wine and put the bottles into the fridge.

He washed and roughly tore up the handfuls of spinach and leaves of arugula he'd picked from the garden and put them into his largest salad bowl, adding the spring onions and celery and then the capon, beans and broccoli florets. Then he beat together a tablespoon of red wine vinegar and another of mustard, added two tablespoons of olive oil and another two of walnut oil, salt and pepper, and then toasted a large handful of walnuts in a frying pan.

He poured the vinaigrette into the still warm roasting pan and scraped up the caramel on the base, then quickly poured this warmed vinaigrette over the salad. He washed his hands before tossing everything together gently and thoroughly and scattered the toasted walnuts on top.

Bruno was casting a final eye over the terrace dining table, adding napkins, making sure he had an ice bucket for the sparkling wine and a bottle of *crème de cassis* for the kir, when he heard Balzac's familiar bay, signaling the arrival of a car up the drive. It was Rod, and even before he had halted, the passenger door opened and a small but ebullient bundle of fragrant Caribbean energy was hugging Balzac and then leaping up to greet Bruno. The Bruce tumbled out of the car and raced toward them, jumping on his little legs as if determined to join the embrace.

"Wonderful to see you, Amélie," Bruno said, hugging her in return. "Welcome back."

"Rod told me who else is coming," she said. "I'm dying to meet Joël and his singer and delighted that the naughty old baron is joining us. It's so good to be here again with you. *Voilà*," she said, handing him a warm bottle of champagne.

"You may want to wash up after your trip," he suggested. "I'll have a kir waiting for you."

Outside, Rod was sitting happily on the ground as Balzac and the Bruce clambered over him, until Balzac pricked his ears and darted off to the entranceway again, baying to signal the arrival of Joël and Flavie in the Baron's DS. Bruno opened the first bottle of sparkling wine and put Amélie's warm bottle into the ice bucket.

As they sat chatting around the table with their glasses of kir, Bruno suddenly became aware that he was coming late into a conversation that the musicians had already developed, between Rod, Joël and Flavie in the baron's garden, and then between Rod and Amélie when he'd picked her up at the station. They had already agreed in principle that Rod and Amélie, who had already performed together at Rod's comeback in St. Denis, should also take part with Les Troubadours in the following evening's concert. They would spend the next day rehearsing at the recording studio in Rod's château. It was simply a matter of working out who would sing what and when.

Joël and the baron were continuing a conversation, or perhaps a lesson, that had evidently been underway for some time. The baron kept asking more and more questions about the way the Islamic culture in Spain had transferred much of the knowledge of ancient Greece to medieval Europe. Like Bruno, the baron had never heard of Gerard of Cremona, who moved to Toledo and learned Arabic in order to translate almost a hundred works, including Euclid, Archimedes, Aristotle, Ptolemy and the Arabic medical writing of al-Razi.

"When historians talk of the twelfth-century renaissance, they point to the great cathedrals and the new universities in Paris and Oxford," Joël was saying. "They tend to skate over the way Gerard and the Englishmen Daniel of Morley and Adelard of Bath translated the Arab works and brought back classical learning to Europe. Much of that was transmitted through Catalonia and Aquitaine."

Bruno always enjoyed hearing scholars expound their expertise, but Joël was a born raconteur who could bring to life these long-dead scholars and their passion for their research. And why was so little generally known or taught in his own day of the importance of Islamic culture in this period? He'd heard endless political speeches condemning modern Islam for being stuck in the laws and religion of the Middle Ages. Now he was learning that without the Islamic scholars Europe's Middle Ages might never have ended.

But Bruno had his guests to feed. He excused himself, went to the kitchen and made small mounds of the diced tomatoes in the center of each bowl, poured the cold tomato soup into six bowls, then added a generous spoonful of his herb mousse to the top of each tomato mound. Then he took the bowls out on a tray to the terrace with the bread, opened a bottle of Chardonnay and called his friends to dinner.

As the evening wore on, Bruno brought out the huge bowl of capon salad, went back to whip up a caramel cream to go with the peaches, almost grudging each moment he spent away from Joël's endless seminar. He had never seen the baron so rapt, scribbling down names and notes as Joël spoke. At last, the plates cleared away, Rod brought his acoustic guitar from the car and began plucking at the familiar chords as Amélie sat back and began crooning the song that had launched Rod's comeback, "Watching You Sleep." How fortunate he was in his friends, thought Bruno.

Chapter 31

Bruno was at Fauquet's café shortly before nine to meet Joël and Flavie for breakfast before they went to Rod's château for the rehearsals. He had woken early and checked his phone. A message from General Lannes confirmed a final videoconference at nine. Armed with croissants and coffee, Joël and Flavie were holding court, being welcomed by the mayor and Stéphane as well as other friends who came to embrace Flavie. Bruno left her to her admirers and strolled down the rue Gambetta to greet Yveline and Sergeant Jules and take his place before the big screen.

Lannes began with congratulations for all those involved in the arrest of the sniper, adding that, since there was no news of Africa and Major Garay, they would start with a forensic report from J-J's team at the Police Nationale.

"The Russian-made sniper rifle we found, the OSV-96, is relatively new and most probably was obtained in Syria where it was used by both sides in the civil war," Yveline began. "We also found at the villa two five-round magazines. An attempt to clean the villa of fingerprints was only partly successful. We have prints confirmed as those of Major Garay and another set which we believe to be those of the Russian operative Africa, alias Madame

Van Diest. There were two bedrooms at the villa, one used by Sergeant Jaudenes, which contained several empty bottles of Alfonso brandy, one of the cheapest Spanish brands. The other bedroom seems to have been shared by Africa and the major, and there was evidence of sex on the sheets, which has given us a good DNA profile of each one. We'll check that with the Belgian police who have been searching Africa's apartment in Brussels. The tire marks at the fire match those of the camper that exploded at the Périgueux station. That's pretty much it, except for a Spanish newspaper photo of the songwriter Joël Martin that we found in Jaudenes's bedroom."

"I have a short report," said J-J. He explained that each conductor on the trains from Périgueux during the four hours before the explosion had been contacted and interviewed. Not one was able to confirm that the two suspects had been seen, neither together nor alone. He'd also checked airline personnel and security cameras at the airports of Bergerac, Périgueux, Limoges, Brive and Bordeaux but found no trace.

"We suspect, therefore, that they had access to a second, unknown vehicle, and could still be in the region," J-J said. "They may also have alternative methods of attacking this concert as well as other personnel we don't know about."

Colonel Manzaredo then asked to speak and reported that his colleagues in Madrid had over the past twenty-four hours contacted all known members of the Novios, and several leaders of Vox, all of whom were still in Spain and claimed to have no knowledge of an operation against Catalan exiles or supporters in France.

"They angrily denied any suggestion that they might in any circumstances be prepared to cooperate with any Russian-backed operation," he added. "One member of the Novios did identify

Africa, or Van Diest, from a photo, saying he believed he had seen Major Garay dining with her in Madrid three weeks ago. Garay's wife added that she suspected her husband was having an affair.

"Last, I should report that on my strong recommendation, the Spanish government has announced the lifting of the ban on the 'Song for Catalonia' on Spanish media. What's more, I have been given to understand that the composer, Joël Martin, will be awarded a medal for his services to European culture for his impressive historical website. There are no charges against him under Spanish law, and he will be a welcome guest should he wish to return to Spain. An official bulletin confirming this is expected later today. We will also compensate the owners of the recording studio for their losses in the fire."

"Very sensible," said Lannes. "Please convey my personal appreciation to your government. Now, Bruno, since I understand that France 3 will be televising the concert tonight, what's the current status of the preparations?"

"The stage is being erected as we speak, to be shielded by trucks blocking the sides and rear," Bruno explained. "The sound system is being set up. And since you kindly agreed that your budget would finance the rental, the strobe lights and searchlights have arrived, and I will personally supervise their placement. We're expecting a full house of around five thousand people, perhaps more after all the publicity."

"So short of strong evidence that a new attack is planned, it would be logistically difficult as well as highly embarrassing politically and diplomatically to cancel the concert at this stage," Lannes said. "And I gather that sniffer dogs are still available to check the stage and venue for explosives?"

"Yes, sir," said Bruno. "What of Sergeant Jaudenes? Is he likely to survive?"

"He's in intensive care in Bordeaux and is expected to live, but he's lost one lung and much of his digestive system," said J-J. "The *procureur de la République* is preparing several charges against him once he is well enough to stand trial, including attempted murder."

"Thank you, everybody," Lannes said. "I assume that you and the gendarmes will be taking the usual security precautions for the concert?"

"Yes, sir," said Yveline. "We have extra gendarmes being sent from Bergerac and Périgueux, but no other specialized personnel except for the sniffer dogs."

"Thank you, everybody. And I trust that strenuous efforts will continue in order to find the two missing suspects. I think we can leave that to the Police Nationale, but I should be informed as soon as Van Diest is apprehended."

Lannes nodded briskly and then the screen went blank.

"So they have declared victory and gone home, leaving us on our own here to clean up," said Yveline, shaking her head in disbelief. "And to deal with whatever comes next." She turned to Bruno and asked, "What do you think?"

"I suspect Africa and her major might still be in this region, perhaps with an alternative base," said Bruno. "Let's hope Lannes hasn't blown the final whistle before the match is over." He rose. "I'd better go check on the concert preparations."

With Balzac at his heels, Bruno walked back past the *maternelle* and the post office, over the bridge and down the steps beside the medical center before continuing along the riverbank to the big open space. Dozens of temporary toilets were being delivered from trucks and erected in rows at each side. The flatbed truck that would provide the stage was in place, and the three trucks intended to protect the sides and rear were backing and edging into position. Another truck was unloading banks of amplifiers and loudspeakers, all being controlled by Michel of the *mairie*'s public works department. Armed with a clipboard and walkie-talkie, Michel was yelling at a distant gendarme not to let any of the food trucks into the area until the stage was complete.

The last time St. Denis had hosted an event of this size had been Rod Macrae's comeback concert; Bruno had been told that the food trucks alone had cleared more than sixty thousand euros that evening. The public had contributed almost twenty thousand euros in the big cash boxes installed to solicit donations to help fund the "free" concert, which had more than covered the costs of setting up the event and the overtime for *mairie* employees. He knew for a fact that the town vineyard had sold more than thirty thousand euros' worth of wine and handed out more than two thousand plastic cups. This time Bruno had insisted that they use only paper cups that could be recycled.

He turned to look back at the river, dotted with tourists drifting and paddling down in rented canoes. He smiled to himself as he recalled how crowded with canoes that stretch had been when Rod gave his concert. Then the stage had been open. From time to time Rod had turned around to wave to the people on the river and the far bank. This time the view from the rear would be blocked by trucks. With a start, Bruno knew that this was a vulnerability. If Africa and her Spanish major obtained a canoe and had weapons, they could come from behind to attack the stage. He'd have to do something about that.

He pulled out his phone and called Antoine, a friend who ran the local canoe rentals, and asked what he thought should be done.

"I'll be stopping my rentals at seven tonight," Antoine said. "I want to see the concert. But you might talk to the river marshal at Montignac: the gendarmes there run the flat-bottomed security boat. They're the only ones allowed to use an outboard motor. The rest of us are stuck with oars or feeble electric motors."

Bruno called Yveline and asked her if she could arrange for the river marshal to block the river upstream. She said she'd take care of it. He was putting his phone away when he saw the mayor coming along the bank to check on their progress. Balzac trotted up to greet him, and Bruno followed as the mayor sank to one knee to caress the dog.

"I'm glad the concert is going ahead, a tribute to the work you've put in this last week," he said, and then paused. "The prefect called me, asking what was going on."

"Yes, I noticed that once General Lannes took over, the prefect was no longer brought into the videoconferences," Bruno said. "But by this time they were mostly about operational matters and diplomatic ones, too. Choosing who would join the conferences was hardly up to me."

"Well, now that the emergency is over, you might give her a call," the mayor said, and then added, more hesitantly, "Perhaps I could sit in."

"Let's do it from your office," said Bruno. "I'm sorry I wasn't allowed to tell you more. And I need to tell you what happened with Florence's ex-husband."

"I heard about your tussle at the *maternelle* and Casimir's arrest, and of his stealing the priest's car in Bergerac," the mayor said. "I went to visit Millard, the fireman he knocked out. You might do the same, when this concert is over."

Bruno felt suitably chastened. So many things he could have done, should have done.

"Some council members are pointedly asking why the concert wasn't canceled when our own chief of police knew there was a dangerous sniper running loose," the mayor went on. "The prefect might also want to hear about that. She told me that you were the one who had made the argument that it should go ahead as the best way to catch the sniper."

"That's not what I said," Bruno protested. "I explained how we could use lights to blind the sniper. And announcing that the concert would go ahead gave us time to catch him, which is exactly what happened."

"Welcome to public life, Bruno, where every good thing you try to build for the community provokes resentment among some people, and the more you manage to achieve, the more enemies you make until there are enough of them to band together to defeat you. That's politics."

"That makes it the more impressive that you have remained mayor for so long," Bruno said. "There must be a trick to it."

"Indeed there is," the mayor said. "Divide your opponents. If they get hurt by one thing, find something else which will benefit some of them and make them your allies. But remember that while you can ensure that all your enemies will be temporary ones, the same is true, in politics, of your friends."

"I'm glad I'm just a policeman, and not a politician."

"Don't try that tired old cliché with me, Bruno," the mayor said, smiling. "Of course you're a politician. Every policeman ought to be in a democratic society that's ruled by consent."

Following Balzac, Bruno arrived in the mayor's office feeling he'd just sat through a short master class on the nature of politics. He accepted a coffee and tried to marshal his thoughts as the mayor sent his secretary, Claire, to hunt out some obscure document in the archives so she would not be able to eavesdrop. The mayor put his phone on speaker and called the prefect's private number.

"Madame Prefect," the mayor began, "the chief of police has asked me to arrange this call to brief you on the progress of this security problem we've been dealing with, if you have a moment to talk."

"Thank you, Monsieur le Maire. Is Bruno there now?"

"Yes, madame," Bruno said. "I'm here and please accept my apologies for not keeping you informed so far. I hope you'll understand that I was acting under orders."

"Understood. I'm aware that General Lannes is renowned for running a very tight ship. My congratulations on dodging that bullet yesterday, by the way."

"Thank you, madame." Bruno began to explain the progress of the case since he'd sat in the prefect's study the previous Sunday. The role and background of Africa; the testing of the sniper weapon; the blackmail of Alba over her Ukrainian lover; the arrival of the French Special Forces; the tracking of Africa to the villa; the shooting of Jaudenes; the disappearance of Africa and Garay and the explosion in the station parking lot.

"So we don't know where this female mastermind might be, nor her Spanish lover, but General Lannes deems it safe for the concert to go ahead. Is that right?"

"Yes, but with full security precautions, including extra gendarmes and the river marshal," Bruno replied. "And the informed consent of the musicians, who are all eager to play."

"All? Are there more than just Les Troubadours?"

"Yes, the rock star Rod Macrae, and Amélie, who did that wonderful televised performance of Josephine Baker songs at Château des Milandes. I was with them yesterday as they discussed their roles. They're rehearsing together right now."

"You make it sound like an event not to be missed," she said. "Do I need a ticket? I was hoping to bring the mayor of Périgueux and the gendarme general."

"Of course," said the mayor. "You will all be my guests. We may even have chairs."

"Thank you both," she replied. "I'll see you tonight, then. Goodbye."

"Good, now you have her blessing," said the mayor. "Letting the concert go ahead is not just on your head, but the responsibility is shared with me and the prefect and it's also shared with General Lannes. That's politics, too."

Chapter 32

Millard, the volunteer fireman who had been felled by Casimir's punch, lived on the outskirts of town near the railway station. Bruno found him sitting in front of a TV with his feet up, watching soccer, a bottle of mineral water at his side.

"Tell me when you can drink something stronger than water, and I'll bring over some beers," Bruno said. "I'd never have been able to tackle that big guy if you hadn't distracted him first. How long will you be off work?"

"Distracted is one way of putting it." Millard grunted. "The doc says I can go back Monday, after she looks deeply into my eyes again. I'm hoping it means she likes me."

"Dream on," said Bruno, and they chatted for a few minutes before Bruno went back to the concert ground. The food stalls and the wine tent were in place, while dreadful howls and electronic burps came from the loudspeakers as the sound system was tested. The four big searchlights had been set up, two at each side of the stage, and Michel was supervising the placing of some other contraption much farther back, which Bruno had been told was artificial smoke.

"Looks pretty much ready," he said to Michel. "What's our access route?"

"The entry beside the bank. There'll be an armed gendarme there with a list of approved entrants: you, the mayor and his guests, the musicians, the TV guys, preaccredited press and technicians. Nobody else gets in that way. We have a secure lane that brings you right beside the stage."

"That sounds great. Any problems?"

"I have to set up the strobe lights, but that's all. You might take a look inside the truck to the left of the stage," he replied. "We've put some chairs and a table for the artists in there, beers and mineral water, a few snacks and a mirror for the girls to do their makeup."

"Sounds good, I'll go and round them up," he said.

"Oh, and I almost forgot," Michel said. "The vet asked if you could drop by his office. Something about sniffer dogs."

Bruno drove on the Route de Campagne to the new complex: the vet's office, dispensary and kennels on one side, and a medical laboratory on the other, with a parking lot in between. Parked there was a large military vehicle, empty and with its rear doors open. Bruno went in to the office and found two men in military uniform who looked profoundly miserable. Giselle, the vet's receptionist, greeted him by name and opened the door behind her that led to the kennels.

"Bonjour, Bruno. The vet's expecting you," she said. "He's with the poor dogs. But where's your milk?"

"What milk?"

"I told Michel to be sure to tell you to bring two liters of milk. For the eyes."

"What eyes? Michel just told me to come to the vet." Bruno went through the door, hearing Giselle ask the soldiers to fetch milk, and then heard the awful sound of dogs whimpering in pain. The vet was busy bathing the eyes of one large Malinois and a slightly smaller German shepherd.

"Ah, Bruno, look what some bastard did to these poor dogs. Ground red chili pepper, one sniff and they're in agony. Did you bring the milk?"

"Nobody asked me to, but the soldiers have gone for it. How do you use it?"

"To bathe their eyes. I'm using distilled water, but milk would be better. Lord knows what I'll do about their sinuses."

The Malinois gave an enormous sneeze and whined pitifully as fluid leaked from its nostrils. Bruno felt tears start in his own eyes.

"That's an unspeakable thing to do to a dog. Where did it happen?"

"Somewhere near Bara-Bahau, I don't know exactly. Ask Giselle." He turned back to the dogs, and Bruno went back to ask her.

"The parking lot at the Bara-Bahau cave was all the soldiers told me when they brought the dogs here, and now they've gone for the milk," she said. "How's Balzac?"

"He's fine, in the van outside."

"He's one of our favorites. Make sure you keep him well away from Bara-Bahau."

Bruno had already made the connection to the path that led from the parking area below the cave to the hunters' cabin on the ridge overlooking St. Denis, the spot where Balzac had tracked the Spanish sniper. Presumably Africa and her major knew the French soldiers had gone, and the sniper threat and the location were now assumed to be no longer relevant. Maybe they were hiding out up there and putting down the pepper in case Balzac came sniffing? If that was their plan, he'd like to kill them with his bare hands.

"I have to go," he told Giselle. "I'm helping organize tonight's concert."

"The Catalonian guy? I'm coming with a bunch of friends."

As Bruno settled Balzac into his van, his phone beeped. He checked the dial and it was a text from Colonel Manzaredo, saying, "Announcement made in Madrid: Joël Martin has been awarded Order of Civic Merit for his contribution to European culture and will forever be an honored guest in Spain."

Bruno whistled in appreciation and drove out to Château Rock, Macrae's home, where he'd converted an old tobacco-drying barn into a recording studio. The front door was open and the house was empty, so Bruno and Balzac strolled down to the studio, wishing as he had so often before that he could play an instrument and join in this constant feast of music with which Rod, Amélie, Flavie and the others filled their days. What he heard as he approached, however, was something strange, the sound of a medieval instrument being played as if it were a modern guitar. Was it Vincent's rebec or Flavie's citole? He had no idea.

The door was ajar, so he pushed it open and saw Les Troubadours standing around Rod, laughing as he tried to make sense of an instrument that had been developed more than a thousand years ago. It was designed to produce a drone, the chords changing but constantly running into one another, while Rod was trying to play individual notes and chords and making a caterwaul version of one of his own songs. Amélie was laughing helplessly while trying to hold some kind of beat on a medieval drum.

"I'd like to say I'm glad you're all having fun, but it certainly doesn't sound like it," Bruno said, waving a greeting. "It's getting toward showtime. Are you all ready to go?"

"That's a song composed by King Richard the Lionheart himself, 'Ja Nus Hons Pris,' while I in prison lie," declared Joël, laughing. "Have you no respect?"

"I hope you all stick to your own music onstage tonight," said Bruno. "I don't know if any of you has eaten, but there are some snacks for you in a truck by the stage, and you won't have to put up with my cooking tonight. Ivan has offered to feed us all when the concert's over. One more thing . . ." He paused until he had their full attention. "Spain will pay to rebuild the recording studio."

Bruno watched Dominic embrace Vincent, and then each of them hug Arnaut and Joël and Flavie. Then Bruno went on, "There's more news from Madrid. The ban on 'Song for Catalonia' has been officially lifted. I think we can say there is somebody very smart in the Spanish government who understands that you don't make war on culture, you simply admire and enjoy it."

He read out Manzaredo's message, and a strange silence fell as everyone turned to look at Joël, who bit his lip and nodded two, three times. "I'm glad it's for European culture," he said, then paused. "I'll accept in my own name and that of my late wife."

Bruno began to clap and the others joined in, applauding Joël and slapping him on the back. Flavie moved up to kiss his cheek.

"Right, time to go," said Bruno. "Who has the playlist and is there an intermission? The guy on the sound deck will need that."

"We'll put that together on the drive over," said Rod. "Thanks, Bruno. And, please, can we leave the Bruce somewhere with Balzac while we're playing?"

"We'll leave them at the stables, in my horse's stall. They're used to that," he said.

By seven, all the tables in the eating area were crammed, and the space between them and the stage was becoming increasingly packed. The parking lots of all three supermarkets were full, and so was the big square in front of the gendarmerie as well as the one in front of the train station. Yveline reported that cars were lined up along the roads back toward Campagne and Le Buisson. She had arranged for a bus to go back and forth to Limeuil and Le Buisson as a shuttle service. Farmers were making a small fortune renting out parking spaces on their harvested hayfields at five euros apiece.

The food stalls were doing a roaring trade, and Julien was ferrying supplies of wine between the town vineyard and the big tent. It was too busy for wine to be served by the glass, so only bottles were being sold. With a roving TV camera and radio reporters running nonstop live interviews with the crowd, and with the prefect and the gendarme general arriving, there was a sense of occasion. The mayor was interviewed and the great space along the riverbank was alive with noise and laughter, and tiny, flashing neon lights were being sold by a strolling vendor. The air itself added to the convivial mood, combining scents of roasting meats and spices, French fries and Caribbean curries.

Bruno had taken his sidearm from his office safe, the nine-millimeter SIG Sauer Pro that had replaced his familiar PAMAS. He had coordinated the patrol system with Yveline, and gendarmes were now stationed at each side of the stage, at the front and at the rear along the riverbank. Yveline herself kept out of sight around the stage, carrying the gendarmerie's only automatic weapon, a Heckler & Koch UMP 9.

"*Merde,*" she said to him, the traditional good luck word before action. It covered all eventualities from a sports match to an artistic performance and was so universally used as a swear word that it had lost all sense of affront. "*Merde,*" he replied as the stage lights went up, followed by a friendly groan as the mayor appeared, rather than the musicians, to give a short speech of welcome and introduction. But the vast and still swelling crowd fell silent as the mayor said Les Troubadours' "Song for Catalonia" had become a worldwide phenomenon thanks to the support of the people of France, despite the ban by the Spanish government.

"You have spoken and Spain has heard you," he declared to cheers. "The Spanish government has today announced an end to the ban on the song, and its author, our own Joël Martin, has been awarded Spain's Order of Merit for services to European culture."

The crowd rose, cheering and whistling, and the loudspeakers howled feedback as the mayor held out the microphone to the crowd so they could hear themselves.

"And to help us all celebrate tonight, we have two of St. Denis's favorite musicians, the lovely Amélie, our Josephine Baker reborn, and the rock legend for the last thirty years and more, a man who lives here among us and sent his kids to our schools, the great Rod Macrae. *Mesdames, messieurs,* St. Denis welcomes you to a historic night of music."

The mayor left the stage to what was probably the loudest applause he'd ever received, swiftly replaced by wolf whistles as Amélie came onstage in a slinky white dress, looking the very image of Josephine Baker, and launched into:

J'ai deux patries,
La mienne et Paris.

Except she somehow managed to replace "Paris" with "St. Denis," and the crowd went wild.

The crowd erupted again as Rod Macrae strolled onstage in his cowboy boots, blue jeans and leather vest, carrying his guitar. He doffed his Stetson to the people, perched on a high stool and began a gentle acoustic accompaniment as Amélie swayed into the familiar melody of "Sous les Ponts de Paris." Then she let the song merge almost imperceptibly into "April in Paris," and by now the crowd was singing along with her.

Gritting his teeth in frustration that he was not there to watch and sing along with them, Bruno patrolled the riverbank. He checked the sides of the stage, the fringes of the crowd and kept watching the river.

Then his phone buzzed. It was Morillon.

"Bruno, can you hear me over that music?" he heard.

"Yes," he said, trotting along the riverbank to crouch down at the edge of the water where the bank gave him cover to hear. "The concert has begun, you can hear it."

"I certainly can. But listen, we've managed to break into some of Africa's phone records. There were two words she used in English, rather than the Russian equivalent. The first one was 'drone' and the second one was 'claymore.' I'm sure you understand the first, but the second one is an antique Scottish sword. You may be getting some kind of drone attack, do you understand?"

"I understand," he said heavily. "The claymore isn't only a sword, it's a modern antipersonnel mine. *Putain*, we never thought of that."

"Good luck," said Morillon, but Bruno was already two decades and hundreds of miles away. He was back in the Balkans when he'd first come across the weapon that the Americans had invented and deployed in Vietnam. He'd seen an entire platoon of Serbian irregulars blown away by a Claymore mine.

It shot seven hundred tiny steel balls, fired at an arc of sixty degrees in a fan-shaped pattern, two meters high and fifty meters wide. Anything within that target area would be shredded. At this concert, Bruno knew, it could take out the stage and dozens of people standing close to it, probably including the mayor, the prefect and the gendarme general. But it could not have been placed here. The sniffer dogs would have found it.

And then he thought of the first word Morillon had used—"drone." Bruno had never heard of a Claymore mine being delivered and fired by a drone, but modern military technology was moving too fast for him to keep up. He'd been thinking like an old man, focusing on snipers and bombs and mortars and forgetting that drones these days could be big enough to carry humans, let alone a two-kilogram Claymore mine. *Putain,* he thought, the sniper had always and only been a false trail. This devastating strike from the air was what Africa had planned all along. Far more than a single assassination by a sniper, it would be an act of widespread slaughter of French civilians by Spanish extremists. J-J had been right all along. The sniper's bullet and the drunken sniper were simply distractions from Africa's far-more-sinister design. Maybe even the two Spanish ex-Legionnaires, including her lover, were cat's-paws, useful idiots who had no idea of her real plan.

Bruno ran back to Yveline and yelled, "Drone—Claymore mine." He saw that she'd understood, and she ran with him to the searchlights beside the stage.

"No time to evacuate," he shouted over the music. "We have to knock it out."

Each of the searchlights was pointing straight up into the sky. He found the handle of the nearest one and moved it on the cantilever to focus on the approach to the stage. He swung it slowly to his right, to the west, where there was still some weak postsunset light in the sky. Yveline was shifting her own searchlight to scan the dark skies to the east.

Bruno hadn't noticed until now, but Amélie and Macrae had been replaced onstage by Flavie and Les Troubadours. They were playing a cheerful folk-style tune and the area in front of the stage was filled with people dancing, some of them the young mothers of the *maternelle* whom Bruno knew, the women who had rallied to Florence's defense.

Perhaps the drone was another of Africa's distractions, like the sniper, and the Claymore had been planted in front of the stage all along. But no, he reminded himself, the dogs would have found it. He caught himself—what if the dogs had already been disabled by the pepper? Surely not, he'd seen them at work when he'd spoken to Michel before seeing what had happened to the dogs at the vet's office. And where had the dogs been disabled? he asked himself. The answer came at once, in front of the Bara-Bahau cave, where the path led to the hunters' cabin, the place with the best sniper position to shoot at the stage.

Suddenly certain that Africa and Garay must be launching and directing the drone from there, he carefully swiveled the search-light a little farther to his right and back again along the ridge. No, you fool, he told himself, higher. Drones have to go high to set their sights.

But what an unmissable target it was, the stage, the lights, the crowd, the river behind, the bridge just a hundred meters away. They couldn't miss it, the best-lit, most vulnerable target there could possibly be.

Bruno tried to remember the range of a Claymore, dredging his memory to recall that its most effective range was fifty meters but that it was still lethal at a hundred. This could be a different version, perhaps Russian, with different characteristics. Fifty meters was damn close. The crowd was still packed fifty meters from the stage. *Putain,* it was still packed at a hundred.

"What the hell are you up to?" came a shout. Michel was at his side, demanding to know what he was doing with the searchlight.

"I think we're under attack by a drone," Bruno shouted in reply. "Get the other searchlights to follow my beam. If we can find it, we can shoot it down. And use the strobes to blind it."

Michel's jaw dropped, then he nodded and darted away, heading for the other searchlights that still pointed straight up at the stars.

How did drones see? Bruno wondered. How did they take in an image of the earth below that they could transmit back to their controller? There was a bulbous lens that scanned the land, he recalled. If that lens could be blinded, overwhelmed by the powerful beams of two, three, four searchlights, they might be able to frustrate it. He had a sudden memory of wartime movies, bombers moving slowly through the skies, one of them caught in the beam of a searchlight and then by several more, weaving and turning but unable to escape as the antiaircraft fire crept closer and the fighters moved in to attack. But there were no fighters in the sky tonight, and the only antiaircraft fire was his handgun and Yveline's submachine gun. But with enough light, they might still blind it, if they could find it.

And then he caught a gleam, a flash or a reflection of something pale and suddenly rising. He followed it with his beam, almost too small to see but getting bigger, swooping up and down to evade his beam, but he kept it there and then came a second shaft of searchlight as Yveline joined him and then a third and then another, a powerful cone of lights that sent the drone jerking as though unsure of what it could see.

He kept focus, even as it swayed and shifted in the beams. But then it suddenly soared upward and he lost it before catching it again and seeing it barreling directly toward him, growing larger by the second. It was no longer jerking but coming as straight as a bullet. He pulled out his handgun, shouted to Yveline to open fire, sighted and waited, almost distracted by the sudden sea of upturned faces that appeared as the crowd looked up. Then he blinked as his eyes were assaulted by a monstrous ice-blue flare as Michel somehow triggered the strobes.

The drone was still coming right at him but jerking with each flash of the strobes, still growing larger. Almost blindly he opened fire, all twelve rounds, one after another, then slamming in another magazine as he heard the metallic tear of Yveline's weapon firing sharp bursts. He didn't have time to fire again, but with another burst of strobe lights the drone seemed to lurch and then jerked upward. It sailed over his head, over the stage and with a monstrous explosion the Claymore fired, lashing the river with seven hundred steel balls.

"Come with me," he shouted at Yveline. "I know where they are."

They ran together up the security path to where the gendarme motorbikes were parked. In uniform, with her brand-new captain's epaulettes attached and holding her weapon, Yveline commandeered the first one. She straddled it and slung her weapon over her shoulder. It almost hit Bruno as he clambered onto the seat behind her.

"Bara-Bahau," he shouted, "fast as you can."

She swung up the slope beside the bank, turned right over the bridge, left at the roundabout, down to the hotel and up the narrow, winding cliff road to the prehistoric cave where bears used to hibernate and ancient people engraved bison, bulls and reindeer into the soft rock. She skidded into the parking lot and braked. Bruno slid off, went down on one knee and aimed his gun at the entrance to the path wondering if the pepper was still there. Yveline edged away to the right, her assault weapon ready.

Bruno's phone vibrated. He risked a quick glance. It was Isabelle, probably watching the concert on TV and trying to learn what was happening. He ignored it.

"Come on out, Africa," he shouted. "Or I send in the dogs."

There was silence, only the sound of distant music from the stage far behind him. And then, after what seemed an endless moment, the sound of a woman's laughter, and Africa appeared on the path, illuminated by the headlight of the motorbike. Her arms were outstretched and from one hand dangled a gun, held by the barrel.

"You will find a dead Spanish major by the cabin," she said in accented French. She spoke it like a Spaniard. "I shot him to save innocent lives. I think we can negotiate an exchange, perhaps for the lover of that sweet little Catalan girl. I hear you are a romantic, Bruno."

She came down to the end of the path, self-assured and looking confident as though certain that she held the trump cards. Then she seemed to lose her footing and stumble on the path, sending up a cloud of red dust toward her face. She sneezed hard, sneezed again, swayed and began tottering to try to keep her balance. The gun was suddenly in her hand and looking dangerous. Yveline fired a short burst that sent Africa tumbling back into the bushes as the red dust rose and fell.

Bruno breathed out hard and put his handkerchief over his mouth and nose. He walked to the sprawled woman and saw the diagonal splashes of blood from her left hip to her right shoulder. The recoil must have jerked Yveline's gun upward as she fired. Bruno put a hand to Africa's throat to check that she was dead. He held his breath against the pepper and used his handkerchief to pick up her gun. He put it back into her hand and fired three single shots into the air and another two into the bushes. Then he took out his own gun and fired once into the dead body.

"Fire another burst, quickly, into the air," he said to Yveline.

She did so, the sound suddenly very loud. He fired his own weapon again.

"Now we have a firefight," he said. "We fired in self-defense. That should be enough for the inevitable inquiry and to save your career. Get some gendarmes up here with lights and an ambulance. We'll draft our report together tonight."

"She was trying to surrender," Yveline said. "But when I saw her aim the gun . . ." She broke off, and suddenly leaned over to vomit heavily.

Bruno waited until Yveline had wiped her mouth and was standing up again, remembering how he'd felt when he had first killed a man. And every time since. He sighed, walked toward Yveline and shook his head.

"No, Yveline, once that woman knew the drone had missed, she shot her tame Spanish major and came down to make a deal. She got caught in the pepper that she'd laid down to disable the sniffer dogs. Don't mourn her. Think of those who didn't die tonight."

He waited until Yveline had phoned the gendarmerie and asked for an ambulance, lights and reinforcements. He glanced back toward the town, surprised that the music was still playing, the spasmodic glare of strobe lights still slashing the air.

Had the crowd not noticed? Had the musicians not heard the shots? Who could have missed the explosion of the Claymore? Or had it all been seen as part of the light show, fireworks and rockets? But how had the audience not seen him and Yveline firing into the sky? Because they'd been behind the glare of the searchlights, of course. Had any of their bullets hit the drone and made it jerk upward, or had it or its operator simply been blinded by the sudden explosion of the strobe lights? Perhaps they'd find out tomorrow when they dredged the river for whatever was left of it. But no matter; it had worked somehow. And the show had gone on.

Bruno pulled out his own phone to return Isabelle's call.

Acknowledgments

This is a work of fiction and all events and persons are figments of my imagination except that the original Soviet woman spy called Africa, who is buried beside Kim Philby, was real; the Russian cyberwarfare center, Unit 74455 at Ulitsa Kirova in the Khimki suburb of Moscow, is real; and they did indeed attack with cybertools a U.S. presidential election campaign, the Brexit campaign and the electoral bid of France's president Macron. Perhaps it stems from my own background in journalism, and as a former Moscow correspondent for Britain's *Guardian,* that I focus on these facts that underpin my novels and make them all the more real to me.

The background of the Catalan independence movement is much as described here, but I was delighted when completing this novel to learn that the Madrid government had decided to pardon nine of the Catalan separatist leaders. Joël Martin is an invention, a concocted amalgam of several scholars, poets and enthusiasts whom I have met through SHAP, the Société Historique et Archéologique du Périgord. I have learned much from them about the history of the region and the importance of the civilized and relatively tolerant culture of medieval Islam in Spain.

Even more than the contacts made by Crusaders in the Holy Land, the intellectual centers of Toledo and Córdoba passed on to Europe their own medical and musical skills as well as the heritage of ancient Greece and Rome. This has transformed my own understanding of Europe's cultural history and our emergence from the Dark Ages.

In that sense, the baron's awe at learning from Joël Martin how much we owe to our Islamic neighbors, in music as in philosophy, matches my own. I have found delight in the knowledge that the Périgord played such a crucial role in music and poetry and in civilizing the brutalities of the feudal era. Without Eleanor of Aquitaine and the Occitan culture she brought to the tales of Geoffrey of Monmouth, King Arthur might have had his Merlin, but he would not have had the Knights of the Round Table. Nor would he have had the sword of Excalibur, the Lady of the Lake, the tale of Sir Tristan and Lady Iseult, the passion of Sir Lancelot nor his son, Sir Galahad, to whom Lancelot bequeathed the Périgord. And Germany might not have had the great opera *Parsifal,* drawn from the tale of Sir Perceval. Our European history and culture have long been more closely entwined than we tend to think.

The Occitan culture is alive and well in southwestern France, with a thriving institute in Toulouse for the study and teaching of the language, and local clubs and associations in every *département* of the region. Flavie and Les Troubadours are an invention, but there is a healthy musical and literary heritage in the region. I am grateful to Jean Bonnefon, musician and writer, who has introduced me to much of this rich and fertile vein of poetry, history and music. For a sense of its resonance and power, I recommend the CD *Pretz et Paratge* by Rai d'Honoré, recorded at St.

Timothy's Episcopal Church in Greenhill, North Carolina, and published by www.OccitanCulturalInitiatives.org.

It is to the Périgord itself, its people and history, its food and wine, that I owe a great debt for this novel. So my special thanks to Julien and Caline Montfort, who have helped bring my Cuvée Bruno wine to life, and to all the winemakers of the Bergerac *appellation* whose wines have given so much pleasure to so many people. Thanks also to my dear friend and neighbor Raymond Bounichou, who translated my own "Song for Catalonia" into the Occitan of the Dordogne Valley.

I am indebted far more than I can say to my wife, Julia, without whom Bruno's meals would be so many burnt offerings, and to our daughters, Kate and Fanny. I am more than fortunate that my literary agent, Caroline Wood, and my editors, Jonathan Segal in New York, Jane Wood in London and Anna von Planta in Zurich, have all become dear friends. They have all been guests at our Périgord home, where Julia's cooking explains why our Bruno cookbooks (in German) have each won the Gourmand International award for Best French Cookbook in the World! A composite volume of the Bruno cookbooks will soon be published in English by Knopf. *Bon appétit*!

—Martin Walker, the Périgord, 2021